MASKED

INNOCENCE

Alessandra Torre

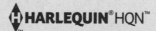

Recycling programs
for this product may
not exist in your area.

ISBN-13: 978-0-373-77837-9

MASKED INNOCENCE

Printed in U.S.A.

Dedicated to Mom.

Thank you for raising me to be independent, and for always letting my imagination run free. Thanks for gnomes in the forest, walks through cotton fields, and your unwavering acceptance and support.

I love you.

Having two men at one time is a strange experience. My first time in a threesome, I was blindfolded, my senses heightened and restricted to touch, scent, sounds and taste. *Touch.* The feeling of their hands on my bare skin, caresses, grips, slaps and fucks. God, those long strokes of pure animal ownership. *Scent.* Fresh linen, candles, Brad's unmistakable combination of God knows what that drove me absolutely crazy, my own sweat, the strange new scent of the stranger in the room. *Sounds.* Their ragged breaths, my own heartbeat pounding in my head, a primal groan, whispered words of reverence, the sound of flesh on flesh, of my own wetness. *Taste.* Tight, stretched skin in my mouth, Brad's mouth on me, my own taste on their tongues, the eroticism of it all. And finally, the taste of completion when I milked them dry, the flavor of victory and carnal satisfaction. I had done it. I had gone there. And I had loved every minute of it.

One

"So, what's next?"

I turned my head, glancing at him, his dark profile hiding the grin that I knew played over his features. I reclined in the passenger seat of his car, snug against the warmth of the seat heater. He reached his hand over, offering it to me, and I grabbed it, running my hands over his huge palm and strong fingers. "What's next with tonight?"

He chuckled, the sound unfairly sexual. The man could make a sneeze sound carnal if he wanted to. "I'm taking you home with me tonight, unless you have an objection to that. I meant in regards to us."

I yawned. "Your home sounds good for tonight." Yes, his huge home with its big, luxurious bed, worth-giving-up-carbs-for shower and stocked fridge would be welcome tonight, especially since a night in that wonderful bed normally led to a morning of orgasms. "As far as with us, that's in your ballpark. I tried the threesome, and I'm cool with that if that's what you need to be faithful."

"You're 'cool' with it." His wry tone elicited a frown from my side of the car. "You seemed a little more than 'cool with it.'"

I rolled my eyes. "Fine. I loved it, can't wait to do it again, I will worship at the shrine of Brad from this day forth. Happy?"

The light changed in the car, and this time I could see the grin that stretched over his face. "Well, if you insist. You know I strive to please."

Yes, you certainly do. I never thought I would appreciate one singular quality so much. Competitiveness is great in a partner. *Sexual* competitiveness, I've learned over the last several weeks, is holy-freaking-God amazing. I watched the curve of his mouth, loving the transformation it caused to his powerful features. "So, tonight was it, right? That's the sexual extent of your freakiness?"

"Well..." He shrugged, glancing over at me.

"Well?" I sat up, turning in my seat to fully face him. "Well what?"

"I will never need anything more 'freaky,' as you like to say, than what we just did. But the point of this is not just my pleasure. It's to awaken your sexuality, to find what turns you on and to explore that. Chances are, tonight wasn't your single perfect fantasy." I shifted slightly at the statement. *Uh, yeah— it pretty much was.* "As we grow in our relationship, you may find you like completely different things than you do now. As your sexual boundaries expand, your preferences may change."

I smirked at him. "So, what you're saying is, if I keep dating you, in three years I'm going to be licking whipped cream off a bearded lady and loving it?"

He laughed. "If it reaches that level, you're not going to be still dating me."

I relaxed back into the seat. "Well, for now, that was plenty hot enough for me. I don't know how much more sexual exploration my mind can take right now."

"So, if I receive any invitations, I should turn them down?"

I paused, midsnuggle into the leather cocoon that the BMW's seat had become. "What? What *kind* of invitations?"

"You know, parties, cruises or threesomes like we just did." His offhand tone was ludicrous considering the events that he was so casually discussing.

Parties? Cruises? I swallowed, unsure if I was ready for more. Brad read my silence and looked over, the passing streetlights revealing concern on his face. "Too much?" he asked.

I braved a smile. "For now. Let's take it one freak show at a time, okay?"

From the other side of the car came that delicious chuckle, and I clenched my core in an involuntary response.

The car slowed, making the turn onto Brad's road, and I looked at the stately homes that passed, each one more impressive than the last. Then we pulled into Brad's drive, the suspension smoothing the rough ride of the pavers below us, and taking us to his home.

Two

I entered the lobby of Clarke, De Luca & Broward on Monday morning at seven-thirty on the dot. Waving at Ancient Dorothy, I pressed the elevator call button and waited for the car. My early morning wait was interrupted by a clattering of heels from somewhere behind me. The clattering had speed and determination that made me tense in anticipation. I risked a glance over my shoulder and came in full eye contact with an Amazon of a woman. I was wearing three-inch heels and she still towered a good six inches above me, coming to an abrupt halt so close to me that I was forced to look up just so my face wasn't buried in her breasts. I smiled hesitantly in greeting and stepped to the side, turning back to the bank of elevators, now in the awkward position of whether or not to make polite conversation on the ride up. I was already terrified of this woman, and didn't know why, other than the fact that she was clearly sizing me up and not being the slightest bit shy about it. I almost expected her to ask me to open my mouth so she could inspect my teeth.

The doors slid open, and after standard overtures, she

stepped onto the car, her strong mass dominating the elaborate space. My inner turmoil over whether or not to converse with her was solved by the moment the doors closed.

"So," she announced with gusto. "You're Julia."

"Beg your pardon?" I asked.

"Julia Campbell," she said, grinning at me, her face beautiful despite the extra weight it carried. As a failed makeup study, I recognized quality makeup when I saw it, and this girl had enhanced an already beautiful face to model-quality, an attribute that many men probably overlooked because of her size. "That's you, right? I hacked into H.R.'s file and got a copy of your driver's license. Your pic is a few years old, but pretty damn close."

If there had been room to take a step back in the elevator, I would have. If I had been scared of her before, I was sweating bullets now. "I'm sorry...I don't believe we have met. You are...?"

She laughed. "Sorry. I'm Rebecca. Brad's assistant."

Brad's assistant. Suddenly I could breathe a little easier. "Oh. I thought all of his assistants were..." I tried to find the words to describe the three secretaries that reigned over Brad's wing of the firm.

"Old, wrinkly bitches?" She grinned at me as the doors opened, and I burst out laughing at the description, one that probably fit the three elegant senior citizens that had stuffily dismissed me the one time I had dared to approach their desk. We stepped out of the elevator together and she followed me as I pressed on the door to the West Wing. Surprised, I glanced over at her. "You coming over here?"

"Just for a sec. Brad wanted me to introduce myself, and a thirty-second ride won't do that justice."

I doubted a three-day road trip would do that justice, but

I smiled at her and unlocked my office door, ushering her in. It was early, but the rest of the staff would be filing in soon. I hoped she wasn't planning on staying long. Rebecca's presence was as subtle as a giant sign screaming *I'm dating Brad De Luca!* hung outside my door.

"I can't stay." Her quick words made me wonder how transparent my inhospitable thoughts were. "Let me just get your email address and I'll be on my way."

"My email?"

"Yeah. Your personal one. I'll need to send you some stuff that shouldn't go over the company intranet."

I blushed, hoping the attachments weren't of the adult variety and wondering how much Rebecca knew about our relationship. I scribbled down my email address, passing it to her with a smile that I hoped communicated my friendly intent. "It was nice to meet you, Rebecca."

"Hey, you, too. Maybe I'll see you around." She waved cheerily and swung out the door, her heels pounding down the hallway, and I breathed a sigh of relief when I heard the double doors close behind her. I plopped down in my chair, spinning slightly as I stared at the ceiling. Rebecca sending me "stuff." This would be interesting.

Three

"Julia, can I borrow you for a moment?" Broward's voice floated through the open doorway into my office, four hours later. He had politely used the office phone system for the first three weeks of my internship, but had abandoned that practice and now simply yelled for me, like I was his puppy roaming somewhere in the house, looking for a place to pee. I sighed, sliding back from my desk and working my bare feet into heels and standing. I was in his doorway a moment later, barely in time to stop another interoffice yell, his mouth already opening in preparation.

"Yes, Mr. Broward?" I asked politely.

"Come in, Julia, and please shut the door."

I cringed, stepping forward and grabbing the handle, pulling it closed behind me. Broward seemed to have this misconception that "closing his door" actually afforded him some measure of privacy. While the heavy, oak door probably did have excellent sound-deafening qualities, the one-inch gap that ran along the bottom allowed almost every word to come through in crystal-clear quality. This had to be about Brad, and thanks to this poorly hung door, someone was bound to walk by and hear the entire conversation.

"I'd like to extend your internship, assuming you are interested."

My jaw literally dropped, an involuntary relaxation of muscles that I struggled to contain. *Okay—guess this isn't about Brad.* "Extend?" I said dumbly.

"Yes. I've been very impressed with you so far, and would like to expand your duties here, maybe bring you to court, let you see more than just the inside of a file." He grinned at me, a worthless exercise of muscles, because as soon as he had said that word, everything else had disappeared.

Court. The word hung, in gold glittery letters, above my head, blinking on and off like a Vegas sign advertising half-priced buffets. I tried not to lick my lips but could feel saliva pooling, and my jaw started itching to do that damn dropping motion again. "That would be wonderful, but I—um…I just need to check my class schedule for next semester."

He shrugged at my response, picking up his phone and cradling it to his ear. "Check your schedule and let me know, I'll speak to H.R., see if we could take you on part-time, give you some hourly rate that would make it worth your while."

Monetary compensation? Court time? I smiled at him and turned quickly, wanting to get the hell out of there before slobber shot in all directions out of my mouth. I fled his office and collapsed into my chair, an expression somewhere between a grin and a grimace contorting my face. My excitement over the job prospect fought with the predicament it would cause. *Court. Money. Brad. Broward. Certain disaster. Court.* Ugh. I laid my head on my desk and groaned.

IT WAS 4:00 p.m. before I thought to check my personal email, remembering that Rebecca was going to send me something. I had one new email, from Rebecca Cray, titled INFO. I opened the email, and read the one-line message.

When you get a chance, please complete the attached and scan it back to me. Thx—Rebecca

I opened the attachment, an Excel spreadsheet, and scanned it quickly, my eyes narrowing the further down the document I read. *No fucking way.* Then I printed it, closed out the email and picked up the office phone, dialing Brad's extension and waiting.

He answered in a way that expressed he was not alone. That was fine. I had aspirations for my bitch-out session, and the minimum requirement was that it be in person. "Dinner, tonight? The bistro on Sixty-ninth at six. Okay?"

"Do I have a choice?" His voice held a hint of wariness.

Damn. I had wanted to blindside him with my tantrum. More dramatic that way. "Not really."

"The bistro is fine, at six, but be aware that I don't do subservient very well."

His voice was almost dangerous in its authority, and my feminine side swooned a little despite my best efforts to project more of a dominatrix side.

I tried to come up with a witty response, but struck out. "Whatever," I finally snapped, hanging the phone up glumly, feeling, as I often did with him, that I had been outmatched.

Then I stood, going to ask the other dictator in my life if I could run out for thirty minutes at six. I really needed to do something to get the men in my life under better control.

Four

"What, pray tell, could I already be in trouble for?" In the brick-walled restaurant, Brad's face could only be described as pained as he ended a call and stood from a four-top at my approach, stepping aside and pulling out my chair.

I sat, accepting the kiss he placed on my cheek, a kiss that moved, traveling down my neck before I pulled back with a squeal, a smile fighting me tooth and nail to reach my mouth. "What makes you think you are in trouble?" I purred, crossing my legs and reaching forward, dipping a carrot in some hummus and crunching down on it, Brad looking at me in barely contained disgust. "What?"

"That stuff. It looks disgusting."

I snorted, all sexy purrs now gone. "Disgusting? You ordered it!"

"I ordered it because women everywhere seem to eat it, and I was trying to find something you'd like in this granolified tent that they call a restaurant."

I smothered a smile, looking around. He had a point. Birkenstocks and deodorant-free patrons seemed to be the vibe this place was going for. It had been a recommendation from my roommate Alex, and was one of the few downtown restaurants that was avoided by the staff. Now I knew why. "No steaks on the menu?"

"Barely any meat on the menu. One free-range chicken dish, the rest all vegetarian. I'll eat at home, but you need something. Here." He pushed a laminated menu across the small table, and I scanned it quickly, fighting my own urge to curl an upper lip. The items were all healthy, all organic, and all…unappetizing. I spotted vegetable soup and decided to go with that, setting the menu aside and looking at Brad.

The man was sinful. Tan skin, thick black hair, with bits of silver littering it. Dark brown eyes that held every emotion possible, with the tendency to smolder and cloud at just the moment when it drove me the craziest. Strong features that worked perfectly together to make every grin, grimace and glare heart-stoppingly gorgeous. But honestly, you could run his face through a blender, shave his head bald and starve the man out of his amazing, too-built-for-mortal-men build, and he would still be stop-you-in-your-tracks sexy. Because it wasn't the looks that really made him sizzle; it was the pure sex that reeked from his pores, the cocky confidence that dominated every move, every touch. And the horrible yet ecstatic fact about the whole package is that he could back it all up with mind-numbing sexual prowess. He knew what he rocked beneath those dress pants, and he knew exactly how to use the damn thing. It was, as I had thought a thousand times before, ridiculously unfair.

"Stop smirking at me." I spoke through a half-eaten carrot, hoping that my mental drool-fest hadn't shown in my face, which I fixed into an irritated scowl.

"I'll smirk at you until you tell me what I have done wrong.

I assure you, I have not fucked anybody since you left my house last night." He leaned back, placing his hands in his pockets, his legs spread. He looked relaxed, which was the last thing I wanted him looking.

Our waitress, an overall-wearing blonde, swung by and I handed her the menu, requesting the soup and a glass of ice water. Then I took him out of his not-even-present misery and reached into my bag, pulling out the spreadsheet Rebecca had emailed me and slapping it onto the table.

He leaned forward, his hands still in his pockets, and glanced at the document before leaning back and shrugging. "So?"

"So? *That's* your response? Do you *know* what this is?"

"Yeah. It's the questionnaire. Rebecca sends it to all of the important women in my life." He gave me a grin that indicated that I should thank my lucky stars and dance around hugging myself, so grateful that he graced me with receiving his ridiculous spreadsheet. I wanted to take the hummus and shove it all over his face.

"Let me read this shit to you, Brad. Birthday, time of monthly cycle, favorite authors, favorite clothing store, shoe size, bra size, name of four closest friends, favorite band—"

"Where are you going with this, Julia?" he interrupted my rant, which was too bad, because I was just getting to the good stuff.

"I'm not telling her—or you—all this shit! This is Lazy Boyfriend 101. This is her cheat sheet so that she can buy all the right presents at all of the appropriate times! Text you during social events, reminding you of my friends' names. This is the stuff we are supposed to discover about each other during dates—things that you are supposed to care enough to find out, and then remember!" I slammed my hand on the table, the noise loud in the small restaurant.

He didn't move, studying me from his seat, his head tilted as his eyes burned through me. "Okay."

"Okay?"

He shrugged. "Okay. I'll tell her to throw away the list, as far as you are concerned. You're right."

My mouth threatened to drop open again. *That was easy.* From the man whom I had expected to fight me tooth and nail, on principle and stubbornness alone.

My astonishment must have shown; he gave a quick laugh and leaned forward. "Rebecca doesn't know, okay? I told her I was dating someone, and she probably assumed you are like the other girls. I don't need that list, I know half the shit on it already and will know the rest soon enough. Forget it. I'll talk to Rebecca and make sure she leaves you alone from here on out." He grinned at me, reaching across the table and grabbing my arm. "Now, am I forgiven?"

I tried to glare at him, but my anger had abandoned me somewhere around his admittance of fault. My face contorted in a variety of expressions before I finally returned his grin, accepting the tug of his hands and meeting him across the table for a quick, panty-melting kiss.

We parted, the connection broken, and he grinned at me as he settled back into his chair.

"What?" I asked warily, leaning back as the waitress set my soup down.

"Boyfriend." My quizzical look caused him to elaborate. "Lazy Boyfriend 101—you referred to me as your boyfriend."

My soup steamed hot before me, and I broke saltines into it and stirred, avoiding his cocky stare. "You're reading too much into my word choice—I was trying to explain, in simple caveman terms, your gross error in judgment."

"I'm ready to be exclusive."

The statement surprised me, and I looked up to find his eyes on me, serious and intense. "Really? Now?"

"Yes, now. We had wanted to see if you were okay with my sexual lifestyle. You've had a chance to experience it, you enjoyed it, so let's move on."

"Together," I said, my word more of a question than a declaration.

"You seem to have trouble grasping this concept."

"I have no problem grasping the concept. I'm just shocked you are pushing the subject. You seem like the type to run from commitment, not seek it out." I took a sip of soup and watched as he shifted in his seat.

"Julia, what I said to you three weeks ago in the stairwell was true. I don't like being alone. While I enjoy the flirtations of being single, I would prefer to be in a committed relationship."

I grinned at him. "So the promise of a relationship wasn't just to trick me into ditching my inhibitions?"

He had the good grace to look wounded, reaching over and tugging on my hand. He brought it up to his mouth, kissing it gently and looking at me. "I am a man of my word, and ready to commit fully to you. With the obvious exceptions."

"The exceptions being our group sex partners, not random women you screw on the side."

His mouth twitched under my fingers and he nodded, returning my hand. "Correct."

"Fine, I'll accept your offer of servitude," I said, glancing at him while blowing on the soup, his amusement visible through the steam. "*Since* that grants me the power of possession, exactly how many women does Rebecca have a dossier on?"

He shrugged. "Not many. I've had five or six extended

flings that have stretched for a few months. Rebecca has files on those women."

I growled through the first spoonful of soup, wanting to march up to her office right now and feed those spreadsheets through the shredder myself. Not that I, with my still-had-the-tags-on-it new relationship, had any right to be territorial. "Well, I was going to hire a pushy assistant and have him, for the sake of invasiveness, send you an STD pee kit, but I guess I'll cancel that, seeing as you have agreed to drop the question-naire and keep your pit bull of an assistant at bay." I grinned at him and dipped my spoon back in the bowl.

"Oh….speaking of that." The hesitancy in his voice caused me to look up, my body tensing at whatever disaster was lurk-ing.

"Speaking of what?"

"STD tests." *Crap.* I was afraid that's where he was headed. "If you are going to be part of this lifestyle, we need to get you tested."

Never mind, not where I thought he was headed. "Me?" The incredulity in my voice caused another grin to cross his face.

"Yes, oh patron saint of virtue. You. I know you are prob-ably clean, but for future planning purposes, and in order to get access to the elite clubs and parties, we have to know for sure, and be able to provide documentation." He lowered his voice, leaning forward. "Everyone, and I mean *everyone*, wears condoms, but you have to be clean in order to participate. Do you have a doctor that you use?"

Gynecologist. That had been one of the blanks on Re-becca's spreadsheet, and I had planned on its being my argu-ment's grand finale—a shining example of the utter invasion of privacy that the questionnaire had been. Now it made a little more sense.

"Yeah," I muttered, scooping up a combination of noodles and vegetables.

"Do you mind?"

"Not particularly. I mean, I want everyone else there tested, but…" My mouth curved on its own, my own mind realizing the double standard that was about to come out of my lips. "No. I need to do it anyway. I'm due for an annual exam." I glanced at my watch, swearing at the time. "Damn, I gotta go." I stood, grabbing my bag, and leaned over, kissing him briefly before glancing at the table.

"I got it, babe. Go. Call me when you're done for the day."

I thanked him with my smile, trotting out the front and onto the downtown sidewalk. I made a mental note to call my gyno and see if I could get in to see her this week. As I stood at the busy street and waited to cross, I realized that I hadn't mentioned the job offer that Broward had extended.

Five

The invitation came, as so many did, by private messenger, a tuxedoed male with the bone structure of a model. He wound through the halls of Clarke, De Luca & Broward with familiar ease, taking the elevator to the fourth floor and swinging through the heavy doors of the East Wing. Approaching the elevated semicircle of secretarial desks, he stopped in front of the middle one, waiting patiently until the elegant women raised her silver head and looked at him.

"Yes? What can I help you with, sir?"

"I have a courier item for Mr. De Luca, ma'am."

"You can hand it over. I'll be sure that he gets it."

"I apologize, but I am under strict instructions to deliver it only to Mr. De Luca."

The woman pursed her lips, fixing him with a stern gaze that did nothing to alter the confident grin on his face. "I believe you have been here before, Mr...."

"Martin. And yes, I have made deliveries here before."

"Then, Mr. Martin, you are quite aware that Mr. De Luca is a very busy man. I will try to reach him via phone, but if

I fail, you will have the option of leaving the item with me or returning at another time. I will not have you wandering around this lobby waiting for his return, understood?"

His grin still in place, he nodded. "Yes, ma'am."

She turned, the wrinkles in her neck smoothing for one moment, and placed the phone to her ear.

BRAD WAS MIDSWING in the third stroke of a par four when his cell rang, vibrating inside his pocket, the one distraction he didn't need at that point in time. He swore loudly as he watched the ball fade to the right, headed exactly where it shouldn't, a loud splat confirming his error. He yanked his phone from his pocket and glanced at the display. "De Luca."

"Mr. De Luca, there is a gentleman here, a Mr. Martin, who has an item that he will only deliver to you."

"Let me talk to him, please."

There was a rustle, silence, then, "Hello?"

"This is Brad De Luca. Who is the item from?"

"Beverly Franklin, sir."

Brad chuckled. "Okay. Just a moment." He lifted his chin, going through the possibilities, then came to a decision.

"I'm going to give you a set of instructions, but I want to make sure that the secretary in front of you does not hear them. Do you understand?"

"Yes, sir."

"Leave the wing you are in and return to the elevator banks. There will be an entrance there for the West Wing—Kent Broward's name will be visible on the door. Enter there and ask for Julia Campbell. You can deliver the item to her. Just her."

"Gotcha, Mr. D. See you later, sir."

"Thank you." He hung up the phone and approached the

cart, nodding to the three men standing there. He would give anything to see Julia's face when she opened the card.

I WAS ELBOW deep in transcript review when Chace Crawford, in a tuxedo, appeared in my doorway. Okay, so it wasn't *the* Chace Crawford, but enough of a lookalike for me to momentarily forget Drueit vs. Pace Contracting, which was a feat unto itself. I collected myself and waved him in.

"Can I help you?"

"I'm looking for Julia Campbell."

"I'm Julia." I stood, stepping forward and shaking the hand he extended.

"I'm Jeff Martin. I have a couriered item for Mr. De Luca, but he isn't in. He said that I could give it to you."

I looked at the embossed envelope he extended, my fingers reaching out and taking it before my mind had a chance to process the situation. "Thank you," I said, smiling at him.

"Certainly." He gave a small bow and smiled, turning and leaving the room.

I sat back down, leaning the envelope against my computer monitor and staring at it for a brief moment. Being Brad's girlfriend was turning into a full-time job.

I ignored the envelope and returned to the depositions, reading line after line of transcripts until my contacts started to dry out and I leaned back to take a break. The envelope stared at me, beautiful calligraphy dancing beneath exhausted eyes. I reached for my phone and called Brad's cell.

BRAD PARKED HIS cart, tipping the bag-drop boy and stepping up the wide steps of the hundred-year-old clubhouse. It had been built at a time when opulence and masculinity ruled the design world, and every ounce of the building reeked of old money and tradition. He walked through the wide hall, oil paintings and trophy cases, seeing his group of friends at the entrance to the cigar bar. His phone rang and he paused, glancing down and seeing Julia's name. *That took longer than expected.* He smiled, holding up a finger to the men and stepped aside, leaning against the wall and answering the call.

"Hello, beautiful."

"Hey. You got something."

"And…did you open it?" He raised his eyebrows, waiting for her response.

"No," she said indignantly. "It has your name on it."

"Well, I had the courier bring it to you for a reason. It's an invitation to a party."

"And…?"

God, the woman was feisty. "*And* I'd like you to come with me."

She sighed into the phone. "As your secret girlfriend, I think I'm exempt from any of the boring social events you old people go to."

Brad smiled at her words, moving off the wall and stepping forward. "It's an orgy."

Her breath caught, and he wished he were having this conversation in person. "Oh."

"But…if that's too dull and old-mannish for you, I can invite someone else."

She hissed into the phone, "You wouldn't dare."

"Oh, I most definitely would."

There was silence for a minute and Brad stopped walking and waited.

"Where's the party?"

"Does it matter?"

"Humor me."

"I'm assuming it's at the hosts' home. In Irongate."

"Oooh…fancy. Do you know anyone who will be there?"

"I know the hosts. They typically throw a relatively small party, fifteen or twenty couples, a few singles. There will be group play and private rooms. If you feel up to it, we could just observe, maybe hook up with a single or a couple in a private room if you want. Or we can just stop in, let you see how it works and leave."

There was a pause, rustled papers, then an abrupt response. "Okay."

Her agreement came quicker than he expected, and he grinned into the phone.

"Okay. You officially have a date. Read the invitation. We'll talk later." He smiled into the phone, then looked up as one of his friends walked by, slapping him on the shoulder. "I have to go."

"Okay. *Wait!*" The urgency in her voice made him pause. "What?"

"It's this week, which doesn't exactly give me time to shop. What's the dress code?"

"Something sexy. No panties." He hung up the phone and walked forward, sliding it into his pocket.

I MURMURED SOME form of parting and hung up the phone, flipping the envelope over and running my fingers over the wax seal. I grabbed a letter opener and worked it gently under the flap, careful not to rip the paper as I opened it. I slid out a card, stiff and folded, Brad De Luca printed in perfect calligraphy on the front. Dropping the envelope, I opened the card, almost afraid of what was inside.

Big surprise, an invitation. I pushed away from my desk, spinning the chair in a small circle as I read it.

What: Masked Innocence
When: This Friday, 10 p.m. till dawn
Where: The Franklin Estate, Irongate
Attire: Masked Sexy
Consideration: $5,000/couple

We welcome you to our quarterly party. The theme is Masked Innocence. Please dress accordingly. As always, we must have your current credentials on file. Party rules are standard but are listed below for your reminder. We look forward to your presence.

Ladies make the rules.

No means no.

Men cannot approach women.

Proper credentials and protection required.

Well, this is convenient. Twenty-four hours after Brad mentions a sex party, a hot man shows up in my office, envelope in hand. I tapped the invitation against my desk and thought. I had shot out a response to Brad, not really thinking through the implications of what I was signing up for. I wasn't ready for this. A threesome was one thing. A masked orgy was something entirely different. I had to remember what Brad had said. We could *just stop in, see how it works and leave.* I could handle that. Piece of cake.

Six

Broward kept me at the office until ten that night, and every night that week, promising me a short day on Friday. Friday, the night of the party. It loomed, mysterious and expectant before me, and I was filled with equal parts anticipation and nerves. By the end of the week I was exhausted, having stumbled inside my house each night, ignoring the crowds that sometimes filled my living room, even the sounds of Zach's thumping bass failing to delay my immediate slumber. I'd spoken to Brad sporadically, quick conversations squeezed in between Broward's incessant orders, and Brad kept me fed and hydrated, sending in catered meals every night. The evening deliveries raised more than a few eyebrows, but as soon as everyone realized there was enough to share, the brows dropped and chewing began.

I was able to sneak out for a doctor's visit on Wednesday, a nerve-racking thirty minutes in which my most private areas were explored and a vial of blood was drawn, with results promised in twenty-four hours. I returned unnoticed, the never-ending pile of work marginally bigger. Broward was abnormally irritable, working with his door closed, moving files out of my line of sight when I would enter his office. Something was wrong, but I couldn't figure out which case was the source of his angst. From my side, everything seemed to be moving smoothly. He didn't mention my job future once, a fact I was grateful for, since I hadn't had time to come to a decision. Thursday, the doctor's office called, giving me a clean and unencumbered bill of health. And, before I knew it, it was Friday at 6:00 p.m. and I was stepping outside, the dusk light unfamiliar, Broward's promise of an early day fulfilled. I walked through the garage, glancing toward Brad's spot, bare pavement meeting my quick-to-roll eyes. *Shocker.*

A glance at my watch got my mind off Brad's absence and focused on the night ahead. Brad had texted me that he would pick me up at nine-thirty. Three and a half hours didn't seem like nearly enough time to physically and mentally prepare for the evening's activities. I increased my pace, headed for my Camry, a small quiver of excitement running recklessly through my body.

I STARTED IN the shower, begging each roommate to leave me and the bathroom alone for the next hour. I shaved my legs, underarms and all but a thin strip down below. I exfoliated vigorously, soaked in a hot bubble bath for twenty minutes, then exfoliated again. Getting out, I wrapped a towel around my body and put light makeup on. I then went to my closet.

The idea of a sex party was foreign and, as much as I hated to admit it, exciting to me. Images from *Eyes Wide Shut* filled my head, though I doubted any event of Brad's would be as cold and reserved as that scene had been. He said we could stop in, see how it works and leave. That was what I needed to keep in mind. That this was a sightseeing expedition and nothing more. My mind wandered back to the threesome that Brad had orchestrated a few weeks ago. How I had agreed to "try it" for ten minutes and at that point I'd be given the opportunity to back out. How, when that time frame had been reached, and his voice had come through the darkness, offering me an escape, I had never been so aroused, and the thought of stopping had seemed pure insanity. I suddenly realized how drug addicts became addicted. The threesome had been my gateway drug, and I now hovered at the edge of the cliff, ready and willing to jump into the dark depths below. More than willing, soaking wet at the thought of it. I knew, without even entering the party, that I would stay.

Nothing in my closet screamed *Sex Party*, so I aimed for club wear instead. I chose a red minidress that was tight on the bottom, loose and flowing on top. I ignored Brad's directive and put on panties, a black lace thong. Slathering my legs in lotion, I was spritzing on perfume when I heard the doorbell ring. I grabbed small faux diamond studs and a black clutch, then headed for the door.

My roommates Alex and Zach were smoking weed on the couch when I walked through the living room and opened the front door. Brad stood there, dark, delicious and sexy in a white button-up shirt and dark dress slacks. His dark hair and tan stood out in stark contrast to the white shirt. I leaned against the door frame, and his eyes swept over me with an appreciative grin. Stepping forward, he braced a hand on the frame and kissed me, trailing his free hand down my open neckline.

I pulled away from the kiss and blushed, flicking my eyes inside at my roommates. He chuckled and put his mouth to my ear. "You know people are going to see a lot more than that tonight." My cheeks burning, I waved to my roommates and pushed him out, toward the limo idling at the curb.

"Good night, gentlemen," Brad called out. Alex and Zach giggled in response, and I shut the door, taking Brad's outstretched hand. We walked to the car, his hand exploring my bare back and short dress along the way, and I swatted his hand as we arrived at the car. Brad opened the door and I ducked inside.

"YOU SHOULD MOVE." I turned to look at him, confused. We were moving, the limo driving north through town.

"What? Why?"

"Your roommates. Weed? You don't need to get caught up in that."

"I'm not gonna 'get caught up' in anything."

"If the cops bust your house, you are just as likely to be arrested as they are." I glowered at him, avoiding his reasoning by opening my clutch and pulling out lipstick.

"I don't think cops 'bust' houses over weed. Besides, I like my house."

"Really? What's your favorite part? The mildew in the shower or the worn-out carpet?"

"It's the finicky hot water pressure I adore, thank you very much."

I stuck out my tongue at him, uncapping the lipstick and carefully applying it.

He laughed, grabbing my knee and squeezing it gently. "We have a stop to make on the way."

"What kind of stop?"

"Hair and makeup." His cell rang and he straightened his legs, reaching in his pocket to pull it out. Glancing at the screen, he silenced the phone and put it back in his pocket.

"Hair and makeup? I already did all that."

He glanced at my worried face with a reassuring smile. "And you look absolutely gorgeous. This is more for the mask aspect of the party. Jessica and Marco are masters of creative disguises. As much as I hate costumes, it does add to the ambience of the party, as well as relax a lot of inhibitions."

I gripped my purse and thought of the peephole mask I had tucked inside. Not the sexiest thing in the world, it was the only thing I had that would be considered a mask. I was grateful for the opportunity to choose a different one. "I'd think you would have a closet full of swinger costumes. You know, velvet capes, top hats, canes?"

He fought a smile and leaned over, brushing my lips with his, the brief contact not nearly enough for me. "I prefer a more discreet approach. And that is pimp attire, not swinger."

"Oh, that's right. Swingers wear suspenders and fedoras, right?" My smart response earned me another silencing kiss, and I grinned against his mouth, stealing an opportunity to grip his hair and deepen the kiss.

"So." I tilted my head and looked at him. "You'll be fine with us just popping into this party, watching some stuff and then leaving?"

He turned in his seat, my eyes finding mine and holding them hostage. "Of course. Are you getting cold feet?"

I frowned. "Not cold feet—I'm just a little nervous."

"Okay. That's normal. What are you nervous about?"

I shrugged. "Just the fact that it's an organized sex party. I get uncomfortable at being approached. I don't like the pressure of turning someone down. I think that's what stresses me out."

"First of all, all of Beverly's parties have one cardinal rule. Women do the instigating. Men can't approach you, and you will make any decisions about what will occur. Think of it as a feminist's wet dream."

I turned that over in my head, leaning against him and trying to figure out what I would want if it was all going to be up to me.

He frowned, running a hand down my hair and rubbing my neck gently. "I don't want you to be stressed. This party, this lifestyle, is about enhancing our sex life—not causing it or you discomfort."

"But if I'm not okay with the swinging, then we break up."

"I don't expect you to be okay with everything from the get-go. You can ease into this. We are taking the fast route, and we don't need to do that. I just didn't want you to miss out on this party and have to wait three months for the next one." He frowned at me. "We don't need to go. I have no issue with saying 'screw the party' and going home."

I shook my head. "I'm not going to know if I'm okay with it until I'm there. I want to go, but I want you to know that I'm not going to want to do anything that I don't feel comfortable with."

He stifled a laugh and quickly brought my hand to his mouth, kissing it quickly. "I have no interest in scaring you away. If you want to leave, we'll leave. If you want to stay, we'll stay. Tonight, you are the boss."

My eyes flashed at his in the darkness. "Hmmmm.... I like that."

He laughed. "I'm sure you do."

I watched his face as he ran his lips over my hand, squeezing it briefly before dropping it to his lap. "Will this work out?" I asked suddenly, shifting in my seat to face him fully. "You and me, exclusive?"

"At this party?"

"No—in normal life. Us having an exclusive relationship, with you being so…" I grimaced, trying to find the right word. "Slutty," I finally managed.

He smiled, his gaze traveling over my face, the depths of his soul staring out through those dark, confident eyes. "This isn't my first relationship, Julia. I know you think I will whip my cock out at the first woman who breathes my way, but I assure you—I can handle commitment."

"As long as you have additional stimulation. Beyond me."

"Well, there is that, yes. But your involvement in the activity is what makes it so stimulating."

I snorted at that. "Bullshit."

He cocked his head at me. "The other night, if I hadn't been involved in that threesome, would you have enjoyed it?"

I frowned. "If you hadn't been there, I never would have had sex with him."

"Ignore that logic for a moment and envision the situation as two different possibilities. One, just you, me and him. Then imagine the situation with you, him and another guy. Would the experience have been the same?"

I leaned back against the seat, closing my eyes and envisioning the scenarios. When I removed Brad from the equation—my trust in him, his sexual presence that made every touch electrifying, his ability to somehow know exactly how much I could take, how far to push my boundaries in order to give me the most mind-shattering experience that I was willing, at that point in time, to experience. I finally sighed and opened my eyes, meeting his. "No. It wouldn't have been the same."

He grinned, pulling me in one quick motion onto his lap. "And you make things different for me. You don't know it, but you captured me quickly, with your faux innocence, the nerdy-glasses, pencil-skirt look that you were trying to pull off. When I saw you later, dressed to the hilt, pure sex from your stilettos to your hair, I didn't believe it. Saw you as playing a part. But—" he breathed, reaching out and trailing a finger over my open lips "—you *are* pure sex. When you are in your element, which is typically when you are stuffed full of cock, I've never seen a more sexually perfect being in my life." His mouth twitched, and he pulled me to him for a soft, gentle kiss. "I fell for the feisty, smart-ass Julia that calls me on my shit. But I'm owned by the vixen that you become behind closed doors." My response was lost in his next kiss, a heady, desperate kiss that consumed both of us, hands fisting in hair, an erotic fusion between two captive souls. I was glad that he took my response, because I didn't have a coherent thought in my head.

Seven

Our kiss was interrupted by the limo's slow turn into a short driveway, the suited chauffer waiting an appropriate amount of time before opening our door. The makeup stop turned out to be a small bungalow in an established neighborhood, a black Porsche Boxter in the driveway. Lights were on in the house, and Brad rang the doorbell, holding my hand on the front porch.

"Be patient with Jessica," he whispered. "She gets a little excited if given too much free rein."

I laughed. "Patient? Every woman wants free rein with a makeup professional. I'll just try not to have too much fun."

"*Hola!* I'm Marco!" A small muscular man in skintight black jeans, a white tank top and a hot-pink boa opened the door with a dramatic flourish. Behind him, I could see a curvy brunette, tattoos covering her arms and neck, and she waved enthusiastically. They moved aside for our entrance and between the hugs, handshakes and introductions, I discovered that the two were roommates, and seemed to be familiar with Brad; he headed past them to the living room.

Talking a mile a minute, Jessica pulled me into the dining room, where she had a long table covered with every makeup, hair care and skin product known to man. I saw what looked like the entire MAC lineup, as well as half of a Sally's Beauty Supply store. I was shocked the table didn't cave in under the weight of it all.

Brad collapsed into the living room couch, crossing his ankles and settling in. He picked up a remote and starting flipping through the channels, Marco scurrying around him, fluffing pillows and chatting him up excitedly. I saw a brief look of pain cross his face, and then I was gently pushed into a chair by Jessica. She turned on a mirrored spotlight, illuminating my face, examined it closely, then sat back with a satisfied smile.

"What look do you want to go for tonight?"

I shrugged. "I don't know. I've never been to a party like this before. Won't the mask hide a lot of the makeup?"

She clapped her hands and smiled at me excitedly, and turned and grabbed a thick binder from a nearby stool. "Tonight, the *mask* is going to be the makeup. Let me show you some examples. Then you can pick out what you like."

Fifteen minutes later, I was ready to move in with Jessica and Marco. She was a freak of makeup nature, able to create distinct and beautiful masterpieces on ordinary faces. I did my best, but was torn between six different looks in her binder. I couldn't decide—they were all so beautiful and different— but finally chose the one that I thought would camouflage my looks the most.

Marco had given up on Brad, and stood at a clothing rack that was pushed against a back wall. He was going through clothes, occasionally pouncing on an item and bringing it to Brad. Brad so far had rejected all of Marco's suggestions, which was causing increased agitation to the small man. "How can you like none of these?" he complained. "I am showing you some beautiful pieces!"

Brad called to me from the living room. "He wants me to wear a jeweled thong, Julia! Talk some sense into the man."

I frowned at Marco and shook my head, causing Jessica to swear at me. I went back to being still and tried to behave while she continued to apply eyeliner.

"I'll just wear the same thing as last time," Brad called to Marco.

"There is something wrong with a man as beautiful as you hiding your face. If you're going to go that route, then at least let Jessica bejewel you."

"Real men don't get bejeweled," Brad said, turning up the volume.

FIFTY MINUTES LATER, with air kisses and monetary gratitude expressed, we left the small bungalow different people than had arrived. If I can say so myself, I looked amazing. Not Julia anymore, I was now a mysterious, exotic siren. I still wore the red dress and strappy silver stilettos that I had been picked up in, but everything else had changed. Jessica had added extensions, thickening and lengthening my dark brown tresses. On my face, she had created an eye mask, with shadows, liners and a faux lace pattern. She added fake lashes and had painted my lips movie-star red that she promised would stay on "no matter what I did with my mouth." I planned on testing out that theory.

Brad looked, well, exactly the same. Gorgeous, sexy and feral, and the closer we came to the party, the more intense his eyes became. He was aroused, I realized. He had taken only one item from Carlos, a black executioner's hood. I was both scared and excited to see what it would look like on.

We got in the car and I waited till the driver shut the door before I turned to him. "I—"

His mouth was on me before I got the second word out. He cupped my chin in his hand and took my mouth with his. He pulled hard on my neck and I leaned forward, his other hand grabbing to pull me onto his lap. I straddled him, grinding against his crotch while we kissed. His hands gripped my ass and then traveled in between my legs, and he pulled away from my mouth with a sexy scowl when he felt my panties.

"What's this?" he murmured, sliding a finger underneath my thong and dipping inside me, causing my eyes to close and my breath to hitch.

"I think they're called panties," I whispered, pushing against his hand, wanting more than his finger inside of me.

"You are already wet…" he breathed in wonder, sliding a second finger in with the first, stretching my pussy tight around his digits and moving them together in wonderful unison.

I groaned and ground against him, and he slowly withdrew his fingers, sliding his wet fingers over my clit and then away, and my eyes popped open, missing the pleasure. I pouted down at him.

"I want to keep you hot for the party," he said gruffly. He looked up at me, smiling in the darkness. "You look so different."

I tilted my head, grinning. "Good different?"

"I like the normal you better. This is good, though, makes me feel like I'm with a strange woman."

I bit my lip and looked at him deviously. "Strange women can be bad."

"I like bad," he whispered, and I felt his fingers brush my sensitive skin, once again tugging at the lace of my thong.

Eight

The limo came to a stop at a large metal gate, monitored by a valet with a clipboard. After he'd conferred with our driver, the gates opened and we moved forward. Brad pulled on his hood, and I shivered at the transformation the simple black fabric created. All I could see was his eyes, and I hated not seeing his mouth. He expressed so much with it, from the tightening of his jaw to the curve of his grin, and I felt lost without that road map. I reached up the neck of the hood and felt his lips, curved, and I smiled back at him. He pushed my hand down and I looked out the window, fascinated by the upcoming events.

The driveway was curved cobblestone and lined with lit palm trees. Pieces of the house were visible, but it wasn't until the limo came to a stop that we saw the full home. It was a huge, sprawling, Mediterranean-style estate, with an ivy-walled courtyard and a modern fountain in front. Two more men with clipboards straddled the entrance to the courtyard, though I think they were there more for effect than purpose. Brad gave them a name, "Ano," and we were waved through.

"Ano?" I whispered, gripping his huge biceps tightly and trying not to trip on my heels.

"It's an alias. One I use for swinging. You should think of a name to use tonight."

I wrinkled my forehead, trying to think of a name that sounded sexy, but still realistic. There are so many pronounced differences between men and women. If I had attended this party with a woman, she would have given me ample time to prepare for something as important as my false identity. *I should have asked more questions.* A dozen names flitted through my mind, but they all sounded wrong. I finally discarded the task, figuring I'd have time to pick an alias later.

The courtyard was gently lit by the flames of two white stone fireplaces, one on either side. We walked through the dramatic area, going up a few steps and entering the home through two large ornate doors. The party was apparent as soon as we stepped inside.

Brad had mentioned fifteen or twenty couples, but there had to be at least fifty people in this room alone. It was a wide room, with huge columns and towering ceilings, colorful silks and lace tented above us, creating a ceiling of passion. The room had two dark leather sectionals, facing each other, with big gold and cream pillows scattered on them. A food bar was on the left side of the room, a wet bar on the right. Beautiful people were everywhere, wearing everything. Masks ranged from small black cat eyes to huge feathered ensembles. Women wore everything from sheer dresses and lingerie to Oscar-worthy evening gowns. The common denominators seemed to be rich and beautiful. Huge diamonds glittered from ears and fingers, and the normal factors of life—wrinkles, cellulite, imperfect features—seemed to have left these women alone. I wasn't sure if it was the low lights or the masks, but everyone looked beautiful here. At close examination, there were wide hips, small breasts, and big noses, but those imperfections turned to perfect individuality beneath the overriding wave of sexuality and confidence displayed.

We seemed to have arrived at the precipice between friendly mingling and hot sex. As I watched, a woman pulled two men to a sectional and knelt between them. I quickly adverted my eyes and heard Brad chuckle next to me. "You don't have to look away. They want to be watched. Otherwise they wouldn't be here." He grabbed my ass, sliding his hand up my dress and squeezing my bare skin. "You look stunning."

I smiled at him, glad for the reassurance. He reached for my hand, and we entered the crowd. Brushing through the crush of bodies, we approached the bar, manned by a shirtless Adonis wearing only a bow tie and dress pants. He smiled appreciatively at me and nodded to Brad.

Brad asked for two glasses of champagne and we walked out the French doors to the pool, a massive blue-lit expanse of carnal opportunities. There was a couple already inside, naked bodies latched together in the lit water. I blushed and we walked to a lounge set and sat, looking back at the house and the crowd inside. More people were starting to spill outside, and soon we would have company. But for now it was quiet, except for the moans of the couple in the pool.

Brad pulled off his cloth hood, his hair mussed and sticking up, looking adorably hot. He took a swig of champagne and ran his hand down my bare back.

"You okay with this?" he asked quietly.

"Yeah." I flashed him a smile. The party felt refined, classy with a strong undercurrent of sex. "What's the deal with the party, the hosts?"

"The hosts." He smiled. "Dan and Beverly. I represented Beverly a few years ago in a divorce. We fucked a few times during the process. When she married Dan she reached back out to me. Figured this would be up my alley. They host a few parties a year and are very selective about their invitation list. That's what I like."

"Do they personally know all of the guests?"

"I'm not sure. They probably met most of them through AFF."

"What's that?"

"It's a social networking site. Think Facebook for Swingers."

"Are you on it?"

"Not right now. I go through phases, depending on what's going on in my life, who I'm dating."

"Everyone here is so attractive. I kind of expected..."

He laughed at the uncomfortable expression on my face. "There is an application process involved to be invited to events such as this. Photos are one requirement."

I tilted my head, raising my eyebrows questioningly.

He smiled, running his hand through his mussed hair. "I didn't send any photos of you, not that I have any. They know my taste, and trust that I wouldn't bring an unacceptable guest."

Unacceptable? I shifted uncomfortably, playing with the hem of my dress. "It seems like a lot of money in there."

"Dan and Beverly are kind of snobs in that respect. Money also weeds out a lot of the crazies."

"Good. I don't let crazies fuck me."

He laughed and pulled me to him, kissing me deeply. "Let's go back in. If you see something you want to do, just let me know. This will be a good test for us."

"In what way?"

He stood, towering over me, and flashed a grin, pulling his hood back on. "Because I plan on enjoying the party also."

Nine

We walked back into the house, my stomach in nervous knots.
I was glad for the disguise, for the layer of protection it gave
me. Brad held my hand firmly, guiding me as we moved
through the noisy crowd, chatter, laughter and murmurs surrounding us. There were a few long glances, a few friendly
smiles, but no one approached us or said anything as we passed,
and I was grateful for that. I needed some time to adjust and
figure out what was going on. We left the packed foyer and
walked down a few steps into a darkened great room. The
couches were set at different angles, some facing the windows, some open to the center. A round stage had been set
up in the middle of the room, a chrome stripper pole coming out of the middle and stretching all the way to the top of
the vaulted ceilings. Two women, both nude, danced on the
stage, twirling around the pole and caressing each other. This
room had a definite club atmosphere, laser lights creating a
harmony of colors on the ceiling and techno music pumping
from speakers. A woman untangled herself from a sea of bodies on a couch and stood, walking over to us. She had fire-

engine-red hair and wore a black leather mask and matching minidress. I took a discreet peek at her feet and tried not to swoon. Black spiked Louboutins. She gave me a big smile and wrapped Brad in a tight embrace, brushing her hand lightly over his package in the process.

"I'd know this hunk of meat anywhere, even with that creepy hood," she cooed. Reaching out a hand to me, she gave me a blatant once-over, causing a blush to spread over my face. "I'm Beverly Franklin," she said, with no trace of snobbery. "I *must* say, you are utterly gorgeous. Not that I'd expect Brad to show up with anything else," she added with a grin, squeezing his big arm. "Brad, you go sit down, I'm going to give your friend the grand tour."

I had a brief recollection of a strip club tour, one that had conveniently pulled me away from Brad a few weeks earlier. My eyes flickered around the room, at the numerous sexual possibilities in front of him. I felt momentary panic at the thought of being alone, away from him, and him away from me. "I, um…" I faltered, looking to Brad for rescue.

"Stick to her, Bev," he said, stepping backward, his face impossible to read behind the black cloth. "She's new. Remember that." He nodded at me and lifted his glass, and I frowned at him, swearing that I could see his shoulders shaking in a laugh. I turned to Beverly and smiled tentatively, downing the rest of my champagne with a strong gulp.

BEVERLY, THOUGH IN her forties, had an ass like a supermodel's, and the leather clung to her perfect body as if it had been painted on. She was bubbly and friendly, not the stoic and snobby host I was expecting. She wrapped her arm in mine and navigated us out of the laser-filled great room.

"I didn't catch your name, sweetie."

I tensed, my thoughts bumping around in my head until I grasped a hold of a name and blurted it out. "It's Jessica." The tattooed makeup artist had unknowingly rescued me.

"Jessica, Brad said you were new. Is this your first party?"

"Yes. At least, of this sort."

She laughed, a musical giggle that floated away as we walked through the kitchen, a granite-filled masterpiece, full of chefs and shirtless men who were filling hors d'oeuvre platters. Off the kitchen was a hall, and she pulled me down it, the lighting discreet and dim.

"This is what I call the sex hall—there are four bedrooms off it, and if you want to play privately, or with other couples, these rooms are available." We peeked in the first room and I froze.

A man knelt, naked and beautiful, his back a chorus of tanned muscles, candles throughout the room creating flickering shadows on his skin. In front of him stood another man, black and naked, a dark leather mask, similar to Beverly's, obscuring his face. The black man was huge, Brad's size, but not as cut or defined as Brad. His cock was long, dark and *in* the kneeling man's mouth. A woman, stunning, dressed in an azure-blue floor-length evening gown and a huge feathered mask, stood on the other side of them. Her elegant attire was contrasted by a leather riding crop, gripped tightly in one hand. As I watched she stepped forward and slapped the kneeling man, hard along the buttocks. Her voice, calm, controlled and authoritative, rang out in the quiet room.

"Suck it harder. All of it."

The man obliged, and the black man groaned, his legs tightening. I saw a cock twitch in the darkness and realized the white man was hard. *Very* hard.

I felt Beverly tugging on me, and I blinked, stepping back,

but not before my eyes locked with the woman in the room. She smiled, slowly and securely at me, and then I heard her speak to the men. "Now. Get up, both of you, on the bed. I want you to use those hard cocks on me."

I tried to stifle a gasp, and followed Beverly, her hand tugging, pulling me to the next room. For a reason I couldn't explain, I felt my panties sticking to me, wetness pooling.

Ten

Brad leaned against the wall, obscured by the shadows, invisible. He watched the two women walk away, watched Julia, her face as she looked in one of the bedrooms with Beverly. He saw her expression change and wondered what she saw. Maybe it had been a mistake bringing her here. Maybe she wasn't ready.

Movement in his peripheral vision caused him to turn and he watched as a girl entered the room. Alone, wearing white, her face covered with a veil. Even in the dim light he could see through the sheer fabric of her dress, erect nipples and bare skin underneath, nothing else. She was nervous, tentative. She gripped a glass of white wine tightly in her hand and looked around the room. He stood upright and moved out of the shadows, his steps sure and confident.

"I'M SORRY, WHAT did you ask?" I had missed whatever Beverly had said, my mind still filled with images from the first room.

"I was saying that we decorated the four bedrooms in color themes—kind of to fit different fetishes. Me, myself, I just like straight sex with different men. I don't travel too far outside that box. But I like watching all sorts of things. That room back there was the red room."

I nodded, vaguely remembering that the room had a red theme—dark red walls, cream carpet, red lamps and bed coverings. In another world it might be considered designer disaster, but in this setting, it fit the mood of excess.

"This next room is the blue room. I find more mellow couples tend to use this area," she whispered, pushing the door open farther. We peered in.

Now, aware of the color schemes, I noticed the room itself first. It sported robin's-egg pale blue walls, white furnishings, and large abstract art on the walls. There was discreet uplighting, but the room was mostly lit by candles. Two couples occupied this room, one on the bed and one on the floor, cushioned by large pillows. Both couples seemed to be caressing and kissing each other, hands gently moving everywhere. We moved on, me needing less encouragement this time.

The black room was next. "Whips and chains?" I asked, reading into the color choice.

"Not here," she laughed. "S and M is a whole other culture, one we don't participate in. Not because we don't agree with it. It just has its own groups and parties. What you saw in the first room—that's as dominant as it gets here. The black room is mostly for GB stuff. It's the largest guest bedroom we have."

I didn't have a chance to ask what GB stood for, and didn't need to, once we peered in. Six men surrounded one girl. She was voluptuous, with large natural breasts, a soft but slim stomach and wide hips. She was bent over, on a large bed, two men at her feet, one in her pussy, another in her ass. She screamed, loud and in pleasure, and they both moved in unison, fucking her deeply, then pulling slowly out. She supported her body with one hand, and used the other to jack off a skinny man who knelt, naked, before her. The other men touched her, squeezing her breasts, smacking her ass or waiting impatiently for a chance at her mouth. Everywhere I looked in the room, there was movement, skin-on-skin, mouth-on-skin, and sounds filled the space. Slaps, moans, muttered phrases.

I watched, transfixed, as the woman came, long and loudly, her body shaking with the exertion and clear juice squirting from her pussy. The man who had been fucking her, a thin man with a cock like a fucking Clydesdale's, swore in amazement at her gushing pussy and pulled out, using his fingers to finish her off. He wore a dark green mask, and pulled the mask up to get a better view. His handsome face was filled with desire and wonder and sex, and I felt sudden familiarity, as I realized that my emotions matched his. What was I doing? Standing here gaping! I had an image of what I must look like and turned away suddenly, ending the view of the room and my hidden fantasy.

KATE WAS RUSSIAN, in the States on a six-month visa. A visa that could be extended if her boss—and sponsor—Mr. Gunter, agreed to continue her employment and fill out the necessary paperwork. Mr. Gunter had strongly suggested that Kate accompany him tonight. Her hesitancy at his request had displeased him, and the request had turned into a demand, complete with consequences if she did not comply. So she had yielded, and now here she was.

Earlier she had stood in front of him, naked, washed thoroughly by his staff, and he had picked out this outfit, a ridiculous white mesh dress that showed every part of her, and a white veil that did nothing to disguise her young face. He had dressed her, slowly, touching her skin and groping her curves as he pulled the material over her body. He had not tried to have sex with her. Not yet. But tonight must be the night. Here, at this party, where Americans were having sex everywhere, on couches, in pools, against the wall right next to her. She saw movement in the shadows; then a hulk of a man appeared, stepping into the light.

He had impossibly broad shoulders and muscular arms that his expensive dress shirt couldn't hide. Standing, silent and sure, he looked straight at her, waiting. She took a few steps forward, tentative, wanting to see more but needing to be closer to do it. He turned slightly and was fully illuminated by the light.

He wore a black hood, simple dark loose fabric with two eyeholes cut out. She wasn't sure if it was the hood or his body, but danger radiated from this man. His eyes, the only part of his face she could see, were dark brown pools of sexual intensity, blatant arousal in them. She paused, scared of him and the sexual heat that emulated from him, even with ten feet between them. Then she felt a hand on her back.

Mr. Gunter's voice purred in her ear and she stiffened, closing her eyes briefly. Thin hands ran down the sides of her body and then moved up her front, squeezing her breasts and massaging them. She opened her eyes, looking into the eyes of the hooded stranger briefly, then looked away, ashamed, her lip trembling. She tried to be strong, tried not to cry. The hands moved up and gripped her neck, turning her face, and she felt Mr. Gunter's pursed lips on hers.

I WHIRLED, RUNNING into Beverly's big breasts, our faces almost colliding, and she took a step back with a wince. "Sorry," I whispered. "Are you okay?" The girl's squirting pussy was imprinted in my mind, and I clenched my legs together, wanting Brad here, now, instantly.

"Sure," she said slowly, looking at me intently. "Is this too weird for you? It can be a lot to take in—"

"No," I interrupted her, shaking my head and trying to smile. "I like it here. I just remembered something I wanted to ask Brad about."

She shrugged. "Okay. You don't need to see the last room. I can just tell you about it." She looped her arm through mine and leaned close, her breast touching me. "It's called the snack room, and is a lot of fun to visit during the party. It has lots of fun food you can eat off each other, or you can lie on the buffet table and have everyone nibble and lick things off you."

I smiled politely, trying to listen but not able to get my mind off the woman in ecstasy and the circle of hard, waiting cocks.

The bedroom hall led back to the crowded foyer, and as we eased through, Beverly was stopped by several people. I finally leaned to her and whispered in her ear that I would see her later. She nodded gratefully to me and started chatting up a couple by the bar. I moved quickly through the crowd, avoiding eye contact and beelining for the great room. I stopped at the entrance, my eyes adjusting to the change in lighting, trying to find Brad in the dark, pulsating, room.

I saw him, alone by the window, huge and imposing, and felt a flood of relief. He was watching a couple on the couch—a young blonde with an older man—Brad's eyes unreadable but dark. I quickly walked to him, and he slid an arm around my waist, pulling me to him.

"How was the tour?"

"Good. Interesting."

"Good. Interesting," he mocked, his hand trailing down my hip, teasing the skin at the bottom of my dress.

"Stop that," I muttered, trying not to lean into his touch. "Yes, it was interesting. Beverly is very sweet." A breath caught in my throat as his hand traveled higher, pushing up my hem. His attention was focused on me, thoughts of everything else disappearing, and the intensity was unnerving. "Why don't we find a private place and—"

He grabbed me, shoving me hard against the wall, yanking my dress up till my lace panties were exposed, and spread my legs expertly with his knees. I sputtered a protest, but all that came out were whispered curses, my desire to not draw attention to us overriding my need to get him to keep his fucking hands to himself.

"Why don't we skip the private place?" he said, his voice strong in my ear.

He slid two fingers in me, his eyes flickering at my soaked wetness, his fingers moving in and out, his thumb gently making delicious circles around my clit, the sheer fabric increasing the pleasure. I protested, quietly but fervently, but my words dropped off and my legs weakened. Sagging, I let my head drop back as I entered an unworldly plane of pleasure and arousal. He pulled on my dress, sliding the red fabric off my shoulders, and I felt the silky material fall away from my skin, leaving my breasts exposed, my nipples puckering in the open air. I looked around desperately, worried about who might see. My eyes met with one man, then two, who watched with aroused interest before my head dropped back and I felt an orgasm hovering.

Brad did incredible things, his fingers and thumb making my clit stand hard and juices ooze from between my shaking legs. I gasped, gripping his shoulder and looking gape-mouthed into his smoldering eyes. "Do you like people watching you?" His voice was authoritative, demanding, and my rebellious side tensed at the tone. I protested weakly, my words turning into unintelligible moans, his words ringing true in my slutty core. "Do you?" His voice was now a rough whisper, and I moaned, opening my eyes for a moment, long enough to see another face, another pair of eyes on me. A man walked by slowly, close enough to hear, and I let out a strangled cry despite myself.

His fingers disappeared for a moment; then I heard a ripping sound as my panties became victim to his strength. I sagged against the wall, waves of pleasure growing in time to the vibrating bass, the slow circle resuming around my clit, the fingers sliding back inside my soaking pussy.

"God, you are wet," he growled in my ear, and I could hear the wetness, the slick sound of his actions. "Almost as wet as I'm going to make that sweet little blonde on the couch." Opening my eyes wide, I saw carnal activity all around and tried wildly to focus, to see who he was talking about. Perverse snapshots of different possibilities battered my mind. *Brad with me, Brad's hands, cock, mouth on someone else, her pleasure, my possession.* My mind desperately tried to grasp on any form of sanity, but the sexual need, the slutty side of me that was in full unadulterated glory, took the thoughts and savored them, the competitive side of me feasting on the challenge. Then I saw her, the young blonde on the couch, her body lying back, perfect cream tits exposed. The sight, the thought, the jealous arousal sent me over the edge, and an explosion of pleasure erupted in my core, my screams bursting out, unable to control myself.

My orgasm was long, hard and insanely good—visions filling my head, my eyes opening intermittently, seeing faces, hearing words, knowing that a room was watching—the knowledge stretching out the orgasm, and I was close to sobbing when it ended, my body collapsed against him, legs useless.

I sagged in his arms, my thighs wet, body quaking. I had just come, in front of this whole room, men staring, my breasts hanging out, my panties ripped and tossed on the floor. I should have felt like a slut, a dirty whore. But instead I felt liberated, aroused. It was an interesting discovery, to know that I liked being dirty. I wanted to be stared at, pointed to, to have men lining up to fuck me. Inside, I felt a release of some tie, some leash undone, and I knew my descent into sexual awareness was just now starting. I wasn't sure if I could ever tie it back into orderly place.

Eleven

Kate watched the hooded man as he stood in front of the brunette beauty. She slumped against the wall in front of him, her legs shaking, small breasts heaving. Her scream had broken through Kate's mental block and caused her to look over, to see his fingers inside her, his mouth at her ear. Her face a masked vision of orgasmic pleasure.

The image caused Kate to tighten, aroused despite herself, and Mr. Gunter groaned, feeling her body twitch. His hands on her breasts, squeezing and pinching them, moved downward, and Kate winced, shutting her eyes tightly. "No," she said softly, too softly, and he laughed above her. "No!" She said it louder, pushing on his shoulder, and began to cry a bit in spite of herself, her body shaking and tears beginning the path down her face. She tightened her eyes, and willed herself to be strong.

When she heard it, loud and clear despite the noisy room, she froze, body stiff and rigid. The sound of him unzipping his pants, the rustle of clothing as he pulled out his cock. She glanced down, whimpering slightly, his thin, stubby dick already hard, sticking out like a dagger from his body. He was leaning over, his hands at her opening, preparing it for his bareness, and then he was gone. She blinked her tear-filled eyes, and saw the hooded man.

He had Mr. Gunter by the throat and was pressing him back, against a column at the entrance to the room. He whispered something in Mr. Gunter's ear, something that made the old man's eyes go wide in response. Kate sat up, pulling the sheer dress quickly down and standing, the room spinning briefly from the sudden movement. She sat, willing the room to still and searching for the strength to be able to go over, stop him, fix this. Whatever the big man was doing, he had to stop, had to leave Mr. Gunter alone. She couldn't go back to Russia. Couldn't go back to her family.

The brunette, beautiful, her eyes still glazed in euphoric pleasure, her skin flushed, sat down next to her, taking her hand. "I tried to stop him," she whispered. "When he saw your face..." There was a loud crack and they both looked up. The big man stood over Mr. Gunter, his hand bloody, Mr. Gunter limp on the floor. A redheaded lady appeared and spoke urgently with the hooded man. The brunette put her arm around Kate and gripped her tightly. "Don't worry," she whispered.

They carried Mr. Gunter away. Kate saw him move, in their arms, and wondered what was going to happen now. The big man appeared in front of her, his eyes dark, and Kate felt a curl below her stomach, a tightening in her body. He bent, a question in his eyes, and when she nodded, he picked her up, cradling her small body against his. He carried her through the party and out the back doors.

BRAD CARRIED THE blonde, her head curled into his chest, her hand gripping his large biceps. She was Russian, from

the sound of her accent. He took her outside, down the side
of the pool, and headed to a pool house at the end. I opened
the door for him, and we walked inside miniature opulence.
The pool house was a baby version of the mansion, identical
in style and appointments. There were two bedrooms, and he
laid her on the bed in the smaller room. I hung back, not sure
what was going to happen next.

Brad's earlier words, his muttered threat to pleasure the
Russian, now, in the elegant light of the bedroom, seemed
as insane as the bloodied man that they had carried away. So
much had changed in that one instant. He had been standing
before me, my eyes struggling to focus, legs trying to stand.
Then a sound had come from behind us, a cry. Out of place,
asexual in tone. Brad had frozen, his eyes meeting mine, face
hardening below his hood, a coldness coming over his entire
being. Who he became, in that instance, was almost scary. It
was a hardened Brad, the light gone from his eyes, his hands
turning unintentionally rough. He had lifted me, helping me
find my balance, ensuring that I could stand on my own. Then
he had turned, taking in the scene in one glance, as did I. Then
he was gone, a blur of movement, violence and protection.

What I had envisioned during the throes of my orgasm,
the images of Brad and the Russian that had taken the fire of
my arousal and doused it with gasoline, wasn't this. Wasn't
her lying damaged on the bed, him as her protector. I had
actually wanted him to be with her, wanted to see how I felt
when his hands touched her skin, when his lips brushed hers,
the feeling of possessiveness when I watched his cock claim
her tight body. I had, as ridiculous as it sounds, embraced the
opportunity to watch him, to feel that competitive drive as
it warped my arousal into new levels. But this, his concern,
her vulnerability, was too personal, and I felt the evil ten-

drils of jealousy snake into my mind. He could fuck her, but he couldn't care. My psyche wouldn't allow that, despite the compassion I felt for her.

Lying back on the bed, she stared up at him, confused and wary. He started to speak, his words muffled, then reached up and pulled off the mask.

KATE INHALED INVOLUNTARILY. The black fabric pulled away to reveal an Italian god. He had olive skin and a thick head of black hair. Strong, handsome features, he would have been too beautiful if it weren't for the overwhelming strength of his features. The man smelled intoxicating, and reeked of masculinity and sex. He spoke, his voice deep and gruff.

"Beverly said you can stay here. Get some rest. In the morning she will help, find you a new place to stay. It will be okay. Are you Russian?" His voice had gentled but was still dangerous to her, to any clear thoughts in her head.

She nodded. "My visa is almost expired." Her voice sounded weak, broken, and she hated her stilted English.

He nodded. "That's fine. Don't worry." He brushed his hands lightly, almost accidentally, over her as he pulled a blanket over her body. She pushed herself up, grabbing his shoulder, a question in her eyes, and he shook his head.

"I'm not here for that. I was just trying to help." He pushed her gently down, his fingers caressing her almost imperceptibly and she inhaled, his touch sending desire in hot streaks throughout her body. He turned, his strong silhouette filling the doorway, and closed the door gently, sending the room into darkness. She lay back and stared at the ceiling, her thoughts jumbled and fighting for attention.

Twelve

We spoke in hushed tones, in the second bedroom of the pool house. Beverly had joined us, hanging up her cell as she entered the room. I paced, worried. "Is that man okay? Did you really need to punch him? Are the police being called?" I asked rapidly.

He leaned back against a dresser, his arms crossed, looking impossibly sexy despite his bloody knuckles. "Julia, everything is fine. That scumbag will be fine, and will not press charges." His wry tone calmed me down somewhat, but my nerves were still on edge. "Beverly, can you assist her in the morning? Get her clothes and breakfast, give her a ride?"

Beverly straightened, fixing Brad with a glare. "I'm not tossing her out like a lost puppy. She can stay her indefinitely. The guesthouse is available. I can always use someone to help out around the house."

"If you need my help..."

Beverly waved off Brad's offer. "Stop that, Brad. You're a guest! I never should have allowed him to come with her. The invitation was a favor to my husband, and we didn't know who he was bringing. This is my fault, and I'll fix it." She covered her mouth with a manicured hand, thinking, and then walked over to us, kissing me briefly on the cheek and squeezing my arm. "I'll let you two enjoy the rest of the party. Brad, I expect a bill for your security services." She winked at him and left the room, closing the door behind her.

I walked over to him and he took me into his arms, holding me tightly, and I relaxed against his chest. I wondered if he was still in the mood. A noise caused me to turn and I rotated in his arms, still pressed against his body.

The Russian stood, now naked, in the doorway. Her tight body and firm tits were goose-bumped in the cool room. Her eyes were pools of dark want and she stood, unsure, nervous in cheap heels. "I need you," she said clearly, only a slight accent in her voice, her eyes locked with Brad's. "Please." I felt his thickness harden against my body and I stepped aside, watched him walk forward and stop in front of her. *Guess that answers my question.*

Brad looked down at the girl, his eyes sweeping over her naked body before coming to rest on her face. Her lips were full and pink, her eyes dark and longing. She licked her lips, her tongue lingering before disappearing in her mouth. He grabbed the back of her hair gently and pulled, tilting her head back so that she looked into his face.

"Why?" he whispered.

She frowned, confused. Her lips moved without speaking for a moment, and just a small gasp of air escaped her mouth. He loosened his grip on her, and she relaxed slightly, then spoke.

"Why what?" The accent was still there, her voice young and sweet.

"Why do you need me?"

"I don't know. I just, watching you, with her in the other room..." Her eyes darted to me, then returned to his face, her expression searching him to understand. I understood. I knew the effect that Brad had on me, how I yearned for his touch, for the release he could give me. But I also knew what Brad was asking, what he was worried about.

"You don't owe me anything," he said, his hand releasing her hair and traveling down, trailing on her skin until he broke contact, almost brushing her nipples. She sagged a little, exhaling softly, staring into his eyes.

"This isn't for what you did. I wanted you earlier, thought of you then. Please," she begged, her small hands reaching up and unbuttoning his top button. "Please," she whispered again, moving down to the next button, her hands exploring his strong shoulders and sweeping under his shirt.

Yes. This was what I had wanted. I understood his concern, his desire to not take advantage of her vulnerable position. But I wanted my Brad back, I wanted the sex god who had taken my innocence and turned me into this deviant slut. I saw the need she had and my pussy panted for him to fill it, to be the man who I was falling uncontrollably for.

I took control, making the decision for him, closing the door and locking it, the loud click causing him to look up and meet my eyes. Staring at him, I tugged on one strap and then the other of my red dress, sliding it down my hips until it dropped to the floor, nothing but me underneath. Stepping over to a plush chair set in the corner of the room, I sat, facing the bed. Spreading my legs, I ran my hands over my inner thighs, squeezing, then gently teasing my already wet slit. I raised my chin and stared defiantly into his eyes. *I know you are in there, baby.*

He looked at me darkly, his eyes following the motion of

my fingers, then studying my eyes, reading them, my confident stare meeting his. A slow, sure smile spread over his features. He shook his head, looking upward as if to heaven, then down at the petite blonde still grasping his shirt.

He walked her around to the far side of the bed, laying her backward onto it, her bare skin creamy white against the bloodred duvet. He ran his hand down the center of her body, her skin quivering from his touch, and she gasped as his fingers reached the place where her legs met. My gaze felt physically glued to the scene, and I blinked, the intensity of my stare drying out my eyes. I looked inside myself, tried to read the swirl of emotions that filled my core. Had I been right? Was this what I wanted? Jealousy was there, a hint of it, wandering outside the peripheral of my mind, trying to decide if she wanted to join in on this party. But a stronger emotion, lust, was first and foremost. It was like watching a disaster, and not being able to turn away. You know you shouldn't look, but you ache for it so badly. *Yes.* I wanted to watch. A perverse, competitive part of me wanted to see him in action, to watch, and then join in the passion. Brad lifted his hand from her body and spoke, his words quiet, commanding. "How many men have you been with?"

She stiffened, tried to speak, then licked her lips, and words came out. "I never been with a man."

Uh-oh. This might be a problem. My dreams of a hot and heavy sex fest faded slightly. Brad's eyes darkened at her response, and he looked over at me, meeting my eyes, his face unreadable. *Don't stop, baby,* I begged with my eyes, taking my fingers and pushing them inside me, my breath increasing in time with the thrusts of my fingers. *Please. Just give her something.*

He reached forward again, running his hand from her

knees, up her inner thigh, past her apex, over her stomach, and brushed it lightly over her breasts, her nipples standing at attention under his strong hands. He exhaled deeply, placing a hand over each breast and squeezing them, watching them swell under the pressure. She gasped, arching her back a bit, and a sound close to a whimper came out. He straightened, looked at me again and beckoned with his hand.

"Julia. Come here." I shook my head at him, my fingers moving slowly inside me, and he frowned, his expression unyielding. I finally stood, stepping over the crumpled pile of my dress and crossed the room until I stood next to him, and looked into his face questioningly. He turned, looking down at my nakedness, my breasts upturned to him, my heels tilting and displaying my body in a way that made beautiful all my curves. He ran his hands over me, not gentle and discovering, as he did with her, but possessive and demanding. *Yes.* He grabbed me as though he needed me, as if he were a man in the desert and I were his mirage. He pulled me tight to him and feasted on my neck and mouth, and when we finally separated, we were both panting. "On the bed," he ordered, and I kicked off my heels and climbed onto the softness, brushing against the soft skin of the girl. On my knees, moving farther onto the bed, I paused, over her body, our eyes meeting.

There is something extremely sensual about eye contact. It is often more penetrating than physical sex. I looked into the pale blueness of her, and saw only wanton need. Need that, ever since I met Brad, I was very familiar with. I smiled, and her mouth curved in response, her eyes glued on me. Then she gasped and they shut, our connection severed. I looked back and saw Brad, his fingers moving with slow and steady precision in and out of her.

I turned, straddling her body, facing him, my ass to her

head, and looked into the depths of his eyes. He was aroused, and I smiled at the dark look on his face. Possessiveness and desire lay in the lines of his face. I leaned forward, claiming his mouth with mine, and ground softly against her writhing stomach, my pussy leaving wetness on her skin. I felt small, soft hands tugging from behind me, pulling me back, and I parted from Brad, staring into his eyes as I allowed her to pull me, and lay back, atop her, my back hitting her soft breasts.

Her hands explored me, and I felt her lithe fingers running down the gully of my stomach, up the curve of my breasts, squeezing the flesh of my nipples. She was unashamedly curious, and her soft pants increased in cadence with Brad's fingers, her body arching beneath me.

"Switch places." The order was gruff, and Brad's eyes were black with need. "I want to fuck you."

I rolled off her, and he unbuckled his belt, watching us hungrily as she climbed on top of me, not lying as I did, but instead faced me, her knees on either side of my stomach. Brad groaned, his pants gone, moving close to us, and pulling me slightly so that my pussy lay flush against the edge of the bed. He ripped open a condom packet, his cock popping hard and ready, and my world went black when he entered me.

I came up for air, my senses reengaging all at once, her beautiful face above me, her breasts soft against my mouth, long hair tickling my neck. My legs, up in the air and spread, Brad inside me, then out, then in, the delicious friction of his pelvis on my clit. She moaned above me, eyes closed, and I realized he had fingers in her once again.

"God, she is so tight." Brad's voice floated down to me, and I looked up at the girl, her moans growing as she rocked her body above me. She looked down, her eyes meeting mine, then focusing on my mouth, and she hesitated, then leaned down to me. Brad's statement was so erotic, the sum of all things present too much for me, and as her breasts touched mine, her mouth so close, I came, one of those stiff, tight, every-muscle-in-my-body-is-immobile orgasms. I gasped against her mouth, tightening around his cock, and he groaned my name as he increased his speed. It was long and hard, and I lost reality for a while before coming back to earth. My senses regained, I reached up and pulled her head down to mine.

She tasted like peppermints, her tongue small and delicate in mine, so different from the possessive kiss I had shared, moments before, with Brad. Then her body stiffened and her mouth was gone, and she threw back her head, her rigid body telling me what was coming.

When she came, it was strong, her moans turning to yells, a string of Russian words that we instinctively knew the meaning of. Brad somehow managed to keep up the furious rhythm with his fingers till she collapsed, shaking and quivering, ragged breaths on top of me, and he never stopped the delicious rhythm of fucking me, his speed increasing once she rolled off my body. He reached the point of pounding, my body shaking with the force of it, his face beautiful in its sexual intensity, and I was close to coming again when she finally recovered from her climax. She propped herself up, watching me, watching my face as it clenched and I bucked, and as my hands reached out to grab on to something, anything, she was there, her hands on mine, her greedy mouth on my nipples, and I exploded again, every muscle in my body tensing as waves of pleasure rocked my core.

Thirteen

After Brad thoroughly touched, licked and coaxed the Russian through three orgasms, she fell, exhausted, on the bed, a smile plastered to her face. She reached for me, pulled me to her lips and kissed me once, gently. Her hands turned my head and I felt her breath on my ear, her accented voice speaking. "Thank you. For sharing."

I tried to think of an acceptable response, but my mind was useless, drugged with champagne and sex. I smiled, and she rolled over, reaching for the blanket and pulling it over her body. Brad gathered our clothes and pulled my arm, tugging until I was upright and naked in front of him. He looked down, staring at my nakedness, then leaned over, kissed me gently along my cleavage, scooped me up and carried me out of the room and into the other bedroom. He avoided the bed, setting me on the floor, and I looked up at him in puzzlement.

He lay on top of me, completely bare, his arms keeping him light on my body. "I haven't come yet," he whispered.

I smirked. "I know. But I'm a little tired. I was thinking about going to bed."

He nuzzled my neck, biting it gently while he pushed against me, his shaft sliding up between my legs, almost inside me, but a fraction too high. I groaned, untangling my legs from underneath his body and wrapping them tightly around him, my pussy now impossible to avoid, my need wet against him.

"Going to bed, huh?" His arrogance in my ear, my moan in response. His cock, so close, so teasing, *there* but not yet inside, lying hard against my ass instead.

"Maybe I'll stay up a little longer." I gasped as he was finally there, just the tip of him inside me, and I dug my heels into his back, panting, trying to push him farther in. He leaned down, whispered something against my mouth, then kissed me, softly, sweetly. As un-Brad-like as anything I could imagine. He tasted my mouth, trailed kisses along my jaw, sucked gently on my bottom lip. And when I finally relaxed, finally surrendered to his mouth and kiss, my legs going slack, he pushed his cock all the way in, taking my breath. I almost orgasmed right then, my need had been so great, then so fulfilled, his cock insanely perfect inside me. It took about a minute of deep slow strokes, almost painful in their perfection, and then I was done, shattering into pieces in his arms, my mouth open, frozen, as the swells washed over me. I was whimpering by the time I was done, and he held my face in his hands, looking into my eyes, his fire burning into me.

What had just happened, in the other room, that had been us, an experience we had shared, the blonde somehow an extension of our union. But now, alone in the room with each other, I was captivated, held in his arms, him filling me, his strokes quickening, our eyes locked in identical pools of lust. Then he took in a quick breath, closed his eyes and buried himself deeper, his thrusts stronger. I wrapped my arms and legs tight around him, riding his wave of orgasm, burying my face in his neck, his strong heat inside me.

He rolled over, pulling me with him, and I lay limp across his chest. I ran my hands down the clefts of his body, his skin damp with sweat, his muscles tight from exertion. His eyes were closed, and I pulled myself up until my face was above his. I ran my fingers lightly over his face, awestruck at the beauty in his strength. God, I was in trouble. In more ways than I could count. I didn't know what I would become if I stayed with him, to what further depths I would plunge inescapably into, a slave to his sexual drugs. And I didn't know what I would become if we parted, and how I would ever again find sexual satisfaction without the man.

We could just stop in, see how it works and leave. I made a mental note not to fall for that one again.

Fourteen

The limo moved quietly through the dark streets. Curled into a ball in Brad's arms, my body limp, weakened by orgasms, four-inch heels and champagne, I watched passing streetlights flickering by, softened by the car's dark tint. I closed my eyes and let my body go limp, kept warm by Brad's jacket tented over me.

A few minutes later, on the verge of sleep, I heard him talking, softly, and my ears strained to catch his words.

"I need you to take care of something." Brad spoke into his cell, looking out on the passing lights.

"What, a body?" The voice laughed roughly, loud enough that I could hear it. He shifted, and I saw his jaw tighten, face hard.

"There's a Russian girl, at 42 Hemingway Drive. In the morning, have Maria call Beverly Franklin—I'll text you her number. Tell Maria to offer assistance to Beverly, see if there is anything she can do to help out with the girl's situation. Have her mention our contacts in immigration."

There was silence for a moment. "You fucking this girl?"

"No. Not that it matters." Brad's voice changed when he was on the phone. Softer in volume, but harder in tone. The smooth cadence and cultured voice were gone, replaced with a rough brogue and steely tone. He ordered rather than asked.

"Okay, okay. I was just asking."

"If I was fucking her, I wouldn't have left her there. Just tell Maria and call me when it's taken care of." Brad ended the call, tapping his phone to his mouth and then looking down at me.

I shifted, turning onto my back and gazing up at him. "What's going to happen to the girl?"

He smiled down at me. "Don't worry. Beverly won't abandon her. She will be fine."

"Who's Maria?"

He looked away from me, out the window for a brief moment. "My sister. She is the saint of our family. She is the one person I would trust with something like this."

"Why don't you just take care of it? Doesn't someone in the firm deal with immigration?"

He shifted underneath me, looking down again, locking me into his stare. "Julia, one danger of our type of relationship is the risk of getting involved with a sexual partner. I don't ever want to worry about you falling for someone that we meet with, and vice versa. We have to be very careful to separate ourselves emotionally. What happened tonight, everything that went on, it was too much already. I shouldn't have touched her, shouldn't have done that."

I frowned up at him. "Because you're worried you have feelings for her?"

He chuckled. "No. It is very rare for me to have 'feelings' for anyone, which is what makes my relationship with you unique. But I'm not the only person involved in a threesome, and other people don't have the same cavalier opinion of sex that I do. I shouldn't have done anything with her because of everything else that went on. The fact that she was a virgin was a whole other moral issue, but in her state tonight, upset and scared, there was more of a chance for her to take that experience as more than it was. All I'm saying is that there are a billion people out there for us to meet with, to fuck. We have the means to be picky, to isolate our experiences, to only be with other people or couples who are emotionally safe. Some couples in this lifestyle like to 'hang out' with their outside partners. I don't follow that philosophy. I feel like that is a dangerous game, not to mention a colossal waste of time. I don't want to 'care about' or 'become friends' with the people in this lifestyle. That leads to nothing but problems."

I laughed at his serious expression. "Yeah, you like to skip the talk and go straight to sex."

He leaned over, pulling me up to him for a kiss. "When I can." He laid me back down and ran a hand through my hair, snagging my extensions, and I winced. "Sorry."

I swallowed, closing my eyes and trying to focus my mind on anything other than what lay beneath my head. I liked what he had said. The "getting involved" part seemed to be what my feminine jealousy had the most trouble with. I relaxed, pushing my hands underneath his legs, the warmth of his body comforting. "I didn't know you had a sister. Just one?"

"Yeah." His tone was short, and the stress in it caused my eyes to open again. I turned to him with a question in mine. "I have two brothers."

It didn't answer my question, but I sensed the land mine behind the simple statement. I reached up, capturing his hand before it went through my hair, and brought it to my mouth, kissing it softly. He ran his fingers over my lips, and then looked out the window again.

"You mentioned that you rarely have feelings for anyone. What did you mean when you said I was unique?"

He looked at me carefully, his eyes a cluster of competing emotions. "You are unique in that I am developing feelings for you."

"Developing." I pursed my lips and looked at him.

"Fine. There may be a few already developed. Little ones."

I rolled my eyes and shifted, burrowing deeper into his lap and putting his hand back on my hair, his fingers obediently resuming their movement. Little, barely developed feelings, he said. I did a spot check of my own warm and fuzzies. *Hmmph.* Well, Mama always said I developed ahead of the others.

I closed my eyes, the gentle feeling of his fingers wiping any thought from my head. I must have fallen asleep, because I woke up in Brad's arms, being carried like a small child, up the inner stairs of his home. At the top I untangled myself, standing up and stumbling to the bathroom, where I ran hot water over a washcloth and wiped down my face, turning his white terry cloth nine shades of colors. After thoroughly rinsing my face, I flipped off the light and shuffled toward the bed. His grip stopped me, and his hands brushed down my body, grabbing my dress and pulling it up and over my head. He then helped me into bed, pulling the covers up and over my naked body.

I awoke when he got in the bed, sometime later, smelling of fresh soap and toothpaste. He wrapped his arms around me and we fell asleep, our bodies spooned together, the hum of the fan the only sound in the dark room.

Fifteen

Brad's hand was on my cheek. He traced the curves of my face, gently, light, his soft touch a strange contrast to his muscular hand. I smiled, my eyes still closed, and felt his fingers move to brush my lips. I opened my mouth and sucked on a finger, opening my eyes to find his handsome face, close to mine, his eyes on mine.

I gave a contented sigh and closed my eyes again, his fingers leaving my mouth and traveling back up, smoothing my hair back and tracing their way down my shoulder and back.

"It's late." His voice, husky and dry, sounded in my ear as he leaned over and gave me a soft kiss on my neck. I pulled the blanket over my head in response, burying down deeper into the soft down. He tugged on the blanket, trying to pull it off, but I held firm, locking my fingers tight and using my body to pin the edges down.

I was no match for him, though he went easy on me to begin with. My giggles finally lost the battle for me, and when I finally came up for air he was there, playful and sexy, pushing me back on the bed and smothering my body with his hard bare chest. I kicked and screamed, pushing against his hard chest, and he leaned down, silencing me with his mouth and tongue, till my muffled screams subsided and I wrapped my arms around his neck and my legs around his waist, losing myself in the kiss.

Then, in the soft sheets and morning light, I had my seventh, eighth and ninth orgasm in twelve hours.

"I DON'T UNDERSTAND the problem," Brad said.

I sipped my lemonade and looked at Brad over the rim of the glass. We had driven three ridiculously short blocks from Brad's home, and now sat beneath teal umbrellas at a restaurant on the edge of a large park. "There isn't really a problem, per se. Not now, at least. But it's only a matter of time before someone finds out about us. I am one week from that no longer hanging over my head. If I stay on, and Broward finds out…" I couldn't finish the sentence, the idea too bleak to even consider. Brad's snort brought me out of my pity party and I looked up at him, frowning. His bemused expression only increased my exasperation. "Don't give me that look— you have no consequences if they find out about us. He already hates you."

"He *won't* find out. How long is this…extension he offered you?"

"I don't know. This next semester, I think."

"He'll still get a new intern. We all do. So, if he's keeping you on, it probably means that he'll expand your duties."

I nodded enthusiastically. "Yes, he mentioned expanding my duties, and even bringing me to *court*." I couldn't help it; reverence entered my voice at that word, despite my best efforts to contain myself.

He smiled at me. "You know I take Todd to court with me at least once a week. It's not that big a deal."

I slapped my hands over my ears. "Don't tell me that! I barely got over that fact the first time he rubbed it in my face!" I glared at him, his damn mouth twitching in response.

He leaned forward, tugging my hands away from my ears, holding them in between his. "What do you want to do?"

I leaned back, snatching my hands away from him before his damn sexuality hijacked my common sense. "I don't know. I want the additional experience and money without worrying about death by a Broward staff firing squad."

"So work for me instead." His impossible-to-read eyes stared at me, a relaxed expression on his face as he signaled for the waiter.

"Like *that* would work. We both know you wouldn't be able to keep focused on clients when my delicious self was in the same wing." I grinned at him confidently.

He laughed. "Right. That's me. Easily distracted by beautiful women."

I twisted my mouth at him. "No. *One* beautiful woman. Remember? You're committed now."

"Oh, that's right. How could I ever forget?" he asked, snaring my hand and bringing it to his mouth for a quick kiss. "So. What's your decision?"

I sighed, trying to decide whether the risk was worth the reward. The issue was, I was dealing with multiple risks and multiple rewards. Broward's wrath, a law school recommendation and my professional reputation all hovered menacingly above me. But those threats paled against the danger that had been worrying me the most lately. My heart, and the danger those inexplicable dark eyes brought to it.

MONDAY MORNING, I waited in Broward's office, watching the top of his head as he scribbled on a notepad. He paused, processing my sentence, before responding. "That's great, Julia. Good to hear." His voice did project an air of enthusiasm, an emotion I was grateful for, though my mind was still filled with trepidation about my decision to accept the job. "Human Resources will send you the paperwork, and you may have to take another drug test, but we'll get you in the system by next Monday. How many hours a week can you give me?" A loaded question, since I had no doubt he would push the limits of whatever answer I gave him.

"Twenty hours, sir. I have classes on Monday, Wednesday and Friday, so I can work on Tuesdays and Thursdays." It wasn't *my* fault that those were the days he frequented the courtroom. Okay, so maybe I had shifted my classes around a *bit*.

"Great. You'll work out the rest of this week?" He looked over his calendar, making a notation.

"Yes, sir. And in a few weeks I'll have a form from my professor that I will need you to complete." I shifted in front of his desk, the new heels I wore rubbing a blister on the back of my ankles.

"Great. Just print it out for me when you get it." He nodded at me, a quick smile crossing his features. Then his cell rang. He looked at it, the now familiar stressed look returning to his face. I gave him a quick wave and backed away from his desk, turning and stepping into the hall.

"Julia, please shut the door," he called out. I obliged, grabbing the knob and pulling it tightly closed. The instant the door clicked, I leaned down, loosening the strap of my shoes and unbuckling them, anxious to get the damn things as far away from my ankles as humanly possible. I was working on

my second stiletto when I heard Broward's voice, cold and irritable, a hateful tone that I had never heard from him, seep
out from underneath his set of double doors.

Sixteen

Brad had dialed the number unsure if Kent Broward would answer. It had been years since they had had a civil conversation.

"My wife's not here, if that's who you are looking for," Kent answered.

Talk about holding a grudge. Brad sighed heavily. "Cut the shit. We need to talk about your work."

"Unlike you, I'm in the middle of it. Bring up any complaints you have at next quarter's meeting."

Brad spun in his chair, looking out on the city view. "Not CDB work, Kent. Your *extracurricular* clients."

Kent's voice tightened. "What about them?"

"I came to you three years ago, when I first found out what you were dealing in. You told me then, in simple enough terms, to stay the fuck out of your business."

"I remember it, quite clearly. What's your point?" Kent's voice was hard, a tone that didn't match the spineless intellectual that was on the other end of the line. A man who was playing tough with the wrong person.

"This is the *Magiano* family you're dealing with now. And

I'm telling you to stay out of their business. You were being stupid then, but you're being suicidal now. You will never be good enough for them, and you are just one mistake away from them no longer needing your services."

"Your compassion for me is heartwarming. But I'll tell you the same thing I told you three years ago. The last thing I need from a piece of shit like you is advice. Don't be pissed just because some of the biggest names in town are coming to me for representation. The Genovese turnover was handled perfectly, and I haven't heard any complaints from the Magianos so far." His smugness was infuriating, if only for its stupidity. It was unbelievable that this level of self-destructive egotism came from someone with an Ivy League education.

"This isn't a dick-measuring contest, Kent. This is about being smart. Fuck our history, forget your hatred for me for one humbling, intelligent moment. You need to get out. Before they take you out."

Kent snorted, and then there was pure silence for one long, sobering moment. When he finally spoke, there was an equal level of sadness and disgust in his tone. "I don't know if that's even possible."

Brad didn't know if Kent was referring to his ability to forget their history, or his ability to quit his current clients. It was a moot distinction, because he was right on both counts. It probably wasn't possible.

THE SECOND SHOE off, I crouched in my bare feet on the soft carpeting, my head tilted toward the door. My blistered ankles forgotten, I tried to understand what Broward was so angry about. This man speaking, the cold, scornful tone, wasn't the Broward that I knew. And he had mentioned the Magianos as though he was working with them—or for them. I realized it had been a while since Broward had spoken, and I rose, suddenly panicked, and moved silently down to my office, settling in behind my desk and placing my heels on the floor. Then I leaned back in my chair, looking up at the ceiling and thinking.

The Magianos. It could be a different family. It was probably a common enough name, but in this town, that name translated to one thing: sleeping with the fishes. Broward, with his fastidious flossing, his perfect 2.5-kid family, was as far from a mob attorney as I could ever imagine. Must be a different client, or I had misheard the conversation. I pushed aside my fears and sat up, unlocking my computer and diving back into work.

SINCE IT WAS the last week of interning, the eight of us decided to grab lunch together on Tuesday. Broward had left at ten that morning, stopping briefly in my office on the way out. His face had been hard, no reason offered for his departure, and I had nodded meekly and returned to my work, waiting for the sound of the wing doors to close. Then I had stood, trotting down the hall to his secretary Sheila's desk.

"Mr. Broward just left, but he didn't say how long he'd be gone. Do you know when he'll be back?"

She turned, her face scrunched, an expression that amplified all of her wrinkles. "Julia. I don't know where he headed. He had me clear all of his afternoon appointments. Why? Do you have a question regarding one of the files?"

I blushed. "No, just wondering if I could join the other interns for lunch. We were going to run up to the Chinese restaurant up the block."

She smiled. "I don't think he's coming back until this afternoon. You go on and have a good time."

I shot her a grateful smile. "Thanks."

"Oh, and, Julia?"

Something in her tone made my stomach clench. "Yes?" I asked casually.

"I want to apologize. I was a little cold to you when you started, but you have been an excellent addition to our team. I was wrong to judge you, and I'm very excited about you staying on." She smiled brightly at me and I somehow managed to nod in response.

"Thank you, Sheila. I appreciate the opportunity." I fled her office before she had a chance to say anything else, moving quickly to my desk and sinking into my chair. Getting accolades for not living up to her expectations felt a little sour when I had gone exactly where she had hoped I wouldn't. Flat on my back, underneath Brad De Luca's gorgeous, sinful body.

LATE THAT AFTERNOON, I worked in my office, typing up corporate documents at a furious rate. I wanted to leave relatively early, if at all possible. The girls and I were going out for drinks at nine, and in the interest of keeping their friendship, I really wanted to be on time. Finally, I reached a stopping point and stood.

Broward had returned around three, walking straight to his office and closing the door. After a lunch out, I didn't really have grounds to ask for an early night. But there was a chance he wasn't aware of my lunch. I shifted on the soft carpet, trying to get up the courage to go into his office.

"Julia!"

That ended my internal debate. I stepped quickly out into the hall and into his doorway.

"Yes, sir?"

"Will you tell Sheila to dismiss the staff at seven?"

"Today?" A stupid question, but this was so far out of normal behavior that I was confused. *Talk about good luck.*

"Yes, Julia. Tonight." He gave me a pointed look, his face irritable, and I hesitated before speaking.

"Just the support staff, or the paralegals also?"

He waved his hand in the air dismissively. "Everyone. The whole wing. She'll know what to do."

"Certainly. Is there anything you need me to take care of before then?" I shifted my weight, knowing that I should get the hell out of there before he changed his mind.

"Your normal *duties*. Just tell Sheila." Irritability was *definitely* in his voice now. *Great.*

"Yes, sir."

He grunted in response, and I fled his office, doing a little dance when I reached the privacy of my own. I reached for the phone and dialed Sheila's extension.

At 8:05 p.m. I leaned against the linoleum counter in my kitchen and rolled my eyes at my roommate. "I don't give a damn if she was a bad lay—you don't abandon a chick and then expect Zach and me to babysit her all day."

"I would've given a bad lay a ride, Jules. This girl was crazy! She was talking wedding plans!" He pounded his fist on the counter to emphasize his point, and a spoon bounced off the counter and landed on the dirty floor just as my phone began to ring.

Through a mouthful of chips, I answered on the fourth ring.

"Yes?" I said playfully.

"Nice to talk to you, too," Brad's smooth, sexy drawl sounded through the phone.

I grinned, the motion carrying through my tone. "Don't give me that. I'm in the middle of something very important."

He chuckled. "Likely. Are you at the office?"

"No. Broward let me off at *seven*! Can you believe it!"

"So, are you coming over tonight?" His voice had taken on a suggestive lilt, and I smiled into the receiver.

"*Yes*, but I plan on getting sloshed with the girls first. I'll leave my car at the restaurant and either take a cab or beg my boyfriend to come pick me up." I winked at Alex and grabbed another handful of chips, chomping noisily on them.

"Good. He can join me in defiling you later on." The sex in his voice was delicious, and I couldn't fight the shiver that shot through me.

"Oh, I don't think you want to mess with him. He's a big, scary guy, ripped with muscles, that type of thing—he can be quite intimidating," I teased.

"Well, call your manly boyfriend when you are done at the bar. I don't want you catching a cab."

"Fine, but be ready!" I playfully snapped, and hung up the phone. I looked up at Alex.

"That your sexy man?"

"The one and only," I said, grabbing a final handful of chips and checking my watch. "I have to get ready. We'll take up this conversation later," I promised, giving him a quick hug and skipping down the threadbare carpet to my room.

Seventeen

"So, give me the scoop on Brad." Olivia gripped a cold bottle in her hand and smiled at me over the dark rim. Olivia was my closest friend, though I'd never admit it to Becca, who sat to my right.

I blushed and picked at the label on my own beer, a Michelob Ultra. "Nothing much to tell," I said, evading her direct gaze.

"Come on!" Becca said, tossing her perfectly cut and dyed hair over her shoulder. "We just listened to a fifteen-minute snooze fest on O's history class, for God's sake. Give me something good. Are you guys official yet?"

"Yes. As of last week, yes." I set down my beer and looked into their expectant faces.

Becca squealed and clapped her hands; Olivia's response was, as expected, less enthusiastic. "Are you sure about this, Jules?"

I met her eyes squarely, loving the fire behind them. "Yes, I am. Why are you so against it?"

"Yeah, O, Brad is, like, awesome!" Becca chimed in, though I didn't know that Becca's endorsement was going to help my case with Olivia. If there was a disaster on two legs anywhere in a five-mile radius, Becca would be going after him and frothing at the mouth.

Olivia sighed, setting down her beer and squaring off for confrontation. "First, you don't know much about him. You met him two months ago. Second, you were warned by at least five people to stay away from him, that he was a philandering sex addict. Has anyone who *knows* the man suggested he has any redeeming qualities?"

I blinked, unsure of how to respond. The girl made some good points. There was a reason she, along with Becca and I, would be headed to law school after graduation. I hadn't been completely honest with the girls about Brad, for more reasons than one. But I wasn't sure if giving full disclosure would help or hurt their opinion of him.

"Olivia," I began, trying to formulate a reasonable response. "While I work at CDB, I have to keep our relationship a secret. So I haven't *met* many people who would vouch for his redeeming qualities. But you've known me three years. Do you think I have poor judgment in people? I'm not blindly throwing myself into this relationship with stars in my eyes and blinders on. I'm approaching this hesitantly, and seeing how it goes." I shrugged. "If it doesn't work out, I haven't lost anything but a few weeks of my summer."

"I would have followed that reasoning if you were about to end your internship, but you're taking a job there now. You can't keep this relationship a secret and expect it to work." She had gone past concern and moved into preaching, a transition I wasn't crazy about since her logic was sound.

"*Ignore* her," Becca said, waving a hand dismissively in Olivia's direction. "Tell me about the sex—and don't think about holding any details back!"

Olivia butted in, intent on ruining any fun. "Yes, tell us about the sex. Are you using protection?" Her eyes narrowed, and she watched me closely.

Jeez. "Yes, *Mom*, I am using protection," I spat out. Becca elbowed Olivia and then leaned forward.

"Jules, I say do as much with that beautiful man as you can. And when you are done with him, pass his number on to me!"

I grinned at Becca and stuck my tongue out at Olivia. "Lighten up on me. I'm twenty-one. I'm allowed to make a few mistakes."

Her eyes sharp, she took a swig from her beer and met my offhand look head-on. "I just don't like it. He seems... dangerous."

KENT BROWARD HEARD the elevator ding and looked up from the legal brief, listening for a hint at who had arrived. He hoped it wasn't a member of his staff; privacy was needed for tonight's meeting. His palms perspired, and he wiped them quickly on his dress pants. He clenched and then relaxed his fingers, willing the tension to leave his hands. Shit had officially hit the fan.

The man walked down the carpeted hall, headed for Broward's open door. He glanced in dark office doorways, the wing silent and still. It was as the attorney had said—empty. He held a briefcase loosely in his right hand, an expensive suit hanging perfectly on his muscular frame, the fabric swooshing slightly as he walked. An air conditioner clicked on, the cool air welcome on his hot skin. He was always hot. His stride was relaxed; no tension tightened his body. Killing was not new to him.

The man walked into the office without knocking. Broward was sitting at his desk, his head cocked, and he jerked to his feet when the man entered. The man turned, closing the door, and Broward spoke as soon as the lock clicked into place.

"Jesus Christ, what are we going to do about this?" Broward ran his hands nervously over his shaved head, and covered his face. "This is bad, this is very bad." He pointed to the man. "You. You got me into this!" His voice had reached a shrill level.

"No." The man's deep voice filled the well-appointed room. "The money got you into this. Don't blame me for your poor decisions." He set his briefcase on Broward's desk and unclipped the latches.

Broward wrung his hands and looked at the man. "Look, as soon as you told me, I closed the accounts, I hid the trail. Now you gotta get me out of this. Permanently out. I don't want anything to do with this business or this family anymore."

The gun came out of the briefcase, fast and deadly. The man saved his witty comeback and made his statement by squeezing the trigger.

Eighteen

Kent Broward's body was found in his office Wednesday morning at six-fifteen by Sue Mendoza. Mrs. Mendoza had cleaned the fourth floor for the last three years. It was the first dead body she had ever seen.

His body was facedown on the plush cream carpet, a pool of blood surrounding his head and torso. He had been shot twice, twin holes of death marring an otherwise average body.

When Sue Mendoza discovered the scene, she promptly fled the room, locked herself in the nearest office and called her priest. Three minutes later, she dialed 911.

6:30 a.m., Wednesday

"YOU HAVING PANCAKES ALSO?" The rude voice of Martha interrupted the conversation I was having with Brad. I looked into her wide eyes and pursed lips and shook my head. Pancakes sounded good, but it was obvious from her stance and tone that she did *not* want me to have pancakes.

"I'm fine with just eggs and grits, thank you."

"Good. Brad, I fixed three. That should be more than

enough for you." She unceremoniously dumped three deli-
cious-looking flapjacks on a plate and slid it across the island
to Brad, who was sitting one bar stool over from me. Brad
winked at me, grabbed the maple syrup and poured a generous amount over the top of the pancakes. Martha fixed my
plate, giving me a scant helping of eggs, grits and bacon. I
hopped off the stool and went to the fridge, grabbing orange
juice and two glasses from the cabinet.

"There. You two should be taken care of. Brad, you know
what to do with your dishes." The round woman glanced at
me, wrinkled her nose slightly, then pulled off her apron and
hung it by the door. Without a parting word, she swung open
the back door and stomped through, letting it slam shut behind her. I let out a breath of air and poured the juice.

"I know she can cook, but doesn't her grouchiness get a
little old?" I called over my shoulder as I put the lid back on
the juice.

His hands grabbed my waist, startling me, and I jumped
a little. He stood behind me, nuzzling my neck with his soft
lips and scratchy stubble. I giggled a bit, set the juice on the
counter and pressed back, feeling my ass fit perfectly against
his hard body.

"Easy," he growled, running his hands up and down the
sides of my body, then cupping a breast in each hand and
squeezing gently. My nipples instantly hardened against my
bra, and I pushed harder against him. He spun me around and
used his hands to grip my ass, pulling me tight against him. I
grinned, looking into his face.

"What?" he asked, smiling down at me.

"You know Martha's going to inspect our plates as soon
as you leave for work. Are we eating, or are we..." I reached
down and grabbed his crotch, rubbing it suggestively, feel-

ing his flesh grow under my hand, the outline now visible in his pants.

"You really have to ask that question?" he said, inhaling when my hand gripped him firmly. He suddenly released me, and I wobbled, caught off balance. His eyes were dark, aroused, and he took a few steps back, unzipping his dress pants.

"The sink. Bend over it." His voice was authoritative, deep, though I could hear a slight hoarseness to it, verifying his need.

I wore a black pantsuit, and removed my jacket, shivering slightly in the cold house. I met his gaze, seeing pure authority there. I took two steps to the left and turned, facing the sink and looking out the window that hung above it. Darkness still blanketed the street, and the kitchen light no doubt illuminated the room to anyone on the two-lane road. "Brad, the light—"

"Unzip your pants and drop them around your ankles." His order came from behind me and I heard his footsteps sound on the stone floor. I hesitated, but felt the need twitch inside me, the twinge when my cunt squeezed tight and begged for stimulation. As I heard the familiar rip of foil, I unzipped my pants and pulled both them and my already wet panties down around my ankles. I bent over the sink, resting my elbows on the edge of the counter, and arched my back, offering myself to him.

I felt his rough hands, sliding down the curve of my skin, traveling closer, closer to my apex, and my eyes closed when he reached the wet area between my legs. "God, you are already wet," he breathed, tracing my opening with a finger. I flinched at his touch, tightening my inner walls. He ran his finger over my taint and the place where it met my wetness, playing with that skin, and I gasped, gripping hard granite with my hands. I pushed back against his fingers, wanting something, anything inside me.

Brad pressed against me, putting a hand up my dress shirt. He bit my neck gently, then sucked at the skin, and I tilted my head back, opening my throat to him. "Put your fingers in me," I whispered.

He sucked on the soft lobe of my ear, then whispered into it, the tickle of his stubble driving me crazy. "We don't have much time. I'm gonna have to make this quick."

Before I could formulate a response, his fingers were gone and he shoved himself inside my wet, tight core. I called out in surprise, a twinge of pain hitting me. Recovering, I fucked him back, pushing on the sink with my hands, welcoming the fullness inside me, moaning from the feel of it.

I grounded out a moan, flipping my hair over my shoulder and looking behind me, into his eyes, steel traps of passion. My juices, flowing out around his stiffness, lubricated our movement, and I gritted my teeth and bounced off his hard thighs, pulling my body on and off his cock. He took over, moving both hands under my bra till they cupped my bare tits and squeezed, pinching my nipples in a way that was half pleasure, half pain. I gasped, my head tilted back, and he rammed me over and over in quick succession. I could see our reflection in the window before me, our two faces, his fierce and masculine, mine breathless and on the verge of ecstasy. Knowing that anyone on his quiet street was seeing us lit a fire in my body, and a surge of arousal shot through me. I let go of the sink and ripped open my shirt, grasped the front clasp of my bra and undid it, exposing my pale breasts, the curve of my chest, twin blurs of pink. I saw Brad's hands, clear in the reflection, pinching my nipples, and the image made my legs weak.

He moved in and out of me, long, measured strokes, my body aching with every outward pull. Then he slowed, burying his hardness inside so deep, so strong, and I clenched my eyes tight with the pain of his depth. Then he slowly withdrew, my muscles tensing, squeezing him tightly, feeling his girth as it traveled out and then I was empty, needing, gasping from the vacancy. I pushed back, wanting him again, desperate for the heat and sensation of his cock. But his hands held me, and he bumped me gently, teasing me with the tip. "Do you like me fucking you?" Brad's voice, deep and dark in my ear, his breath hot. I met his gaze in the reflection, his face strong and in control, mine desperate and unrestrained.

"Yes," I gasped. "I need it, dammit."

"Louder."

Yes! I screamed, the effort giving me a burst of adrenaline, and I shoved harder, searching for more of him, needing all of it, instantly, like an animal in heat.

He rammed, my tight wetness welcoming the invasion, squeezing the length of him as he filled every pore of me. I whimpered from the release, the feeling of his skin inside me almost painful in its perfection. He moved a hand, letting go of a nipple and wrapping his hand around my neck instead. He squeezed and my eyes widened, asking his reflection a silent question. He released my neck and instead grabbed my hair, wrapping my ponytail around his hand and pulled, hard and firm, on it.

I could feel my orgasm coming, my walls clenching around his thickness. "I'm close," I gasped, and he grabbed my hips, fucking me without restraint, his balls slapping my clit with a furious rhythm. The orgasm came and took with it every ounce of my self-control. I lost it, crying out and bucking, my legs shaking and hands slipping, my reflection making a ridiculous face before my eyes clenched shut and pleasure racked my senses.

He fucked me through the orgasm, pounding over and over until I could feel his cock twitching, him close to his own explosion. He smacked my ass hard, and I cried out, my spent muscles liking the stimulation. He spanked me again, and then yanked out, jacking his cock fast and hard.

"On your knees," he gritted out, and I turned quickly, trying to navigate with my pants still bundled around my ankles. I knelt in front of him and grabbed his cock, peeling off the condom, taking over the motion, and looked up into his gorgeous, intense face.

His mouth opened and he groaned softly, looking into my eyes and my upturned face, then focused on my lips, his eyes intent.

"Open your mouth."

I did and turned my eyes to his swollen head, bobbing in and out of my clenched hand. I added my second hand, wrapping both of them around him, and jacked him and his orgasm into my open and waiting mouth.

The first spurt came—hot and white and on my tongue. Tasting it, I dove onto his cock, sucking it hard and taking it as deep as I could. I continued jacking, sucking his come and gagging on the hardness filling my throat. Brad moaned and clenched his legs, grabbing the back of my head and pulling it to him. I continued sucking, sliding my mouth up and down. After a few seconds, his hand loosened, and he stepped back, resting against the island and sliding his cock from my wet mouth. He leaned forward, grabbing me under the arms and picking me up. Spinning, me lifted, he set me on the island, sliding dishes and food out of the way and laying me down. I relaxed on the granite, a smile overtaking my face, and he leaned over, spreading open my shirt and laying soft kisses on each of my breasts and then down my stomach, ending at the top of my legs. He breathed in my scent, then placed his mouth softly on me and I moaned, pushing him off with one foot. "Enough," I breathed.

He laughed and traveled back up my body, kissing me and smoothing my hair back.

"Thank you," he whispered.

"Back at ya," I said, grinning at him, delirious with contentment. I closed my eyes, a smile stretching across my face, totally exposed to him, feeling his eyes on me as his fingers trailed off my skin.

"What do you have today?" Brad's voice was muffled as he rounded the island, his voice changing in location.

I opened my eyes, staring at the ceiling. "Another twelve-hour day of secretarial duties."

Brad tugged at my arms, pulling me to a seated position, my limbs lazy and unresponsive. I smiled at him while he buttoned my shirt, looking up into my face as he spoke. "My offer still stands. You could start next week in my wing. You can come to *court*...watch me work."

I made my eyes as huge as possible. "Wow, really? You are so big and important, Mr. De Luca."

He stole a kiss on my neck, nipping the skin gently with his teeth. "If you won't let me steal you permanently, let me borrow you for a day. Let me speak to him. I'll tell him I'm swamped on a case and need more help."

I laughed, taking over my buttons. "Like *that* would fly. He'd accuse you of wanting another sex toy and would keep me under even *more* of a lock and key."

He frowned, grabbing my waist and sliding me off the counter. "You've got to get over your hang-up on Broward.

If you expect our relationship to have any type of a future, eventually he's going to find out about us."

"Regardless of whether we have a future, I need you to keep us secret for now." I grinned at him, hoping my thoughts didn't convey through my often-traitorous eyes. Did I expect us to have a real future? It was certainly something I wanted, but Brad was a wild card. He had professed his intentions, vowed that he could remain faithful as long as I participated in his lifestyle. But I wasn't putting too much faith in him until I saw actions to back up his words. I leaned forward, kissing him lightly on the lips before pulling away, his frown deepening, and he grabbed my head, taking me back to his mouth, his tongue taking mine until he'd had his fill. With a confident smile he released me, crouching down and grabbing my pants, sliding them up my legs, his fingers teasing me the entire way up.

Somewhere in the background, a phone rang.

Nineteen

The call was from Hugo Clarke. Brad took the call from his partner in the living room, and I ate my cold breakfast while trying to redress. I glanced at my watch. Five till seven. I was good on time, assuming that I left in the next twenty minutes.

Brad appeared in the doorway, and I looked up with a smile. My face froze when I saw the somber fix of his features. "What's wrong?"

"You should sit down."

I paused, setting down my fork, my mind trying to figure out what Clarke could possibly have said that would have this effect on Brad. "I'm fine standing. What is it?"

"It's Broward. He was found in the office this morning, dead."

It took a moment to register his words, and I ran the phrase through my head a few times, the unfamiliar concept fading in and out of reality until my vision began to spot in front of me. *Maybe I should sit down.* I gripped the counter, reaching blindly out for a stool. Brad was suddenly there, his hand gripping mine, and he led me to a chair, my legs giving out the moment my ass hit wood. "Bullshit," I finally whispered, a part of me hoping, wishing, that this was his sick version of a joke.

"No." The tightness of his face made the situation real, and I physically swooned for a moment, fainting now a real possibility. He sat down across from me and held my face, forcing me to look into his eyes, to focus on him.

"Suicide?" I whispered, Broward's strained face, his obvious stress, all of the signs, *signs I should have seen*, flooding my mind. Guilt settled on my shoulders, heavy and judgmental.

"No." He leaned briefly away from me and rubbed his temples. "Murdered. Shot in his office."

The guilt, for a brief moment, took a hiatus. It might have skipped Julia-town and landed in Brad-ville; he certainly looked as sick as I felt. His face pale, he stared forward, his body tense. Wherever he was, it was miles from here, miles from me. I reached out, touching his shoulder, and he turned to me, our eyes meeting, a sudden connection forming. I fought to stay still, to not react, but the look in his eyes when they met mine—it scared me. His face was dark and brooding, but his eyes? They were intense, fiery. They screamed pure fury, sparks flying from them, his temple jumping, and I realized, my eyes traveling over his body, that he was a tight coil of barely restrained rage.

Rage? Not the reaction I would expect when someone finds out his business partner is dead.

"Are you okay?" I asked softly.

He closed his eyes briefly, then opened them and looked at me. And just like that, it was gone. The madness dissipated and he was calm and in control. The transformation scared me more than the fury had. He reached out, grabbing my hand reassuringly. "I'm fine. Just trying to understand it." He stood, moving away from me, and yanked open a drawer by the door, grabbing his wallet and keys, his back to me.

My thoughts returned to Broward and the unexplainable situation. *Murdered. In his office.* My mind grasped at straws, trying desperately to convince itself that this was a random act of violence. "Was it a robbery?"

"They don't know. I have to get to the office. The police want to talk to me."

"To you? Why?" I stood up and walked over to my shoes, grabbing them and pulling them on.

Brad ignored my question and came up behind me, his strong arms wrapping around me tightly. "Are you okay?"

I turned to him and sank into his chest, gripping his shirt with my hands. "I don't know. Yeah. No. I'm just trying to understand it." I looked up into his worried face, searching it, the lines, his mouth, his eyes. They stared back at me, concern and compassion filling them, no hint of the fury that had monopolized them just moments earlier. I didn't know what I hated more, when his eyes were unreadable or when I didn't like what I read in them. I wiped away tears that were swelling and stood on my tiptoes, kissing him gently on the lips. "Let's go."

Brad turned to follow, his hand finding the small of my back, the slight support appreciated. He grabbed the door, pulling it closed behind us and locking it. "The police will probably want to talk to you, too."

"Me?" I stepped off the porch, going carefully down the back steps. *Why would they want to talk to me?*

"Yeah. If he was shot last night, you may have been the last person to see him alive." He paused. "Other than, of course, the killer."

Twenty

We decided to just leave my car at the bar, my nerves way past the level of safe driving. Brad drove us to the office, watching me closely the whole time, as if I were a piece of china with a hairline crack.

We didn't speak on the drive. I was shaken, trying to put the pieces of what was happening together. It was as if the last twenty minutes had uprooted my world and set it back upside down. I had too much to think about, too much to process. My mind flipped back and forth between an image of Broward's body, and the words I had overheard on Monday. *The Magianos*. It couldn't be, there must be some other explanation. Not in our office, not with Broward. I clenched my eyes shut and sat back in the seat.

"You okay?" Brad's voice, coming through my thick cloud.

"Yeah," I mumbled, my eyes closed, the feeling of his hand on mine, gripping my palm, a soothing thumb caressing my wrist.

The car slowed and I heard a turn signal. We must be close. I wasn't ready to face the office and all this day would entail.

My stomach tightened at the thought of being questioned. I needed to figure out what to do.

BRAD ENTERED THE East Wing of the fourth floor of Clarke, De Luca & Broward. The East Wing was his domain, the area where expensive marriages came to die. Divorce Central. He was God in this wing. He noted that, despite this morning's events, business was still being conducted. Both conference rooms were full, and two groups of clients waited in the lobby's leather seating clusters. He walked through the elegant space and up to the three elevated secretarial desks that were the focus of the lobby. The only sign of trouble glistened from the blotchy faces and red-rimmed eyes of his secretaries, who rose at his approach. The three women, who ran the wing with iron, liver-spotted fists, were all in their late sixties, and all had been with him for over ten years. He stopped at their desks and nodded a hello.

Carol Featherston, the center and head secretary, spoke first. Never one to mince words, she skipped over pleasantries. "There is a detective waiting to speak with you."

Brad nodded. "Give me a moment in my office, then send him in."

"Certainly." She swallowed hard, her wrinkled neck stretching and straining. "Brad, we were so sorry to hear about Kent. Despite your history, I know this must be a difficult time for you." Her two clones, Diana and Beatrice, nodded in unison, both murmuring soft condolences. Brad nodded and walked around their desks, entering his large office set against the east wall of the building, a million-dollar view of downtown stretching its length. He paused for a moment, collecting his thoughts, then walked behind his desk. Opening up a side cabinet, he set his briefcase inside, then sat in his dark leather chair. He closed his eyes briefly and collected his thoughts. There was a knock at his door, and Carol opened it, ushering in a tall, thin man, with short gray hair. The detective.

Let the games begin.

Twenty-One

The West Wing was chaos. Our front lobby was filled with employees, and I was stopped just inside the doors by one of the firm's security guards. "Julia," he said, recognizing me. "All employees are asked to wait here. The police are conducting interviews in the offices, and the hall with your office and Broward's is closed for the investigators."

I nodded and moved past him, into the waiting area. Looking around, I saw almost every employee of the wing, some huddled in small groups, some standing alone, and others pacing on cell phones. I sought out Sheila. Seeing her leaning against her desk, at the rear of the room, I walked over and touched her shoulder. She whirled at the contact, her elegant appearance marred by her tear-soaked face and shaking hands.

"Oh, Julia!" she gasped, grabbing me and hugging tightly. We separated, and she wiped under both of her eyes, straightening up and trying to remain composed. "I just don't know what to do without Kent."

"I am so sorry, Sheila. I know how close you were." I didn't know if *close* was the right word, but Sheila had been an admin for Broward since he began at CDB eleven years ago. His death had to be hard on her, more so than anyone else in this room. I felt as though I were falling apart, and I'd only known the man two months—she had to be destroyed. "Have the police already questioned you?" I asked, squeezing her cardigan-encased arm.

"Yes. Right when I came in. Now that you're here, I'm sure they will want to speak to you, too."

"Do you know anything? Know what could have caused this…?" *Anything other than the largest mob family this side of Chicago?* I let the question trail off, her watery eyes sharpening in response, looking more like the Sheila I knew.

"No. Absolutely not. But I didn't have a hand in all of his cases. Not like you."

Like me? What cases did I work on that Sheila didn't? I didn't bother arguing with her. She grabbed my arm and pulled, almost dragged me, to a uniformed officer standing by the wall. "This is Julia Campbell," she announced, pushing me in front of him. "Broward's intern."

The man consulted a clipboard, then nodded to us. "Detective Parks will want to speak with you. Come with me."

I followed him down the hall, grief and confusion heavy in the air around us. He took me into the conference room, opening the door to reveal a heavyset man in a cheap suit, papers, notes and coffee scattered on our normally pristine conference table. I sat in front of the man, who said nothing to me, scribbling furiously on a form. The officer left us alone and I wondered where Brad was, and what he was doing.

THE OFFICE WAS long, impressive, a view of the city filling the ornate space with light. "Detective Wilkes." Brad stood and shook the detective's hand over his large leather and wood desk. "I'm Brad De Luca. Please, sit," he said, indicating the chairs that faced his desk.

The detective sat, opened a notebook, uncapped a pen and stared at Brad, assessing him. "Good morning. I'm sure you are quite…busy, so I'll skip the pleasantries and barge into questions. I assume you were close with Kent Broward?"

Brad tented his fingers, looking over them at the detective. He shrugged. "Define close."

The detective sighed deeply, stretching out the action until he was certain Brad picked up on his irritation. "Knew him well. And don't ask me to define *well*."

"I have known Kent for eleven years, but I do not have more than a business relationship with him. We are not friends, we do not confide in each other, we do not see each other unless it is at a quarterly partnership meeting or in passing." Brad paused, picking up a pen and slowly tapping it on his desk. "Does that answer your question?"

The man's mouth tightened. "You seem irritated, Mr. De Luca. Has Broward's death *inconvenienced* you?"

Brad looked somberly at Wilkes. "Grief is not a prerequisite for innocence, Mr. Wilkes."

"Detective Wilkes."

"Sorry," he said shortly. "Look, I am happy to answer your questions, but whether it be insensitive or not, I am a very busy man, and I do have appointments waiting."

"Like it or not, your partner is dead, and I need to ask you some questions."

Brad waved his hand, indicating for the detective to go on.

"*Why* were you not friends with Mr. Broward?"

"For several reasons. I considered him dull. He worked constantly, and probably didn't have any friends to speak of.

Plus, as you have probably heard from other staff members, Broward didn't like me."

"Was the feeling mutual?"

"I didn't really care whether he liked me. I have enough friends. I respected his work ethic. That was all I needed from a business partner."

"Why didn't Broward like you?"

Brad smirked. "You probably already know the answer to that question." He sat back in his chair and resumed the slow tap of the pen on his desk.

"I'd like to hear it from you."

I SAT NERVOUSLY in the big space, the same conference room where I had eaten cold pizza with Brad over six weeks ago. Back when we didn't know each other, and all I had heard were rumors and warnings. The table was where he had talked me into a trip to Vegas, a trip that had begun the erosion of my sexual boundaries and opened up the possibility of a relationship. The same conference room where Broward had opened up to me, sharing his true hatred of Brad and all that he encompassed. The weight of the memories lay like irons on my shoulders, conflicting emotions driving me wild. It seemed surreal, for me to sit here, questioned by police, an overheard phone call I couldn't get out of my head. I never should have eavesdropped, never should have blatantly dismissed Broward's heartfelt warnings, and never should have deceived the good man who now lay dead. Guilt from every angle hit me, but even as I sat there, bemoaning my traitorous actions, I wanted Brad, needed him here, his strength, his arms around me. I was officially a horrible person. *I can't believe he's dead.*

"Ms. Campbell?" Detective Parks in the cheap suit, sitting across from me, had asked a question.

"I'm sorry, can you repeat the question?"

He raised his eyebrows, but looked back down at his notepad. "I said, how long have you been employed at Clarke, De Luca & Broward?"

I wondered if the firm name would change. "I'm not technically employed. I'm just a temporary intern. I've been here a little over two months. But I will be employed—part-time, starting next week."

"And you have been an intern assigned to Kent Broward for that entire time?"

"Yes."

"How close were you to him?"

I frowned at the question. It seemed a little odd. "I worked with him every day for ten to twelve hours. We discussed business, little else."

"So, a strictly business relationship."

"Yes."

"Sheila Ponder says you are intimately familiar with his current caseload."

"I would agree with that. All of his current cases I am familiar with."

"I will need a list from you of which cases or clients might have endangered his life."

I laughed, a small, awkward sound. "You're kidding, right? Didn't Sheila tell you about our cases? We have the most lame, unexciting files on the planet. No one is *killing* anyone over anything Broward was working on. We deal with corporate documents, real estate transactions, civil litigations." I shook my head emphatically. "Whatever happened to Broward couldn't have had anything to do with a client." *At least, not a CDB client.*

"Hmmm." He wrote something down. *Hmmm? What does that mean?*

"At least no clients that I am aware of." I rushed out the words, anxious to speak before my conscience took a convenient vacation.

He set down his pen. "What do you mean by that?"

"Just, ah, if there were other clients, ones I wasn't aware of, maybe they had something to do with it." I was sounding like a complete idiot, a fact I was sure he was picking up on.

He flipped back a page, looking at the notes he had scribbled down. "You just said that you were familiar with all of his cases and clients. So, in theory, there shouldn't be any clients that you aren't aware of."

Shit. This was it, time to put up or shut up. I took a deep breath and told him about the conversation I had overheard two days before. He sat quietly, his pen placed beside his notebook, and listened. When I was done, he tilted his head and looked at me.

"I'm not understanding where you are going with this, Ms. Campbell."

Was the guy daft? "Broward pretty much stated that he was providing some type of services to the Magianos. Then he's killed one night later!" My voice had left the calm and rational level and was now in full-blown hysterical female mode.

"And you think the Magianos are…" He lifted his chin and met my teary eyes head-on.

Was this a damn current events quiz? "The Al Capone of this generation? The most powerful crime syndicate in the Southern U.S.?" I leaned forward, smacking my hand on the table, eliciting a frown from the detective.

"First of all, Ms. Campbell, we don't know that the 'Magianos' that Mr. Broward mentioned is the same family that you are referring to."

I tried to remind myself this was an officer of the law and not someone I could flick off at will. "He's dead. He didn't stumble over a gun and get shot licking stamps! How can you *not* think that the Magianos had something to do with this!"

"Ms. Campbell, lower your voice. You haven't even explored the possibility that you misheard Mr. Broward. He was on the phone. You were outside his office, with the door closed. You could easily have misunderstood what he said." His voice was firm, his gaze direct, and I looked at him helplessly, my hysteria close to returning.

I opened and closed my mouth, trying to put intelligent words into action. I didn't get a chance; he returned pen to paper and went to his next question.

"Are you aware of any upset clients, or anyone who disliked Mr. Broward?

"Other than the possible Magianos?" I asked sarcastically.

"Yes. Answer the question."

"No. No one that I can think of. Broward is…" I paused briefly, closing my eyes. "*Was* a likable guy. I'm sure you will find that out by speaking to all of the staff."

He nodded. Then he set down his notebook and looked at me.

"Ms. Campbell, where were you last night, between 8:30 and 10:30 p.m.?

"Last night?" I was suddenly tense.

"Yes. Are you *aware* of what you did last night?"

I fought the urge to roll my eyes. "Yes. Broward dismissed everyone early. I went home, changed and met my friends for drinks at nine. We stayed at the bar until about eleven."

"I will need to speak with your friends and verify this."

I sat back and folded my arms. "Are you verifying all of the staff's alibis?"

Parks paused and looked at me appraisingly. "*Alibi* is probably too strong a word, at this point. But to answer your question, no. Not all of the staff."

THE AIR HAD gotten hot in Brad's office. He sighed. "Broward doesn't, or didn't, like me for a few reasons. The main one, and what I assume you are hinting at, is that I once slept with his wife."

The man cocked an eyebrow at him, but didn't move otherwise. "You seem awfully cavalier about that—sleeping with another man's wife."

Brad shrugged. "I sleep with a lot of women. I regret that specific experience, because he was my business partner, and because it complicated an already strained relationship."

"Strained how?"

"He was…irritated by me. By my large income and what he considered to be lack of work ethic."

"Did you dislike him?"

"You already asked that. No."

"Hmmm." The detective wrote something down.

"Where were you last night, Mr. De Luca?"

"At home."

"When did you arrive home?"

"After work. I am unsure of the exact time."

"Take a guess." The irritated voice of the man had turned harder.

"I would guess six or seven."

"And you stayed in your home all evening?"

"Until about eleven."

"Where did you go at eleven?"

"Do I need to re-create my entire evening for you? I was told the time of death was before 10:00 p.m."

"By who?"

"Hugo Clarke. Am I done here?"

"Just answer the question, Mr. De Luca. Where did you go at eleven?"

"To pick up a female friend, and no, I will not reveal her name." He stared at the detective, a tic beginning in his cheek.

"Are you aware of any of Mr. Broward's current projects?"

"That's it." Brad leaned back in his chair. "I'm not going to answer any more questions without a lawyer present."

Wilkes snorted, then laughed softly, shaking his head. "I thought *you* were a lawyer."

Brad said nothing, just stared at him over the desk.

"Fine." The detective snapped the notebook shut and stood, scraping his chair backward. He snapped his fingers and pointed at Brad, a stern look on his face. "I'll see you soon," he promised.

Brad smiled and lifted his chin in response, but did not stand. Wilkes turned and stalked out of the office, and Brad watched him leave through the heavy glass. He frowned, then opened his center drawer and pulled out a cell phone that he kept in the back, behind paper clips and Post-its. He dialed a number and waited, listening to the ring in his ear.

Twenty-Two

With Broward dead, we milled like ants through the lobby, everyone unsure of their duties. CSI staff, police and detectives were everywhere, and it was whispered that Broward's body still lay in his office. Finally, the police moved us all to the East Wing, Brad's domain, to get us out of the way. We filled his lobby, the ornate room now a sea of black suits and boring neutrals. I felt a hand tug mine, and turned to see Todd Appleton, six feet of blond and blue-eyed concern. He tugged on my hand, pulling me into a hard hug, his arms wrapping around me and hugging me tightly to his chest, white shirt and black suit smooshing comfortably against my face. A sudden sob welled in my throat, an unexpected breakdown of the walls I had fought all morning to control. He shushed me, bodies and voices crowding us from all sides. "I'm so sorry, Julia. So sorry."

I pushed gently on his chest, stepping back and wiping at my eyes, sniffing back snot and tears. "Thanks, Todd. I'm still trying to work it all out."

He raised his voice to be heard over the crowd. "There

were cops everywhere when I arrived, but we haven't heard any updates over here—they've all been in your wing till now." He looked a little too enthusiastic about the drama, the earlier concern replaced by excited curiosity. The wing doors opened and a new group entered, causing the room to go from crowded to packed. There was pure bedlam for about two minutes, and then Brad appeared at the head of the room, calling out and bringing the room to silence.

"Everybody, go *home*. Sheila and Beverly, you both stay and use Conference Room D to reach out to clients and reschedule appointments. Everyone else, please leave. We will email you tonight regarding tomorrow's schedule." He sought out and met my eyes but gave nothing away, turning and heading back to his office. There was silence; then the din of the room resumed, and we moved as one giant mass to the double doors that led to the elevator lobby. I met Todd's eyes, moving away with the crowd as he stayed in place. I gave him a crumbling smile and waved, turning and looking to the exit. As nice as Todd's embrace had been, I needed a stronger set of arms, the steadiness and security of Brad.

I avoided eye contact and conversations as I moved with the crowd. I wanted nothing more than to be at home and alone with my thoughts. What would happen with our wing? Who killed Broward? Was I a suspect? Was the Magiano family involved? Was I in danger? Most of my thoughts and questions were selfish, and I scolded myself as I moved with the crowd. Beside the elevator was one of the firm's chauffeurs, and he tapped my shoulder lightly.

"Ms. Campbell. My name is—"

"Jeff. I remember. You took me to lunch one day." Me and Brad, but I wasn't about to say that in the crowded lobby.

"Yes. I've been asked to take you to your car. Or to your

home, whichever you prefer." He ducked his head toward the elevator, and I nodded, moving forward when the doors opened. *My car.* I had forgotten about it. It was, no doubt, still two blocks down from the bar, in a metered spot, the windshield littered with tickets.

We avoided the crowd and walked through the lobby. I looked at my watch as I stepped into the morning light. Only nine. The shortest workday on the planet. The town car was idling in one of the reserved spots in front of the building, and we moved toward it. I wondered what time they would email us. Brad would undoubtedly keep me in the loop.

"Ms. Campbell?" Jeff held open the car door, a questioning look in his eyes.

I murmured an apology as I stepped into the car, hugging my purse to my chest. I waited until he got in and started the car, then spoke. "I'd like to be taken to my car, please."

His eyes met mine in the rearview mirror. "Okay. Where is it?"

I gave him the location and we moved, pulling up to the car before I had a chance to collect my thoughts. He was out of the car and opening my door, his pale hands gathering the two orange envelopes off my windshield as I stepped out. I winced, holding my hand out for them, but he shook his head, stuffing them in his pocket. "Mr. D said for me to bring any citations to him."

I opened my mouth to object, thought better of it and smiled at Jeff. "Thank you for the ride. Please pass on my thanks to Mr. De Luca."

He grinned in response and tipped his hat, walking jauntily back to the driver's side. It was as if Jeff was completely unaware that anyone had died. I frowned, getting into my car, the familiar smell bringing a sense of normalcy back into my life. I started the car and headed for home.

THE HOUSE WAS quiet when I unlocked the front door, my roommates still asleep. Their social life didn't accommodate waking before noon, a norm that I was grateful for this particular day. I took out my contacts and changed into sweats and a baggie tee from three boyfriends back, a giant soft number that advertised a fundraiser and would one day soon completely disintegrate in my hands. I crawled into bed, flipping on my TV and scrolling through the stations. I finally stopped on VH1, piling on blankets and adding pillows until I was completely surrounded, in perfect pity-party settings. Then I added a box of tissues and let myself go.

My depressed wallow didn't last too long. Two hours later, my house, in full glory, awoke. I was typically not home when this happened, more by design than default—my lesson learned last semester when I had to endure the morning ritual twice a week because of poor course scheduling on my part. Zach and Alex waking was similar to some type of aboriginal male bonding. One would start blasting music—Insane Clown Posse-style, make-you-want-to-pull-your-hair-out screeching, until it woke the other roommate, who would respond in kind by blaring his own form of musical madness—hard rock. My room was, unluckily enough, right in between the two centers of musical expression.

Three layers of pillows did nothing to soften the effect. I stared up at the ceiling, the frame above my head rhythmically vibrating against the wall. I could scream, yell and pound on doors until they shut the hell up and went about their day, but that typically only started a fight. It was easier to just ignore it for the fifteen minutes it lasted, and then deal with the boys once they had caffeine in their systems.

I sat up, looking around, until I spotted my laptop. Crawling over, I grabbed it off the floor and plugged in some headphones. Putting on a Top 40 playlist to join in the noise, I checked my Facebook account, campus email and then my personal email. All three sites were in sore need of attention, and two hours passed before I logged out of the last account. I shut my laptop and rolled my neck, needing a break. I got up, stretching, my legs asleep and my back aching. Hitting the kitchen, I stole one of Zach's TV dinners, halfway read the directions and popped it in the microwave. While it cooked I flipped through the mail, which had been left on the counter. Junk, bills and more junk. *Yippee.* The microwave beeped, shrill and annoying, and I grabbed the hot plastic dish and pulled it out.

Alex appeared, his dreadlocked head captured under a wool beanie. "What up, chica?" he said, wrapping his arms around me and giving me a quick kiss on the cheek.

"Too much to get into right now," I mumbled, ripping the plastic wrap off the lasagna dish and tossing it into the trash.

"I would stay around and wade into that land mine, but I have class in twenty, so you'll have to lament your woes to me some other time," he said, grabbing a granola bar and snagging his backpack off the floor.

"Thanks, roomie," I called out sarcastically.

He waved, pounding on Zach's door on his way out. "Zach!" he yelled, then spun, giving me a quick grin and jogged out, slamming the door behind him.

Zach appeared thirty seconds later, pulling a baseball cap on his head. "What's up?" he said, eyeing my lasagna as he walked past me into the kitchen. I leaned against the counter and stuck a fork in the dish, waiting, my mouth full of Stouffer's pasta.

He opened the freezer, glanced inside, then looked at the box, sitting on the counter. He raised his eyebrows at me, then his hands. "From the look on your face, I'm not even going to go there. Take as many as you want. I'm not hurting for the three dollars right now."

I grinned despite myself. "Thanks, Zach. Alex just left—he's the one who called for you."

He nodded, opening a cabinet and pulling out a bag of Doritos. Undoing the tie, he grabbed a handful of chips and hoisted himself up onto the counter. Tilting his head at me, he studied my pajamas. "Is your internship already over? I thought you had one more week."

I opened the trash, chunking the remaining lasagna into it. "They let us go home early. My boss was found dead this morning in the office." I moved past him to the sink, washing my fork, my peripheral vision catching his shocked expression. Even in my fragile state, I could appreciate the shock value of my statement.

"No shit," he breathed.

"Yes shit. All sorts of crazy shit. Hence me, in my pj's, eating your lasagna. Which, by the way, sucked. You should buy a different brand."

"It's better when you cook it in the oven," he said through a mouthful of chips. Crunching loudly, he stared at me as if I had something poignant to say. I stared back, our eye contact stretched out until he finished chewing. "Sorry."

"About the lasagna, or about Broward?"

"Broward is, or, sorry, was, your boss?"

God, I really needed to have better lines of communication with these two. "Yes."

"Then I'm sorry about him. Are you gonna start crying or something?" He looked terrified, as if my tears might cause him physical harm.

I fought a smile. "No. Not right now, at least. Though you do seem so adept at comforting."

There was a soft cough behind me, and I turned to see a tall redhead, clad in pink panties and a white tank top. "I can't find my pants," she whispered, as if there were someone else in the house who might hear her. "I think they're in your car...?" She looked to Zach for help.

I turned back to him, fighting a grin.

"Oh—right. Let me go get those for you." He hopped off the counter, tossing the Doritos bag down and bending down to give me a hug. "Find out her name," he whispered in my ear, then bounded out the front door, leaving me and the girl alone. She looked out of place and blushed, covering up as best she could with her hands.

I stepped forward, smiling brightly, and held out my hand. "I'm Julia—Zach's roommate."

"Jen," she offered shyly, shaking my hand. "I met Zach last night, at a party."

"Can I get you anything to eat?" I offered, gesturing toward the kitchen. "There's some really shitty lasagna if that rings your bell."

"No—I've got to run, but thank you," she said, smiling politely.

Zach saved us then, stepping back inside with a pair of white jeans in his hand. Skinny jeans, from the look of them. I had newfound respect for her flexibility if she was able to get out of those in his coupe. I squeezed past them, headed for the hall. "Zach, I'll give you and *Jen* some privacy. I've got to get some stuff done on the computer."

I closed my door to his grateful look, fighting the urge not to flick him and his slutty ways off.

Ten minutes later, I was snuggled under a heavy down blanket with an eye mask on. I had set the alarm for two hours, closed the blinds in my room and turned my television to the History Channel. I closed my eyes and tried not to think of Broward's intelligent face, or the grace in which he had handled the clumsiness of my first day. I remembered Brad's eyes, finding mine in the crowded lobby, his face calm and in control while Broward's body lay in a body bag somewhere. Broward. My mentor, my slave driver. A tyrant that I now, suddenly, missed.

Twenty-Three

I was in the middle of one of those incredible dreams, the kind where you win the lottery, then find out your yard boy is Channing Tatum, and he has just decided to prune your hedges naked, when my cell rang. I reached out blindly, knocking over half of the items on my bedside table before I hit the silence button. I drifted back, seeing his gorgeous profile, his muscular arms reaching up, up—and my damn phone rang again. I reached out, this time connecting with it the first time, silencing it so quickly that dream redemption should have been easy pickings.

I floated down, down, into absolute nothing. My subconscious searched wildly, searching for a fragment, a tendril, anything. I would have been happy with Channing Tatum's chest hair at that point, not that the man had any. But…zilch. It was gone.

I opened my eyes to dark silk and reached up, yanking the eye mask from my face. *Shit.* I groaned, reaching over and grabbing my phone, grumbling as I unlocked it to display my call history.

Brad. Two missed calls. I traded one imaginary hunk for a real one. It should be a good thing. Channing Tatum never brought me to my first orgasm, though I had certainly tried hard enough before chucking my first vibrator into the trash. But seeing Brad's name brought back reality, and reality brought back Broward's dead body and the Magianos' probable involvement. An involvement that Detective Parks had dismissed without a second thought. No matter what he said, I knew what I had heard. And despite Broward's strong words, there had been fear in his voice. And then he had been killed. The circumstances were too strong to ignore.

The phone rang again, startling me.

I rolled my eyes, my mouth curving despite myself. "Whaaaat?" I groaned into the phone, fighting to keep the smile out of my voice.

"You're starting a habit, answering the phone like that." His deep voice weakened my flimsy shield, and I giggled despite my best intentions.

"You're starting a habit of power calling."

He chuckled. "You can't be busy, seeing as how I gave you the day off."

I smirked into the phone. "Don't even start thinking along that path. I'll report to Clarke before I'm under you."

"There are so many places I could go with that statement, but seeing as I'm not alone, I will keep it clean. How are you doing?"

"I'm okay." I stretched, stifling a yawn. "Right now I'm waiting with bated breath to find out what my day will look like tomorrow. Has anyone sent out an email?"

He swore under his breath. "Shit. I've got to have someone do that."

"Sounds like a Clarke assignment to me. He seems by far the most responsible out of the remaining two partners."

"You're right. I'll call him next." There was noise in the background, and then he was back on my line. "Are you mine tonight, or should I make other plans?"

"I'm thinking about it."

He made an unintelligible sound, somewhere between a snort and a groan. "Whatever. I'll take that as a yes. Pick you up at seven?"

"All right. Let me get back to my warm bed. Talk to you soon."

"Bye, baby."

I ended the call, halfheartedly attempted another return to Tatum-land, then gave up, swinging my legs out of bed and standing. Stretching, I headed to the shower, determined to wash away the day's ugliness.

At 5:12 p.m., an email from Lisa Strong, Clarke's secretary, titled "Broward Staff" hit my in-box. It was brief, listing the day and time of Broward's funeral—Sunday, 3:00 p.m. It also stated that the Broward staff would be off on Thursday, but was expected to work normal hours on Friday.

I skimmed the email and then packed an overnight bag. A good dinner, sleeping late in Brad's bed and a home-cooked breakfast sounded pretty good right now.

Twenty-Four

Over thirteen hours later, I woke up in Brad's bed. The smell of bacon was in the air, and I was naked, his thousand-thread-count sheets cool against my body. The shower was running, and I glanced over to the clock. Six-forty a.m. We had stayed up late, talking over dinner, and then, later, sweet, sensual sex, an incredible joining that had given me an emotional connection when I desperately needed one. I fought the desire for bacon and closed my eyes, feeling my body drift back toward dreamdom. The sound of the shower door halted my descent and I rolled over, propping a pillow underneath my head and watching the door swing open, steam billowing out. I smiled when I saw him emerge, butt naked and utterly gorgeous, ripped muscles surrounding nine inches that had become my full-time obsession. I drank him in, his head obscured by a white towel, his hands rubbing it over his head and then down his body. He turned and paused, meeting my eyes, a smile creeping over his face. He dropped the towel and came to me, halting by the side of the bed, my eyes now in perfect eye level with his cock.

I rolled back, looking up into his face, a lazy smile spreading over my own. "Good morning."

He leaned over, resting his weight on the bed and kissing me with a mouth that hinted of mint toothpaste. "Good morning, beautiful. Go back to sleep. I'll be out of here in a few minutes."

I frowned, propping myself up on one elbow, my face close to his. "Fine. If you absolutely refuse to join me." I tilted my head up and he closed the distance, planting a soft kiss on my lips. Then I curled back into the sheets, my eyes closing before he even walked away, sleep beckoning me from afar.

I was wakened by a loud woman's voice.

"I *know* you don't think I'm going to clean around your lazy ass!" I cracked open one eye, then two. Martha stood at the foot of Brad's bed, her hands on her hips and a glare on her face. I propped myself up on one elbow and held the blankets against my body.

"I wasn't aware that you did clean, Martha."

"What is *that* supposed to mean!"

"It means that I thought Helga cleaned, and you 'managed.' And it's…" I looked at the clock. "Only eight-fifteen. Not exactly grounds for calling me a lazy ass." Though I had planned on sleeping till at least ten. *So much for sleeping in late with a home-cooked breakfast.*

She threw up her hands and looked to the ceiling. "Lord Almighty, you test me with these women.…" She stopped cursing whoever was above the ceiling and pointed a finger at me. "I'm not gonna have you talk to me like that!"

That did it. I threw my legs off the bed and stood, dragging the blanket off with me. "What is your problem?!"

"*My* problem?"

"Yes, *your* problem! You have been horrible to me since

the first day I met you! I thought it was just 'your way,' but now I think it's something you personally have against me!"

She pointed at me again and I wanted to reach over and break that finger off. "You're just like all of his girls. You think you're special, but you're not. Why should I bend myself backward to kiss your ass when, two months from now, you'll be back at home, crying over the man?"

I stared at her and pulled my own finger out from behind the sheet. "First, Martha, you don't know a damn thing about me. I *am* fucking special, and I don't cry over men. If I am back at home in two weeks, or two months, or two years, it's because I want to be there, not because a man got tired of me and kicked me out. But while I *am* here, I'm not gonna tiptoe around your grumpy ass. I'll treat you with respect, and don't think it's ridiculous to ask for it in return. Now, since *you*, as far as I know, don't *clean*, how about you give me some privacy!" I turned on my heel, hoping I didn't get tangled in the blankets, and flopped back down, throwing the covers over my head and praying to God, Martha's God, that she wouldn't throw something large and pointy at me.

I heard her laughing, a cruel, mean laugh that grew in volume, and I flung the covers off my head and glared at her.

"Next time you throw that high-and-mighty routine, don't do it under a photo of another naked woman. Just a tip there, Julia baby." She sniffed, laughed again and sauntered off, slamming the door shut behind her.

I flopped back on the bed, glaring up at the gorgeous naked beauty framed above my head. The life-size portrait was of an ex of Brad's, something he told me he hadn't had the time or effort to replace. I'd have to push that higher up on his to-do list.

I rolled over to the other bedside and grabbed my phone.

Eight percent battery. *Figures.* I called Brad, hoping he was still in the house but knowing he wasn't.

"Hey, beautiful."

"Martha is a bitch, you know that?"

He chuckled, sounding way too sexy for 8:00 a.m. "I can't talk now. What do you need?"

"I'm stranded here with your crazy excuse for a… What is her job title again?"

"Ruler of Everything in the House. Martha is part of the package, babe. You're going to have to learn how to get along with her."

"She's the one who's being difficult! She marched in here yelling at me this morning!"

"She's being territorial, Julia. Take whatever attitude she gives you as a compliment. Most women she doesn't even bother being rude to." His soothing voice did nothing but irritate me further. Especially since I now realized whose side he was taking.

"Whatever. I'll let you get back to work."

"Just hang out at the house."

"No, thank you. I hang out at the house any longer and me and her are gonna come to blows. And I'm positive I'll lose that fight."

"Julia, she's not that bad."

"To you! The one who pays her!"

"Look, if you want, I'll have Jeff or one of the other drivers give you a ride."

I slumped back. "Let me figure out my day, and I'll let you know. Maybe one of the girls can give me a ride."

He said something to someone else, then was back on the phone with me, dropping his voice now. "You sure you don't want to just stay? I like the idea of having you there, and I can give you a ride at lunch."

"I'll think about it," I muttered.

I hung up, lay back and stared at the ceiling. *Damn Martha.* Then I closed my eyes and fell back asleep.

Twenty-Five

The third time I woke up, it was to a quiet house. I lay in Brad's bed for a minute, listening for Martha, but heard nothing. I got up, checking my phone. Two missed calls, Becca and Olivia. Becca never called before noon. Something was up. My three percent battery didn't afford me the luxury of calling her back and I crawled out of bed in search of my phone charger. I dug through my overnight bag, not altogether certain I had packed it, and sent a silent prayer upward when my fingers closed around it. I plugged it in, then warily headed downstairs.

The house was empty, the kitchen wiped down and countertops empty, void of anything that could be considered breakfast food. I opened up cabinets, finding cereal, and poured a bowl, sitting at the counter and munching away. The day stretched before me, and I had absolutely no idea of what to do with it. I had lazed away yesterday, doing nothing but feeling sorry for myself, a hobby I was already sick of. I finished off the Frosted Flakes, hefted myself to my feet and washed my bowl, drying it carefully and placing it back on the shelf. Anything I could do to stay on Martha's good side. I returned the cereal box, then headed back upstairs.

I killed two birds with one stone and conferenced Becca in as soon as Olivia answered.

"It's Jules. Was it coincidence, or did you both call because you love me?"

"Ha. The police called me this morning," Becca snapped. "At ten freaking a.m.!"

"Don't be dramatic, Becca. It wasn't the police, it was a detective. Detective Parks, right?" Olivia said.

"I don't know what the damn man's name was!" she retorted.

"Wait, he actually called you guys?" I interrupted their useless spat, my head hurting from the new information. I thought that the detective's request for alibi verification was a line on a form of his, not a lead that he would actually follow up on. Didn't he have more important things to check on? Like the Magiano family? Since when were college interns the most likely murder suspect?

"What happened, Jules?" Olivia's tone was serious, her words cutting into the rant that Becca was starting back into.

"Nothing," I mumbled, grabbing my cosmetics bag and walking into the bathroom. "Well, too much to go into now. What did you tell him?"

"We told him you were at the bar with us until around eleven." Becca's voice was unsure. "Is that okay?"

"Of course. Did he ask you anything else?"

"That was all he asked me," Olivia said. "He just verified, several times, how long you had stayed at the bar."

"Same here," Becca said, her voice subdued.

"Good." I exhaled a sigh of relief. "Then everything should be fine."

"Except that we don't know what's going on, and I was woken up at ten in the freaking morning!" Becca's fire was back, and I wouldn't be able to avoid it this time.

"Fine. Meet me for lunch, and I'll explain everything. Deal?"

"Deal. But you're paying," Olivia said, "in exchange for us keeping you out of the gallows."

"The what?"

"Nothing, Becca. Mellow Mushroom, noon. Work for you both?" I asked.

They agreed, Olivia offering to pick me up, and I hung up the phone with at least one part of my life figured out. I stripped, piling my clothes in the middle of the floor, and turned on the jets of Brad's shower, brushing my teeth as the room filled with steam. Then I stepped in and shut the door, losing myself in the gloriousness of hot water.

"TELL ME THIS isn't about Brad." Olivia had barely allowed me to get both feet in the car before she jumped on me, her tone that annoying level of nag.

"This isn't about Brad," I recited dutifully, digging through her glove box until I found a pair of sunglasses and sliding them on, checking my reflection in her mirror. "But I'm not telling you anything more till we get to lunch. Becca will hack me to pieces if I tell you what's going on before I tell her."

She glanced over, grinning at me, the open window whipping hair over her face. "You always tell me things before you tell Becca. Why change now?"

"I don't *always* do that." I searched my memory for a leg to stand on and, finding none, moved on. "This has jaw-dropping potential, and I don't want your reaction to look fake. We all know your acting skills leave something to be desired."

I studiously avoided her gaze, opening my purse and digging around in it, needlessly organizing and reorganizing it until I felt the coast was clear. I sat back, glancing over at her, a small smile on her lips. Our eyes met and she rolled her eyes.

"I'm going to go easy on you because it's obvious you are having a less than perfect week." She reached over, turning up the radio, and I sat back, happy to avoid conversation, preparing myself for the interrogation that would meet me once they were both in front of me.

I came, I ate cheese pizza, I conquered and I left. Olivia dropped me off at my house, drunk on carbs and gossip, and I stumbled across the yard and through the front door, collapsing on the couch.

The girls had wrung every juicy detail out of me, save the juiciest of all—my walk down eavesdrop lane. They had different theories for Broward's murderer, ranging from his secret gay lover to Sheila, in the study, with a revolver. I hadn't uttered the Magiano name, visions of severed horse heads and smashed kneecaps floating above the Parmesan cheese in front of me. My brooding was noticed, and the girls did their jobs, turning the conversation toward men and shopping, and the second half of the lunch passed by in a sea of lighthearted chatter.

I stared up at the ceiling, feeling the weight in my stomach settle. Maybe the mob wasn't involved. Maybe the detective was right, and I had imagined the conversation. But just to be safe, I was going to keep the information close to my chest and see what Detective Parks discovered.

*Speaking of which...*I sat up, my full stomach protesting, and reached down, grabbing my phone and flipping through my wallet, till I found the detective's business card. I dialed his number and waited, stretching out on the couch and staring at the ceiling.

He didn't answer, and I left a polite but firm message, giving my cell number and asking him to call me. I stewed, my eyes roaming the spiderwebbed corners of the ceiling, going back over the words I had heard that day, the tension in Broward's voice. There was part of the conversation I couldn't recall, some name that had slipped in before the Magiano bomb had been dropped. I pulled deep within, trying to grab the words that had passed through that door. A takeover that had gone well, a name—something that sounded like lasagna. I thought, scrunching up my forehead, and no doubt creating three new future wrinkles in the process. *Ugh.* It probably didn't sound anything like lasagna. It was probably Smith, or Jenkins, or something that had no correlation to the crusty TV dinner box that sat in our kitchen trash.

I dragged myself to my feet, the weight of my current situation too great to handle without endorphins. Carbs certainly hadn't helped; maybe running would clear my head.

The name came to me halfway through lacing up my tennis shoes, as clear and perfect as if it had been stamped on my Nikes. Genovese. Or Ginovase. Italian names always proved difficult, but Google straightened me out, and I stood in my room, spandex-clad, and scrolled through search results, trying to find anything on the turnover that would give credence to my Magiano hypothesis.

Bingo. Eighth result down, a news article dated nine months ago, TAKEOVER, all caps, in the title.

MAFIA FAMILY TAKEOVER, BLOODY FUED ERUPTS

Associated Press, March 16, *USA TODAY*

In one of the major Mafia restructures of this decade, longtime mob patriarch Vincent Genovese is dead,

murdered in his home. Genovese, who has been the
subject of a three-year multi-bureau investigation for
money laundering and extortion, was found Tuesday
morning by his wife, Maria Genovese. The victim was
stabbed repeatedly in the chest and died from loss of
blood. One anonymous source stated Lino Genovese,
a cousin of Vincent, had been questioned by police.
Lino, who has been slowly moving up in Genovese
power circles, has reportedly taken over several family businesses in the last few months. The anonymous
source confirmed that family strife due to Lino's increased interest in their business ventures had grown
to a breaking point. Police refused to comment on
Genovese's death or Lino's involvement, stating that
it was an ongoing investigation. As of press time, no
suspect has been arrested.

Hot fuck. Broward had stated that the Genovese takeover
had gone well, and that he hadn't heard any complaints from
the Magianos so far. I wasn't really up on legal negotiations,
but I was pretty sure that two bullets to the head might clas-
sify as a complaint. My head spun with the new information,
and I straightened, shutting the laptop and thinking. I placed
another call to Detective Parks, left another voice mail, then
grabbed my house key and left, hitting the pavement outside
at a strong pace.

Twenty-Six

The detective entered the East Wing, heading for De Luca's main secretary. He flashed his badge to the elegant, mature woman behind the middle desk. "I need to speak to Mr. De Luca."

The woman didn't blink but fixed the detective with a pointed glance. "Your name?"

"Detective Wilkes. Homicide."

She nodded pleasantly but didn't make a move to her phone. "I don't believe that Mr. De Luca is in, Detective Wilkes, but if you take a seat I will try and contact him."

"You do that."

Her brows raised, she looked pointedly at the nearest seating cluster. He shook his head and sauntered over to the seat, collapsing into it with a loud sigh.

She picked up her phone and dialed an extension.

"Brad De Luca."

"Detective Wilkes just came in, unannounced. He is asking to speak to you."

"Fine. Send him in, then interrupt us after ten minutes."

"Yes, sir."

I RAN, QUICKER than my normal speed, but I needed justification for my pounding heart. Broward assisted in the Genovese family turnover. Broward was working for the Magiano family. His words, strained and hateful, not the man I knew. *"Some of the biggest names in town are coming to me for services... Genovese turnover was handled perfectly...I haven't heard any complaints from the Magianos..."* No wonder he was dead. I jumped curbs, climbed up and pounded down Stadium Hill, my breath coming fast, a cramp in my side, my legs screaming in protest, until I finally wound down, coming to a sudden, gut-wrenching stop. I bent over, feeling slightly nauseated.

What was I doing? Why was I digging into this crap, trying to find proof of the Magianos' involvement in Broward's death? Why was I power-calling Detective Parks to make sure that he explored that angle? Broward, my mentor, a man I had respected, had apparently run a full-page ad in the mobster Yellow Pages. He had wanted the business, bragged about it. And then he was killed. I needed to get the fuck out of this situation and start minding my own business. I had to stop thinking of Broward as an innocent bystander and recognize his part in his own demise. I needed to stop thinking about the entire situation.

"DETECTIVE." BRAD SHOOK Detective Wilkes's hand and sat on the edge of his desk, arms crossed. "I have a meeting shortly. I will only be able to give you a few minutes. Any luck finding Kent's killer?"

"We're working on that." The man looked at Brad appraisingly. "Diligently."

"Last time we spoke, I believe I informed you that I would not answer questions without my attorney present."

"Humor me."

Brad said nothing, just met the detective's eyes.

"We have discovered large amounts of funds deposited into Mr. Broward's bank account over the last three years."

"CDB does very well, I would expect Kent to have a healthy bank account." Brad crossed his arms and looked down at his watch.

"Not from the firm. From other accounts, foreign, untraceable accounts. Do you know where those income streams would have originated, or why?"

"Are you asking Clarke these questions?"

"No."

Brad spread his arms, exasperated. "Then why me? Why assume I know anything about Kent and his money, his clients? I don't have anything to do with Kent or his business. And as you so clearly pointed out, he despised me!"

"Clarke doesn't have ties to organized crimes." Wilkes's eyes glittered triumphantly, as if he had found the cure to cancer.

Brad turned, walking behind his desk. "My family has nothing to do with me, or my business. Don't drag unrelated items into this discussion. If you want to investigate my family, go right ahead. You will have my full cooperation. For now, get out—unless you have something to arrest me for."

There was a knock on the door, and then Carol Featherston appeared. "Mr. De Luca, we need to leave for court."

Brad nodded and turned to the detective. "Thank you for your time, Mr. Wilkes. Carol will see you out." Without waiting for a response, he turned and walked out, shoulders relaxed, but his hands in fists in his pockets.

Twenty-Seven

Detective Parks sucked; it was official. Either he had no concept of how to return a call, or he had no intention on following up on the Magiano lead. Either way, as I had decided on my return jog home, I would leave him one final voice mail, telling him about the Genovese connection, and then I would be done with it. No follow-up calls, no reading the papers, no digging through Broward's stuff. I completed the task, speaking clearly and slowly into the phone, laying out everything I knew in one, concise, forty-seven-second voice mail. Then I hung up, pressing the end call button with reluctance.

Ending that call felt so final, as if I had taken a step off a cliff and couldn't stop my descent. Giving up on Broward felt traitorous, as if I were weak and running from his killer. But I needed to be smart. I had passed on the information to Parks. Now I needed to get back to the land of the living.

I THREW LISA Strong's instructions out the window and decided to go to the office. After reorganizing my jewelry box and flipping through every television station I had, I was going stir-crazy and actually contemplating cleaning, a sure sign that dementia was only a few steps away. I threw on a pullover and grabbed my keys, my mind skipping ahead to the half-finished documents that were currently wasting real estate on my desk.

I walked into the CDB offices at 5:00 p.m., hoping to get into my office and into my work without being seen. Once I knocked out the half-finished items, I could sneak back out. I wasn't sure how tomorrow would play out, or if our cases would get transferred, and I wanted to get a few tasks wrapped up while I had the chance.

Lights were on in the other two wings, but all was dark on our side of the building. Every cop show I had seen prepared me for crime-scene tape and black fingerprint powder, but the halls and offices looked normal, ordinary. I was almost disappointed by the lack of drama. I left the lights off and went straight to my office, unlocking the door, the click sounding loud in the silent halls. Going inside, I pulled the door behind me, leaving it ajar so I would be able to exit in a quiet fashion.

Starting up the computer, I skimmed over the open files on my desk. About an hour of work. Just enough to distract me, without committing me to this office all night long. My computer chimed, loading the desktop, and I leaned over, typing in my credentials and logging on.

I quickly became engrossed, finishing the open files and reorganizing the folders without even noticing. I was starting on a fresh case when the voice came.

"Julia."

I jumped, my breath catching, and straightened, looking at the door to my darkened office. A huge silhouette filled the doorway, and quiet masculinity crept into my small office. *Brad.*

"What are you doing?" His voice was dark and still. Definite.

"Nothing. Working."

He walked toward me, his hands in his pockets, the expensive suit hanging perfectly on his large, muscular frame. His eyes, dark and intense, picked up the light from my monitor and glowed blue in the darkness.

"On what?"

"Filing, typing. Why? Does it matter?" His authoritative tone irritated me, and I pushed away from my desk and folded my arms, my eyes narrowed into a stern look. His tie loosened, a day's worth of growth on his chin, he looked like the perfect late-night distraction. Too bad it was only—I snuck a look at my computer's display—6:30 p.m.

"You aren't supposed to be here."

"Says who? This is my office."

"Says the office email that you received." His voice commanding, he continued moving forward until we stood inches apart. For no good reason, I was suddenly pissed, mad at his invasion of my office, a space he seemed to control and command whenever he damn well pleased.

I looked up at him, feeling ridiculously short in my tennis shoes. He was close enough that his scent invaded me, and my insides quivered traitorously. "Oh, now you want me to follow the rules!" I lifted my chin, meeting his stern eyes, but my response was weakened, standing this close to the damn stern sexiness of him.

We stayed there for a moment, our eyes locked on each other. He looked exhausted, and his eyes finally broke from mine and traveled down my body, his mouth twitching slightly as he took in my tank top and running pants. When his eyes returned to mine, they were almost pained, twin fires flicking hot and cold. "I hate how you make me feel," he whispered, his voice tight.

I recoiled from the intensity in his voice. "What does that mean?"

He grabbed my neck, sliding one hand back and grabbing my ponytail, pulling it hard and tilting my face to him. I growled, low in my throat, and glared at him. I struggled against him, but he held me easily. "Take your fucking hands off me," I said.

He ignored me, walked me backward by my ponytail, hard, until I slammed against the back wall of my office, the chair rail pressing into my back. He released my ponytail and ran his hand firmly and slowly down my body, his eyes burning into mine, his hands groping and squeezing my breasts, stomach and ass as they traveled down. His hands, slow and deliberate, said more than his mouth ever could. *He owned me, I was his to do with as he wanted.* Fuck, I hated that I liked it. He bent down to kiss me, and I turned my head, evading his mouth and trying to push him off with my hands.

They met only rock-hard, unmoving muscle. I employed my best defense and brought up my knee, swift and hard, aiming for his nuts. He grabbed my wrists and jumped back, a hurt look in his eyes. Then he smiled, slow and confident. Slamming my wrists against the wall, on either side of my head, he leaned in close, catching my mouth in his. I stiffened, my body unyielding. Taking my mouth, he kissed me, long and deep, and I sagged a little against the wall. He pressed his body against me, pinning me to the wall, and I felt the hardness of his cock.

"Get off me," I whispered, trying to stay firm.

"No."

"I am not fucking you in my office."

He laughed, kissing my neck, and over his broad shoulders I noticed my office door was still open. I pushed hard against him. "Brad, the door!" I whispered urgently.

"Fuck the door," he growled, grabbing my shorts and yanking them down, exposing my white cotton thong.

I squirmed against him, thoughts running through my mind, too many and too quickly for me to focus on. The dominant and only thought I could grab was the image of his thick cock fucking me right here, right now.

He yanked me forward a step, then grabbed my face, looking at me hard, breathing fast, a tortured look in his eyes. "Please." The word, which should have been a plea, was somehow an order, and I resisted, now for the sheer perversity of it.

I pushed him back and tried to grab my shorts, to pull them up, but he caught my hands and spun me around, grabbing my hips and pushing me forward, till I was bent over in front of him. The speed of his movement caught me off balance, and I reached forward, trying to grab something, anything, to stop me from falling. I grabbed the wall and pushed on it, the motion inadvertently arching my back and pushing my ass against Brad. He chuckled, and I heard a zipper and then felt his fingers, working fast, a ripping sound of condom wrapper, my thong pushed to the side. I realized what was happening and was opening my mouth to object when he shoved hard and was suddenly inside me.

My objection stopped in my throat, quivered there and died. He was so big, so thick, so hard. He pushed deeper, and grunted when he was fully inside me. My hands flexed against the wall and I groaned, low in my throat. He squeezed my ass, hard, then slapped it, the sound loud and animal in the darkness. Then the fucking started, hard and fast, our bodies slapping loudly, too loudly, in the quiet office. All I could think about was the floor full of people, my open office door. What would happen if someone walked by and saw me, bent over, being fucked relentlessly, workout pants bunched around my tennis shoes? The thought turned me on so much that I instantly tightened, an orgasm building around Brad's stiff rod.

He groaned, continuing his fast, furious pace. "What you do to me, Julia; your fucking sassy mouth, your tight little body...I want to make you do such bad things."

I moaned softly, my tits shaking from the pounding he was giving me. He took a hand off me and slapped my ass again, hard, the pain intensifying the pleasure that was growing in my pussy, expanding, taking over.

"Spank me again," I said, breathing hard, needing the release I knew was coming.

He reached down and grabbed my neck, squeezing it. "Beg me," he ordered.

"Please!" I cried, louder than I intended, and I dropped my voice. "Spank me! I need it! Now!"

He spanked me in rhythm with his fucking, and I arched my back, raised my head and dissolved in perfect ecstasy as I exploded around his cock. I screamed, the pleasure overtaking every sense in my head, and he immediately clasped his hand hard over my mouth, muting the sound. He fucked me through the orgasm, until my legs could no longer stand it, my body weak from my release, and he laid us both down, him hovering over me, his body and face a dark silhouette against the light from my screen saver. I kicked off my shorts and wrapped my legs around him, and he moved inside me, long, deep, slow strokes. Leaning down, he kissed me, soft and sweetly, then stronger and more possessively. Our lips finally separated, our breaths ragged, and he rose, looking down at me, his strong face unreadable.

"What?" I whispered, my lips burning from his rough kisses, my body relaxed from the orgasm.

"You look beautiful."

I smiled, meeting his dark eyes. "I thought you wanted to make me bad."

"Oh, I will, Ms. Campbell. I will make you very, very bad," he whispered, his hand gently tucking my hair behind my ear, his cock still moving slowly, deliciously in me. His fingers rubbed my swollen mouth; his thumb caressed my lips, then dipped inside my mouth. I sucked on his thumb, enjoying the light in his eyes as I flicked my tongue over it. I propped myself up on an elbow and thrust my pelvis, squeezing with my legs and burying his cock in me. Staring into his eyes, I spoke deliberately.

"Stop talking and fuck me."

A grin broke out on his face and he growled, pressing down on my chest, flattening me to the floor. He leaned over me, grabbing my wrists and pinning them above my head, then fucked me, hard and fast, pounding me into the plush carpet, my legs popping loose and spreading, his muscular thighs trapping them into place. He was still fully clothed, his dress pants rough against my bare legs and his clothing caused wonderful friction against my clit. I tried to hold off my orgasm as long as I could, but came, my legs bouncing, my arms fighting against his iron grip on my wrists. I moaned, biting into his neck to stop my screams from erupting, the waves of pleasure shaking me from head to toe. He shoved, hard and deep, his strokes continuing. A minute later, he groaned into my neck, his thickness twitching inside me, and I felt his body stiffen as he came.

JULIA CAMPBELL'S REPEATED calls to Detective Parks were acknowledged, discussed and decided upon, her being one small pawn in a game with much bigger fish. She had become annoying, bothersome, a pesky itch in a hard-to-reach spot. And at 5:52 p.m. that Thursday, while mid-orgasm beneath Brad's body, her fate was decided. She was as good as dead.

The man's phone rang, the bright display illuminating on his dash, and he pulled over, answering the cell. "Yes."

"I need you to take care of something. It's regarding Broward."

"I finished that job."

"Yeah, there was an overlooked detail. It's a girl, his intern. She's been calling Parks. She knows we are involved and won't drop it. She lives in some piece-of-shit house near the university and probably has roommates. I'll send you the address. I'm sure the police will make the connection, but try and make it look like an accident."

"Okay."

"Also, find out if she talked to anyone."

He was silent a moment, running his hand along the leather steering wheel. "You want me to make it look like an accident, but torture her in the process?"

"Be creative, Leo. Just get it fucking handled without anyone calling the cops. I don't care if you burn the whole shithole down with the roommates inside."

"Okay. Tomorrow night."

HE STOOD OVER me, zipping up his pants, my monitor now a galaxy of stars. I lay, weak and spent, still on the floor, not wanting to get up, to have to move in any way.

"How much longer will you be *working*?" His dry voice held an edge of sarcasm, and I bristled, raising myself up on one elbow.

"Well, I would be done working, if it wasn't for your interruption."

"You can work tomorrow." His tone had an order to it that I didn't like.

"I want to finish up here."

He sighed, frustrated. I reluctantly moved, rolling over and sitting up, and looked around for my shorts, finally seeing them in the corner of my office. I stood, pulled them on and yanked out my disaster of a ponytail, finger-combing my hair.

"You need to get out of here." I spoke quietly, worried that we would be caught.

His mouth twitched, but he nodded. Collected, his hands in his pockets, he didn't look as if he had spent the past half hour banging the intern. The thought struck me as funny, and I fought a giggle. He shook his head wryly at me, then turned and left the office.

I sank into my office chair, half giddy with pleasure, half furious at myself for yielding to his sexuality. *Good God, I am in trouble.*

I wrapped up the filing, shut down the computer and grabbed my cell and keys, locking my office door and moving quietly through the dark halls, down the back stairwell and into the parking garage. There was a note on the windshield of my Camry. "Call me." Unsigned.

I started my car and headed for home, my stomach growling along the way. I dialed Brad's number, and he answered on the second ring.

"Hey."

"Hey."

"Do you have dinner plans?"

"No, but I think I'll eat at home. I already got what I

Twenty-Eight

Brad was, as always, irritatingly punctual, and I slid into his white BMW in a pair of faded jeans, flip-flops and a scoop-neck white shirt. He gave my outfit an appraising glance before putting the car in reverse and backing out of my driveway.

"I'm sorry, is there a problem with my outfit?" I asked innocently.

"Only that I want to tear it off you," he growled, leaning over and kissing me. I pulled away, playfully smacking him. "Watch the road!"

He laughed and leaned back in his seat, his face dark in the car, lit occasionally by oncoming traffic. I fastened my seat belt and watched him. He seemed distracted, drumming his fingers on the steering wheel in tune to the radio. He glanced over, catching my eyes. "You shouldn't have been in the wing alone. Not after what happened to Kent."

I frowned. "I've been in the office countless times that late."

"I know, but normally there is other staff around. Just, given the circumstances, you should have told security."

needed from you," I teased, putting on my signal and changing lanes.

He laughed, and I heard road noise in the background. "Despite that, let me take you to dinner."

I hesitated for a moment, my heart well aware of the nosedive it was taking into the pool of love. Love that, knowing Brad's history, would never be returned to my satisfaction. I should refuse, fight to keep what distance I could until I figured out what the hell my long-term plan was. "Okay. But somewhere casual."

"Pick you up in fifteen at your house?"

"See you then." I grinned despite myself, hanging up the phone. *Yep. Nose-diving straight into those dark depths.* At least I saw my demise coming. For whatever that was worth.

"If I had told security, they probably wouldn't have let me up there."

He laughed. "Good point. So what, pray tell, was so important?"

I leaned back into the seat. "I don't know. I was just sick of being at home. I needed a distraction."

"Which you got."

I turned to him, grinning. "Yes. Thank you, oh great one, for my distraction."

He squeezed my hand, then released it, putting both hands on the wheel, his face distracted.

"Thinking about Broward?" I asked.

He stopped drumming and looked over at me, his expression serious. "Yeah."

"You don't seem very upset."

"I've had two days to absorb it, Julia. But you already knew that Kent and I weren't close."

I closed my eyes briefly, sitting back on the plush leather seat. Yes, I knew he and Broward didn't get along. We had had that discussion early on, when Broward told me that Brad had fucked his wife, Claire, six years ago on a corporate retreat. The information had caused me to step away, and almost meant the end of our budding relationship.

"I know. Still. You were so...mad when you found out, and were so quiet yesterday. It's just been an odd course of reactions."

He reached over and grabbed my hand, squeezing it reassuringly. "Julia, I have my own way of dealing with things. I don't want to ruin any more time I have with you."

I ran my fingers lightly over our clasped hands, loving how small and delicate my hand looked in his.

We pulled up to a strip mall that had one end occupied by

a restaurant. Navigating the crowded parking lot, he pulled up to the front, lit by a neon light, to let me out. I opened the door and stepped out, moving through waiting patrons as he pulled away to park. I was smiling in anticipation as I pulled open the door and walked into pure, crowded deliciousness.

Despite my Scottish surname, I've always secretly wanted to be Italian. Though no Italian blood runs in my veins, I have gone ahead and adopted their food, lovemaking and overall passion for life. The cheap, strip mall door opened to a wave of noise and smells of Parmesan cheese and marinara. I could barely squeeze in the door, a small crowd filling the small lobby. I took a half step in and waited, trying to see through the crowd for a hostess. I finally saw one, and caught her eye.

"Two. De Luca," I said, and she scribbled it down on a pad.

"You guys sitting in, or out?"

I didn't see any outdoor seating, but the night was unseasonably cool, so I let that be the determinant.

"Out."

"Your car?"

My face must have shown my confusion because she smiled and elaborated. "What kind of car do you have?"

"Oh. White 7-Series." She wrote something else down, and moved to the next person in line. I squeezed my way back through the entrance and into the night air. I saw Brad walking up from a side lot obscured by trees, and met him halfway.

"The place is packed. I said we'd sit outside, but I don't know how long the wait is."

He nodded, flashing a quick grin at me. "Good. If we are sitting outside, then there isn't a wait, they'll serve us out on the car." He gave my waist a quick squeeze and nodded to the parking lot. "Why don't you sit on the hood and I'll grab us drinks? What do you want?"

"White wine—something fruity. Riesling, if they have it."

He nodded and headed in. I wandered to the parking lot. It was a makeshift lot—with cars parked in all sorts of directions, but most facing the overlook. I saw Brad's, the "B D Best" vanity tag clearly identifying it. It was parked close to the edge, and I climbed on top of the hood, which was still warm from the drive. The view from the hood was cut from every sappy movie I'd ever seen—a rainbow of city lights at night—and sitting on the hood I felt like a nervous teenager about to make out. It was almost pitch-black out here, half of the neighboring cars silent and empty, half with couples perched on the hood, or tucked inside their expensive frames. I yawned and lay back, the hood uncomfortably hard but the night sky clear and beautiful. Crickets chirped, and I waited expectantly for the first mosquito to find my juicy self.

Brad appeared from the left side, a red Solo cup in his hand. I sat up, my abs protesting, and grabbed the cup, peering inside. White wine. I looked at him quizzically.

"What—you only drink from fine glassware?" The darkness hid his face, but I heard his smile.

I took a sip. It was chilled, fruity and sweet. *Perfect.* "No. Just not typical De Luca."

He clinked his bottled beer to my plastic cup and sat on the hood next to me, the car noticeably sagging. We sat in comfortable silence for a minute, looking out on the view.

"Are you working tomorrow?"

"Yeah. Lisa Strong emailed everyone, telling us not to come in today, but to be there tomorrow."

"Lisa is Clarke's secretary?"

"Yes." I took a sip of my wine, smiling. "I can't believe you don't know that."

He smirked. "I barely keep my own staff straight." He sobered, thinking of something, then turned to me.

"I met with Clarke today."

I stayed quiet, waiting for him to continue.

"We were never interested in a fourth partner. We always wanted to keep it to three. With Broward…gone…we needed to figure out what was next. If we would stay just the two of us or not. I—"

"Broward's not even in the ground yet!" My voice came out louder and harder than I intended, and he closed his eyes and sighed.

"Julia, I—" He stopped, interrupted again, this time by a thin redheaded waitress in a white button-up, black tie and black pants.

"Excuse me. I am Amber, your waitress. I have your drink orders from the bar. Is there anything else you'd like to drink?" She set a citronella candle on the hood and lit it, depositing two cloth rolls of silverware next to it.

"I'll have bottled water, with dinner," Brad stated, and looked at me.

"I'm fine for now, thank you."

"Would you like to hear the menu?" she asked. I nodded in response, and Brad gave a curt nod.

"It's pretty basic. We have spaghetti, chicken parmesan and lasagna." I waited for more, but from her pregnant pause, that was apparently it. I ordered the spaghetti, and Brad asked for both chicken parm and lasagna. The waitress left, and I looked at Brad, the candle now illuminating his handsome face.

"So they'll serve us out here? On the hood?" The idea seemed preposterous but fun, if not a little messy.

He nodded. "The inside restaurant is pretty small. It fills up quickly. When they first opened, and word started spreading about their food, the line would snake through the parking lot. They started taking drink orders from the waiting crowd… then things just progressed to where they're at now. I should have asked if you like Italian. Their menu is so limited…"

I waved my hand, erasing his concern, and took a sip of wine.

"So. Broward?" I prompted him.

"Right. I understand that it seems cold to you, us discussing this so quickly after his death, but it is a business situation. We can mourn his passing after work, but this is a decision we needed to make quickly. There are clients and cases to contend with, not to mention the necessity to sell his shares so that we can settle with his estate. Claire will need and appreciate the money."

My eyes clouded a bit at the mention of Broward's wife, and I wondered, briefly, if Brad had been in contact with her.

"So, what did you decide? You and Clarke?"

"We decided not to absorb Broward's interest, but to allow an outside attorney to purchase his shares. We don't have the time or expertise to take on Broward's clients, and don't have any junior partners ready to fill his shoes. Today we chose a replacement and extended an offer, which was accepted. Tomorrow we'll make a formal announcement and will introduce him to the team."

I turned it over in my mind, thinking. "Why are you telling me this?"

"Whoever takes his place will be your new boss. There is a chance that he or she won't want to train a new employee— in that case H.R. will either reassign you or terminate your new position."

Terminate my new position. The phrase just screamed *law school rejection*. I sipped my wine slowly. "So. If I was to be reassigned, it would probably need to be to an attorney with a large caseload, someone who would need an additional hand." I looked up at him suggestively, a wry smile crossing his face as he leaned over and looped his arm around my waist, bringing me to him, his lips pressing gently on my head.

"Well, I *would* love to have you under me." His words, a growl against my hair, made me smile. "But, as much as I would enjoy that, we both know I am the last attorney Human Resources would assign you to."

I sighed, his logic solid. "Okay, so scratch my transfer to your office. You're saying if Broward's replacement decides I'm gone, then *poof*, I'm fired?"

"Look at it from his standpoint. A new attorney, coming into a strange office, trying to retain his current clients, plus take on Broward's, learning the staff—he is not going to want to train a new employee or bother getting to know you if you are leaving in a semester. I wouldn't. You would be the first person on my cut list." His face serious, he looked down at me, his brown eyes clear and straightforward.

"But...you're a partner—the biggest one! Can't you keep me there?"

"You mean, since you're sleeping with me?" His voice had a hard edge to it, and I recoiled, glaring at him.

"Fuck you, Brad. This opportunity could pave my way to law school acceptance, not to mention a possible job after graduation. You understand my predicament—I'm asking you to help! I've never asked you for anything!" I fought to keep my voice from rising, but wanted to throw my damn fruity wine in his face.

He met my furious eyes and smiled, disarming me in an instant. The damn man had the most annoying habit of making me want to laugh when I should be choking him. "Julia, anything I do to help you will only shine light on us. As far as they are aware, I don't even know who you are. I can't start campaigning for you without drawing undue attention on us. You are the one so bent on keeping us a secret. I have been, and will continue, going to bat for all of Broward's staff, including you. But I can't make any promises. I just want you to understand that it is important to make a good impression."

I blew out a frustrated breath and kicked off my flip-flops, watching them bounce of the bumper and land on the grass. "Okay. I'll try to make a good impression."

He leaned over and kissed my neck, his delicious scent making me weak. I reluctantly turned my head and we kissed, his hand coming to my chin and his mouth owning mine. I scooted a little closer and our tongues clashed in perfect contrast, his strength meeting my own fiery spirit. He moved his hand lower, played with my breast through my thin T-shirt and then slipped a hand inside the neckline, teasing my nipple with his strong fingers. There was a soft cough and we parted, my face flushed. *Oh my God.*

The redhead was back, this time with a teenage boy who locked his eyes on my chest and caused me to look down, seeing my neckline askew and slight cleavage showing. I hurriedly fixed my shirt and Brad cleared his throat.

"You need something?" he asked the teen, his inflection causing the boy to snap to attention and deposit three foam containers onto our hood, looking everywhere but at me. I felt the urge to laugh, and instead focused on the waitress, who placed two ice-cold bottled waters in front of us. She pulled a wine bottle from under her arm and asked if I wanted more. I held out my cup and she gave me a generous refill. Then they both made a hasty retreat.

Brad smiled and I laughed, and we dug into the containers, opening all three and sharing the contents. The food was delicious, authentic Italian, and I ate quickly, moaning every once in a while at the taste.

After ten minutes, I leaned back, stretching my stomach out, Brad still eating beside me. I hadn't even considered the fact that Broward's death would affect my employment status. And what if his replacement was a jerk? Or didn't want me? I didn't know which would be worse. Somewhere else in the lot, a car radio started, and strands of an Alabama song drifted over to us.

Brad finally leaned back also, and I leaned against him, my head on his shoulder.

"So, tell me about this new guy," I said grudgingly.

"His name is Scott Burge. He has the same area of focus as Broward, and should bring some big clients over to CDB. He seems very intelligent, if a little boring."

"So, basically a clone of Broward." A clone who, hopefully, had better judgment when it came to choosing extra-curricular clients.

"Maybe. You never really know what someone is like until you work with them. As I said, he'll be introduced tomorrow, though he won't take full office hours till next week."

"So I'll meet him tomorrow."

"Yes. I'd dress to impress."

"Is he a horn dog?"

He snorted. "Not that he mentioned in our meetings, but no, he doesn't seem the type. Boring, yes. Sexual, no."

Burrowing into his warmth, I didn't feel like talking, and he seemed content, planting a soft kiss on my head. We sat there, quiet and looking at the city lights and listening to muted country music, till the candle flickered and died and the bugs came and found us.

Twenty-Nine

I stood nervously in the conference room, dressed in a black sleeveless turtleneck, tweed pencil skirt and black peep-toe heels. I had spent an extra fifteen minutes that morning making sure that my hair and makeup looked professionally perfect. The entire West Wing staff, which I still thought of as "Broward's staff," was assembled in the room, ready for an 11:00 a.m. meeting. There was expectant silence in the room as the wall clock clicked to 10:59 a.m.

The conference room door opened. A man in a gray suit strode up to the podium. He was traditionally handsome, the blond-haired, blue-eyed variety that fills every department store flyer in the Sunday paper. He wore glasses, which he adjusted before looking out at the room.

"Good morning. My name is Scott Burge. I would first like to extend my deepest sympathies to you for the loss of Kent Broward. I was personally acquainted with Kent, and had nothing but the utmost respect for him. I know that he has left big shoes to fill."

I studied him carefully, trying to decide what I thought

of him. His clothes hung well on his frame, and his face had just enough strength to be attractive, almost abnormally so.

He paused, clearing his throat and straightening his tie, a gesture I recognized as a nervous one. "That being said, I have come to a partnership agreement with Attorneys Clarke and De Luca, so I will be a permanent fixture in this firm, and the firm name will now be Clarke, De Luca & Burge. I will only be in the office for a few hours today, but will start full-time next week. I would appreciate all of your patience and assistance in familiarizing me with the current caseload and statuses of all ongoing litigation." He nodded once and then closed his notebook, apparently done. There was a scattering of applause, no one knowing whether or not to clap, and Burge left the room.

Chatter started all around me and I moved, heading to the restroom and then to my office, passing Broward's old office on my way. I paused, unsure, and then knocked lightly on the open door, waiting for Burge to look up. He did, and beckoned me in.

The office looked strange without Broward's bald head behind the desk. The office had always been packed with file boxes. That hadn't changed, but now different prints hung on the walls, and Broward's family photos had disappeared. New carpet was underfoot. *Probably because of the bloodstains.*

"Can I help you?" His voice was authoritative, strong, and he looked up at me with clear blue eyes, his skin tan and smooth, his eyes passing briefly over me before they returned to my face.

"I'm Julia Campbell. I was the intern and, starting next week, will be a part-time assistant for this wing. I just wanted to introduce myself." I gestured awkwardly to the doorway.

"My office is adjacent to yours. If you need anything, just call out."

He stood, and I realized he was Brad's height, taller than me in my three-inch heels. "Are you in law school, Ms. Campbell?"

"No." I flushed. "I'm an undergrad. I'm still two semesters from graduation but have already started the process of applying to law schools."

"And what did you *do* for Broward?"

I sensed a hint of sexual innuendo in his question, but brushed it off, meeting his eyes with professionalism. "I worked mainly with corporate document prep. Any basic filings, annual reports, meeting minutes, operating agreements, he would send to me. I prepared them and then sent them back for his approval." A slight exaggeration of my duties.

He nodded, looking pleased. "And you had experience in this previously?"

"No, Broward taught me." I crossed my fingers behind my back, hoping God would give me some leeway given the situation.

He nodded thoughtfully and then smiled. "Thank you, Julia. I look forward to working with you." He reached his hand across the desk and I shook it firmly.

"Likewise, sir." I smiled and left his office, my self-confidence patting my back and smiling broadly. I entered my office and sat down, attacking my work stack with renewed enthusiasm.

THE SOON-TO-BE EX-MRS. Windthorp sat in Brad's large office, facing his desk. She was exquisite, born beautiful and enhanced by the city's top plastic surgeons. She wore a tight white tube top with a cashmere cardigan over it, and had long tan legs barely contained with a black miniskirt. Brad flipped through her file, glancing at her occasionally over the top of it. The file listed her age as thirty-seven, though she didn't look over twenty-six. Her husband was Brett Windthorp, a silver-spoon trust fund baby who had intelligently quadrupled his family's wealth. His current net worth was listed at seventy-two million dollars. Married six years, no children. No prenup. Brad closed the folder.

"Mrs. Windthorp, why—"

"Call me Lisa." A cultured voice, probably from a pageant-queen childhood.

"Fine. Lisa, why do you want a divorce?"

"I'm unhappy." She folded her arms, enhancing her perfect cleavage in the process. Brad looked away, back at the file.

"We're going to need more than your unhappiness to go to the judge with. Tell me about Brett."

"What about him?" She sounded almost petulant in her response.

"Just give me a synopsis."

She delicately sighed, her breasts heaving. "He's boring. All he does is work, and expects me to entertain myself all day. When he's not working, he's either playing golf or spending time with his friends, who he wants me to *entertain*, as well. It's just not what I expected marriage to be."

Brad met her gaze, her response verifying all of the reasons why he never wanted to remarry. "Okay, so irreconcilable differences. And what do *you* want from the settlement?"

She seemed surprised by the statement. "Why, everything, of course. I thought that was what you did."

Brad flexed his hands under the desk, hating his job at this moment. Being good at it made it even more difficult at times. He leaned forward. "You are not going to get everything. You'll be *lucky* to get half. You have no children and have been married less than seven years. You need to take a realistic look at this marriage and reassess your expectations."

The beautiful blonde uncrossed her legs, flashing Brad an eyeful of red lace, and stood, moving forward and leaning on the desk. She tossed her long hair over a shoulder and stared at him, smiling slightly. "Mr. De Luca, I typically get *exactly* what I want."

I bet you do. Brad reclined in his chair and lifted his hands, shrugging. "I'm not the judge, Lisa."

She sniffed and straightened. Patting her hair into place, she lifted her chin at him. "Then make sure you are friends with the one we get." She turned, grabbed her purse and walked out. Brad watched her tight ass as it moved out his door, then shook his head. *Women.*

Reaching forward, he picked up his phone and called Julia's extension.

"Julia Campbell."

"Hey."

"Hey." There was a muffled sound, and her voice dropped to a whisper. "Let me shut my door."

Brad said nothing, watching through the glass wall of his office as Mrs. Windthorp—Lisa—conversed with Diana, one of his secretaries. Then Julia was back.

"I met Burge."

"And?"

"I think he's going to keep me on. He seems fine. Not as nice as Broward, but not an asshole, at least not yet."

"Good. What are your plans for the evening?"

There was silence for a spell, and then she spoke. "I don't know. I had assumed that I'd be working."

"Your slave driver is gone."

"A fact I feel guilty profiting from."

"So feel guilty. There's a concert downtown tonight that Rebecca got us tickets to. Come with me."

"Well, that would depend on who's playing."

"Dave Matthews Band. If that is hip enough for you."

She giggled, a sound that made his cock hard. "You are unhip just from use of the word *hip*. Please, please stop, before you age yourself further."

"So you'll come?"

"Yes. What time's the concert?"

"Nine."

"I'll be ready by eight."

"I'll get a driver and see you then." He hung up the phone, shaking his head and fighting back a grin.

Thirty

The concert was insane. Held at a small, hole-in-the wall bar, it was intimate, fifty of us and *him*—straddling a stool and holding his guitar as if it were an extension of his arm. We dined on finger-size portions of bar food while Dave Matthews told stories, joked around and crooned songs I had committed to memory. In the dim light of the bar, with Brad's grin and Dave's lyrics, it was like being in a dream. I reached over, trailing a hand over Brad's arm, his mouth pressing gently against my neck, strands of sexual harmony floating through the air, a hand sliding up my bare leg.

Dave took a half-hour break and we escaped the smoky air, stumbling into the dark alley behind the bar, inhaling the cool breeze, my cheeks red from too many drinks, Brad's eyes dark embers lit by night streetlamps. We were laughing over some stupid thing, my body folding into his, his strength encasing me, when he gripped me, picking me easily up and setting me on the hood of a parked car, his hands separating my legs, his body sliding perfectly between them.

I laughed at the cold metal against my bare skin, the

thin fabric of my dress now bunched around my waist. He growled against my throat, his mouth kissing and suckling it, making its way up to my mouth as his hands explored my body. My laughter faded as need overtook it, and my hands traveled also, stealing underneath his shirt, feeling the cut of muscles and abs, feeling the shudder of heart underneath my palm. I withdrew my hands, capturing his face in them and planting soft kisses on his cheeks and forehead. There was a strum of music behind us and I heard a voice over the microphone.

"Time to go back," I whispered.

He protested, pulling me tight to him, his need obvious, even through jeans.

"Later," I promised, wrapping my arms tight around his neck, and he lifted and spun me, my legs releasing him and finding ground. Then we ducked back into the bar, the crowd, smoke and music engulfing and drawing us in.

BRAD HAD PURCHASED a CD, and the strands of music danced through the dark limo. I was officially drunk, having polished off five beers along with about two thousand calories of nachos, wings and potato skins. Brad grinned down at me, somehow completely sober despite doubling my alcohol consumption. His image blurred, and I closed my eyes briefly, hoping that a wave of nausea wasn't next.

"You okay?"

"I'm good," I mumbled. "Did I mention I love Dave Matthews?"

He chuckled. "Several times, in fact."

I opened my eyes, his image focused before me. "You did good, De Luca. Even without the cheat sheet."

I felt his fingers, tracing the outline of my lips, rough skin against soft. The limo slowed, turning a corner, and my mind focused. "You're taking me home, right?"

His fingers froze. "I thought you would stay with me to-night."

"I didn't pack a bag, and don't want to go all the way home just to get stuff. Why don't you just stay with me tonight?"

He snorted, the sound causing my eyes to pop open and my vision to sharpen, focusing on a look on his face that could only be described as offensive. "I don't think so."

I sat up, propping my arm against his crotch with more force than was necessary, and glared at him. He winced, shifting in the seat, trying to move my arm. "What, the big fancy lawyer can't stay in my crappy common dwelling?"

He tilted his head to the side and then nodded. "Yeah, that sounds about right." His cool dismissal infuriated me, spawn-ing a sudden surge of anger heightened by my drunken state. Regardless of how much sense staying at his house made, I wanted the upper hand in the relationship, and him giving in to my unreasonable demands was part of that hand.

"I stay at your place all the time!"

"It's hardly a comparison. I live in a nice house, with air-conditioning and running water and—"

I shoved on his crotch, aiming for balls, but must have missed the mark, since his expression didn't change. I gritted my teeth, my chin rising defiantly. "You are such an ass. Now I'm staying at home purely out of principle."

He laughed, grabbing my arms and trying to pull me closer. I fought him, my drunken arms sluggish, and finally untan-gled from his grasp, moving to the front, to the window that opened to the chauffeur.

"Sir?" I poked my head through the window, scaring the man and causing him to swerve slightly on the road. He shot me the most dignified irritated look I had ever seen, and I giggled at the expression. "Sorry. Really, I'm sorry. Can you drop me off at the same place where you picked me up?"

He gave an almost imperceptible sigh, nodded stiffly and put his turn signal on, preparing to turn off on my exit. I was pulling back through the window when he spoke. "Madam?"

I stuck my head back through the opening, causing him to wince again. "Yeees?"

"There is an intercom button back there for your use. So you don't have to crawl through the window."

"Gotcha." I smiled brightly at him in response, no doubt enforcing his perception of me as the village idiot.

By the time I navigated the slippery leather seats back to Brad, his huge arms were crossed and he had fixed me with a stern look. "Why are you being difficult?"

I blew out a breath, trying to organize my woozy thoughts into a coherent response. "You are the one being difficult. It would do you good to sleep one night in a real, imperfect house, without someone making you breakfast or fluffing your pillow."

"Are cockroaches and mildew part of the humbling experience?"

I blew out an irritated breath and rolled my eyes. "Whatever. You're going to regret it when you are sleeping alone tonight." The limo turned down my street, squeezing its way past cars until it was in front of my house. I leaned over, kissed Brad briefly on the lips and pushed open the door, spilling out of the car, my bare feet hitting the pavement, my shoes and my purse clutched tight in my hand. He followed me out of the car, the night air ruffling his hair, his white shirt gaping at the neck.

"You're staying?" I asked, surprised.

He chuckled. "No. Just making sure you get inside safely."

I pouted at that, moving past him down my driveway and up to the front door. There was a voice from the limo driver, who still held the car door. "Sir, I will need to move the car. I'm blocking the street."

Brad turned. "Park in the apartment complex across the street. I'll walk over there when I'm done."

"Yes, sir."

I unlocked my front door, pushing it open to darkness and turning to Brad. "You can go with him. I made it in safely." I folded my arms and leaned in the doorway.

"Aren't you going to invite me in?"

"Nope. It's an all-or-nothing thing, *babe*."

He tugged at my dress, pulled me a step forward and slid his arms around me. "Come home with me. Stay in luxury tonight."

I set my jaw, shaking my head. He kissed the soft curve of my neck, and I pushed back on his chest. "Go. You don't want your fancy house to get lonely."

He sighed, taking a step back and looking at me. "Why are you being stubborn?"

"I'm not the one being stubborn. I've stayed at your place a bunch of times. You've never stayed here and it's the principle of it. This is my house. You should be happy to sacrifice personal comfort for the chance to spend the night with me."

"I'm too old to spend a night in a drug-filled home that might fall around my head if I lean too hard against a wall." He took a step back and stood, the finality of the motion closing the argument.

I shrugged, turning on my heel and wiggling my fingers at him. "Fine. See ya." I shut the door on his handsome frown, flipped the dead bolt and moved through the darkness to my room.

Thirty-One

The man drove down unfamiliar roads, following the map in his head until his headlights illuminated the tin green sign for Cambridge Road. He slowed, turning right and moving slowly down the road, passing the dejected mailbox with the number 2105 pasted on the side. He examined the house carefully as he passed. It was dark, three cars in the drive. One the tan Toyota Camry, which the DMV had verified as belonging to Julia Campbell. Once he passed the house he accelerated, following the road until it circled back to the main street. He took a left and then turned back onto her road, this time looking for a place to park.

BRAD RETURNED TO the limo, waving off the driver and opening the door himself. He climbed in and sat, looking out the window at the concrete block house, sitting beneath a lone streetlight, looking even more pathetic in the fluorescent yellow glow, like an old bald man, his head shining and face in shadow. He could see a ripped screen hanging off a front window, limp and dirty, as if it had just given up one day. A car turned down the street and drove slowly by, obscuring his view for a brief moment. This was a shit neighborhood. She shouldn't live here. She should live somewhere with at least a sliver of privacy, of safety.

A voice spoke, and it took him a minute to realize that the driver was speaking to him. "I'm sorry, what did you say?"

"I asked if I should return to your home, Mr. De Luca."

"Just wait a moment. I may stay here after all. Just let me think."

"Take your time, sir. I have all night."

He blew out a frustrated breath, looking at that damn house. Why should he stay there? He didn't have his car, not that he would leave it parked in this neighborhood. She herself had told him that the place was barely habitable. She was being stubborn, and reminding him of why his life was easier without a relationship. Then that car was back, the same one as before, and he focused on it now, watching as it slowed, braked, then moved forward, pulling into an empty spot on the street, two houses down. *Probably a neighbor.* But the vehicle didn't fit, not in this street filled with Hondas, Fords and Mitsubishis. This car, a black Audi sedan with tinted windows hiding the driver, was wrong. He watched it, leaning forward now, a sense of foreboding birthing in his psyche.

I WASHED MY face, standing in the bathroom, rubbing my skin with cold water and a rough washcloth. The light was bright, harsh in my eyes, and I rushed through the process, taking out my contacts and skipping the whole dental hygiene obligation. I pulled off my dress, swaying slightly from the action, and flipped off the light, opening the door to the hall and stepping into the blackness, lukewarm air hitting my bare skin.

THE AUDI SAT for a long minute with the engine off. Brad watched it, glancing at his watch, willing the damn person inside to get on with his night so he could leave in good conscience. Fuck staying at Julia's tonight. He needed to regain the upper hand in this relationship, something he lost the first damn time he saw her. If she was going to be stubborn and insist on staying here, he wasn't going to fall all over himself to accommodate her senseless demands. The driver door finally opened and a tall, thin man stepped out.

Brad could instantly tell from his stance and stride that this was not a college student. The man had a developed build and a bearing built on years of confidence and experience. Brad's foreboding grew, its arms and legs gaining strength and fortitude. The man moved, walking casually to the back of the car and removing a small bag from the trunk. Puzzled, and with a nagging sense of familiarity, Brad opened the limo's door, leaving it ajar, and moving quietly out into the night air. The man shut the trunk and ambled toward Julia's home.

The coincidence of the whole situation struck Brad as remarkable. There was a chance that this man was not going to her home, but that would be solved soon enough. Regardless, wherever he was headed, he needed to be stopped. What was odd was that this man was here, in this neighborhood. The man was a professional, that much was obvious. A professional didn't hunt for sport, and a job shouldn't bring him to this college neighborhood. Brad moved through the shadows of the street, lengths from the man. The fact that Brad was unarmed brought him considerable frustration. He watched the stride of the man, studying his gait, his eyes sharpening, a sliver of something snaking through his mind. Then the man twisted his leg, a quick popping motion that brought Brad to a sudden stop, the motion familiar. The sliver in his mind turned solid. *Recognition.* The realization hit him hard, and he turned his back to the man, leaning against a nearby tree and attempting to wrap his head around the fact. Reaching into his pocket, he pulled out his cell and dialed a number. Then he turned and watched the man.

The man glanced casually at the dejected mailbox and stepped over the curb, moving onto the grass and across the lawn, heading to the front door. *Julia's front door.* Brad cursed, listening to the phone ring, his eyes glued to the man.

My phone was ringing, the sound muted by my clutch, and I stood in the dark room, feeling around blindly, trying to remember where I had put the damn thing. I felt for the light switch, following the wall, when my foot bumped into my purse. I crouched, opening the metal clasp and pulling out my cell. *Ha. Big surprise.* Brad had cracked first. I smiled, answering the phone with a sexy drawl.

"Where are you in the house?" Brad's voice was quick and quiet.

"My bedroom," I whispered, matching his tone and trying to inject the proper level of husky sex into it.

"Do *not* turn on any lights. Do you have a gun?" His voice was too calm to ask that question, but so calm that I knew something was wrong.

"No. What's wrong?"

"I don't know yet. Stay inside and hide. I'm going to try and take care of it from this end. Turn off the ringer and keep your phone on you." There was a click, and he was gone. I crouched, fumbling with my phone until I had the ringer switched off. I listened, hearing nothing but the wheeze of our air conditioner. I was painfully aware of my nakedness, and had a vision of me running outside stark naked with half of the neighborhood watching. I groped around the floor until I found my discarded dress, pulled it on and crawled on my knees to my closet.

THE STREETLIGHT HAD illuminated for a quick moment the man's features, confirming Brad's suspicion. He knew who the man was. What he was doing outside Julia's house was the fucking question of the century.

Thirty-Two

The man reached the dark stoop, trying the loose handle of the front door, then stepped quickly off the porch and moved around to the side of the house. Brad increased his pace, and entered the dark corridor of the side yard right when the man exited it, stepping into the light of the backyard. The man stopped short, his head tilted a brief moment, and then he turned, slowly, facing the darkness he had just left.

Brad cursed his own size. Cursed his inability to move anywhere without sounding like a herd of elephants trampling through a forest. He stopped, the element of dark on his side, and spoke, a brief staccato of words in Italian.

"Bullshit." The man spat out the curse, his free hand sliding behind him, and pulled out a gun.

Brad stepped forward, close enough that his bulk was seen, his features partially revealed in the partial shadows.

"Wow. It *really* is you. Brad...De Luca, is it?" The last name was said mockingly, the man's tone playful.

"What the *fuck* are you doing here?" Brad's anger was

tightly controlled but seeped through in every word, and he stepped forward, advancing on the man.

"I suggest you stay where you are." The man, his features, the sharp angles in his face, his coarse salt-and-pepper hair, all so familiar. He stiffened, raising the gun toward Brad, who stilled, scoffing and spreading his arms in incredulity.

"What. You're going to kill *me*? That's not going to work, Leo. You know who I am."

"Look, Brad—I'm here under orders, and I'd like to do them and then get the fuck out of here. I don't know how you stumbled upon this, but let me do my job."

Brad's eyes glinted and he flexed his hands, trying to stay under control. "Who's your job?"

"Some delicious little bitch from your office." He started to lower the gun, turning to the house, then paused. "Wait. Is *that* why you're here? Sampling the fucking help?"

Brad stepped forward, ignoring the gun, and stopped a foot from the man. "I'd watch how you speak to me." He locked eyes with the man, who stepped backward.

"Look, like I said, I'm just here under orders."

"Why her?"

"She overheard some conversation of Broward's. Been calling the cops, wanting them to investigate the family's involvement." He smirked, disdain all over his face. A face Brad wanted to pound into the fucking ground.

Brad turned his back to the man, his mind racing, and put his hand on his mouth, rubbing the rough skin. Something Julia overheard. Julia and the cops. Julia on the family's radar. This was bad, very bad. He looked back. "Well, fuck the orders. They've changed. Call whichever piece of shit sent you over here and let him know."

The man hesitated, and Brad lifted his chin, stepping forward a few more steps until they were eye-to-eye. "Understood?"

The man looked away, his mouth working, hatred in his eyes. "Yeah. But you understand if I come back."

"Hey, business is business." Brad put his hands in his pockets and stretched his neck, keeping his eyes on the man. The man hesitated, then turned, sliding his gun back into place and walking past Brad, back into the darkness, his duffel bag rocking gently at his side. "Oh, and, Leo?"

The man paused, his back stiffening. "Yeah?"

"Don't ever fucking talk to me like that again."

The man hesitated, then continued, his feet making no sound on the dead grass. And then he was gone. Brad waited in the light of the backyard, till the Audi drove past him and made the turn onto the main road. Then he walked back to the limo, pulling out his wallet and withdrawing a few bills. The backseat door was still open, and the limo idled quietly in the parking lot. He closed the door and went up to the driver's side. The window rolled down and revealed the driver's lined face.

Brad held out the bills. "If I'm not back out in fifteen minutes, then head home."

"Yes, sir, Mr. De Luca. Understood."

Brad turned, stepped away from the limo and pulled out his cell.

I HUDDLED IN the corner of my closet, an area that I was sure roaches and rodents frequented. My heavy coats hung above me and created a comforting, if not stifling shield around me. I had heard something outside, voices, muffled by the concrete wall of the home. Now all was still, and I tried to control my breathing, which sounded loud and ragged in the tiny, hot space.

My cell, which was clutched in my sweaty hand, vibrated. I answered it quickly, holding my hand over my mouth to quiet my words.

"Yes?"

"Everything is fine. Can you unlock the front door?"

"Are you sure? Are you being held at gunpoint?"

He sighed. "I'm positive. Open the fucking door. Please." Then there was a beep, and he was gone. *Damn man*. I shoved wool garments aside and tried to crawl out, but my drunken mind tangled my feet and I fell in an uncoordinated heap on my floor. I groaned, pushing myself to my feet and hobbling—*damn, I hurt my ankle*—to the hall, moving through the darkness till I reached the front door and unlocked the dead bolt. Brad stood, a dark silhouette in the doorway, no one else nearby. I flung myself into his arms and he gripped me tightly, sliding me backward until he could shut the door and turn the lock himself.

"What happened?" I asked as soon as the latch was turned. "Were we being robbed?"

He reached over, turning on the lamp that sat by our front door, the warm light illuminating his face, which looked stressed. "Is that a common occurrence?"

"It's happen twice, but both times during the day when no one was home. Is that what it was?"

"No. I need to think a moment. Where are your roommates?"

"I don't know. Asleep."

"I want to take you home. To my home. I'll sleep here another night, or tomorrow night, or whenever you want me to—but I need to be home tonight, and I need you there with me. I'll explain more later."

I blinked, confused. Confused over whether there had been any threat of danger at all, confused over the change in his behavior, confused over why he kept running his damn hands through his hair and looking so…worried. I walked over to him, running my hands over his chest and kissing his cheek softly. "Okay. Let me pack a bag."

He nodded, his face tight, his eyes lingering on me. "Thanks. Grab a couple of things, outfits, I mean. In case we go out tomorrow."

I turned, headed to my room, then stopped, the fucked-up-ness of the situation suddenly hitting my drunk mind. Brad calls, tells me to hide, then knocks on the door and wants to take me to his house. I couldn't figure out if this was his ridiculous method of getting his way, or if something serious had occurred, and he was intentionally keeping me in the dark. I turned back to him, my brain working through the events, trying to formulate an intelligent question, a demand for information. Then the room swayed, and black spots momentarily appeared in my vision. *Whoa.* I stumbled, then focused, my eyes meeting Brad's concerned ones. *Fuck it.* My interrogation would have to wait till later, when I was relatively sober.

I turned away from those watchful eyes and entered my room, grabbing a duffel bag and stuffing a few outfits into it. I went ahead and changed into pajamas, twisting my hair into a bun and working my feet into flip-flops. I was ready in less than five minutes, and flashed him a smile as I entered the living room. He didn't respond, the same tense look on his face, and my smile fell as I followed him out, locking the door behind me. I headed for the limo, but he grabbed my elbow, steering me toward my car. "Give me the keys. I'll drive."

"My car?" The idea was so preposterous I almost giggled.

"Yeah. You've been drinking."

Oh, right. I tossed him my keys and looked at the limo. "But what about—"

"Get in." He held open the passenger side, and I ducked in, shooting him an irritated glance and sliding a pile of random crap onto the floor.

My car moved noisily through the city, Brad cramped behind the wheel. He said nothing, so I leaned back in the seat and stared out the window, watching dark homes and empty streets zoom by.

Thirty-Three

With arms of lead, Brad drove, glancing at Julia occasionally. He tried to remember the last time things had gotten this fucked up. It had been a while. Before law school, before Hillary, before life as he knew it. Back when he was a rebellious teenager, and didn't know who and what to stay away from.

She was in trouble, more trouble than she could imagine, trouble he might not be able to get her out of. His blood ran cold at the thought of something happening to her. He had experienced a lot of death in his life, had been perversely conditioned at a young age to accept it, to hold his emotions at bay. But God help him, if something happened to her...he looked over at her still body, slumped against the gray cloth of the seat. She held so much power in her small frame, so much control over his emotions. As much as she scared him by pure existence, the thought of losing her was incomprehensible. It was something he might not recover from. It was a realization that hit him hard, and it, combined with Julia's situation, would keep him up most of the night.

I MUST HAVE fallen asleep, because I woke up in Brad's arms, being carried like a small child, up the inner stairs of his home. At the top I untangled myself, standing up and stumbling to the bed, which I started to crawl into. His grip stopped me, his hands reaching for my glasses, pulling them gently off. He helped me into bed, pulling the covers up around my body.

I awoke when he got into the bed, sometime later, smelling of fresh soap and toothpaste. He wrapped his arms around me and I fell back asleep, our bodies spooned together, the hum of the fan the only sound in the dark room. Behind me, his face buried in my neck, I could feel Brad's thoughts churning.

I WOKE UP to a quiet room, so silent that I lay there for a moment, my eyes adjusting to the room, nothing but blurry colors in front of me. I reached out, patting the bedside table until I felt my glasses, and slid them on, bringing the world into focus.

I rolled over, stretching, my body bumping warm, hard skin, and I turned to see Brad, lying on his side, his eyes on mine. My gaze traveled over his skin, a muscular stomach leading to a glorious upper body, and came to rest on his dark, sinful eyes.

Something was different. His brown eyes were pensive, staring at me with something akin to vulnerable confusion, his soft lips parted, face tight. I felt as if he was on the verge of…something, but I wasn't sure I wanted to know what. Our eyes stayed locked together, and my smile slowly faded as my mind tried to catch up with the change in the air. On impulse I leaned over, grabbing his head and kissing his lips, trying to change whatever was happening with the distraction of sex.

He finished the kiss but pushed me down again, flat on the bed, and I giggled involuntarily at his determination. He trapped me between his arms and stared at me again, as if trying to figure out a riddle.

"What?" I whispered, staring back at him, at his intent eyes.

"You are someone I could fall in love with." His words were surprised, unsure, words that had probably been shelved in a forgotten closet for quite some time.

I flinched and immediately saw vulnerability shudder through his eyes, then disappear. I moved my lips, willing for some intelligent, coherent thought to come out, but apparently my lips were stuck in the same black hole that my brain was taking a break in. I gave up and stared, unmoving, into his face. His jaw tightened, a tic beginning to pulse in his right check.

I reached up, touched the tic and breathed, willing my brain into action. Slowly and rustily, the gears began to turn and I was able to speak. "I love you already, Brad." His eyes closed briefly, resolutely, then opened again, and the tic increased, his jaw flexing. I laughed, my stress gone and my cobwebs clear in my stubborn head. Touching his face, I collected myself and tilted his face to mine, forced his eyes to stare at me.

"I'm not telling you in order to hear it back," I said. "I'm letting you know how I feel, so that you don't have to wonder. I don't need to know how you feel, or care if you love me right now. I just thought you and your delicate ego might want to know." I rolled, his once stiff arms yielding easily, and I was on my feet on the carpet in seconds.

I heard movement in the bedsprings and turned to see Brad sitting upright, staring at me in barely disguised frustration. He spoke slowly, irritated. "What do you mean you don't *care* if I love you?"

I walked back to the bed, rubbing my arms, already cold in the bedroom chill. "I believe I said I don't care if you don't love me *right now*. You will fall in love with me." I turned, heading for the bathroom, and stopped just before the door, turning to him. "But, Brad?" He looked at me, eyes dark. "Just because I love you doesn't mean I won't leave you." I opened the door and was starting to turn on the light when I heard his voice and turned. He stood, gorgeous in tight black boxer briefs and nothing else, his tanned and ripped body looking incredible. I wondered why we were talking and not fucking.

"Why are you so certain I will fall in love with you?" His voice was low, irritated.

I smiled patiently at him. "You just met me. I've had over twenty years to get to know me. Trust me, you will. You're too smart not to." Shutting the door on his scowl, I turned down the lights, turned on the shower and put a towel in the warmer. Stepping into the shower, I buried my face in the hot spray.

It might have been a mistake to show my cards. To tell him how I felt. It was the first time the realization had occurred to me, and the words had kind of popped out. It had been the vulnerability that had shown briefly in his eyes, the confession he had given. *You are someone I could fall in love with.* I hadn't expected it from him, and it had triggered the moment of clarity in me.

I soaped up my hair and body and tried to analyze my feelings. I had certainly thought I had been in love before. Had talked myself into it twice, been convinced enough to accept a marriage proposal just over a year ago. But something had been wrong, wrong enough that I was able to walk from the relationships without tears or regret. True love seems as if it would be a hell of a lot harder to get over. With Brad I just knew it was real, that this was what love was really all about. I was as sure of it as I'd ever been of anything.

Thirty-Four

When I came downstairs, clean, towel-dried and dressed in a yellow skirt and white tank, Brad sat in the kitchen. His head was in his hands and he looked up at my approach. "I need to talk to you. Sit down."

Unsure of what was coming, I grabbed an apple from the fruit basket and sat down at the large teak table, sitting cross-legged in the seat next to him.

"We need to talk about what happened last night, so you are aware of your situation, but first I need to know what you overheard Broward say, the conversation that you spoke to the police about."

I was halfway through a big apple bite when he spoke, and I froze, the unexpected words catching me off guard. I finished the bite, chewing loudly and buying myself some time. *Holy. Shit.*

He continued, keeping his eyes on mine. "Since you haven't mentioned this to me already, I'm assuming it's because you recognized the danger that exists in that knowledge. Unfortunately, it is too late to avoid that. The implicated parties are aware of your involvement. They know who you are and where you live. They came to your home last night, presumably to kill you."

I swallowed, a jagged piece of the fruit getting painfully stuck in my throat, my mind trying frantically to catch up with this information. "Last night. The break-in…or whatever that was." I stopped, my mind following the evening's events, Brad's call, us leaving the house. "So…what happened?"

He frowned at me, his brow lined. "You got fucking lucky. I was unarmed and in the parking lot when I saw the man. By some incredible twist of fate, I knew the son of a bitch."

"You knew him?" I stood, gripping the nearest chair, and turned to stare at Brad, my frantic eyes meeting his calm ones. "Yes."

I tilted my head, trying to process the billion thoughts that were fighting each other for my attention. "I'm sorry—how did you know about what I told the police?"

"The man, last night. He told me that the reason he was there, why he had been sent, was whatever you told the police."

The police…I frowned at that information. "So, what— you just said 'please go away' and he did?" My voice arched and I raised my brow at him, unconvinced.

He shifted uncomfortably. "He was sent by the Magiano family. I have some connections to his boss. I delayed him."

Magiano family. My worst fears, realized. "*Delayed* him. So he's going to come back another time and kill me. Shouldn't we be in a police station right now!" I released the chair and spun, pacing a short path in front of the table.

He laughed, a bitter, short sound. "Sure. Going to the cops worked so well for you so far. Julia, whoever you spoke to at the police station, they are just one cop on a lengthy list of dirtbags. The police cannot, or will not, protect you." His eyes met mine, a hard stare with an edge of despair. Just enough despair to send me onto another level of panic.

"Shit! Then what? I wait around to get whacked?" My heart felt as if it were going to come out of my chest and I stopped pacing, leaning on the table and focusing on breathing. *Magiano. The biggest crime family within a thousand miles. What the fuck was I thinking?*

He stood, his strong hands gripping my shoulder and turning me to face him. I looked up, into his face, stress lining the beautiful lines of it. "Julia. Calm down. I have connections. Let me find out how fucked we are. Go to Martha's. Tell her something has happened, and you need to stay up there for a bit. I'll call my contact at the police, then check on a few things, see what I can find out."

"Why do I need to go to Martha's? Can't I just stay here?"

His hand fell from my shoulder and he studied me with his eyes. "I just dropped a whole lot on you. I'd rather you not be alone, have someone to talk to if need be."

"In case I flip the fuck out?"

His mouth twitched, and he chuckled once before the hard look returned, taking over his face. "Yeah. Or in case you decide to run. Which, I can tell you right now, is a bad idea. The safest place for you right now is on my property." The authoritative tone, one that would normally cause my hands to clench and my voice to rise, was somehow comforting, and I leaned on its strength. I dreaded the thought of spending any time with Martha, but I nodded, my eyes searching his, looking for reassurance, confidence. I found only grim determination and steely resolve.

"Fine," I said, turning on my heel and throwing open the back door. I pounded up the stairs to her carriage house apartment, my shoes making a racket on her iron stairs, my panic growing with every step I climbed. She opened the door with an irritated expression before I even knocked, a small thermos bag in her hand and her purse over her shoulder. Her mouth was open, a smart-ass comment ready, when she saw my face. She paused, her eyes narrowing; then she opened the door wider.

"Aw, hell," she said, her big shoulders slumping and her purse hitting the floor with a thud. "Let me guess, that man got himself in trouble." She gestured with a hand. "Come on in."

Martha's apartment consisted of a small living room, a galley kitchen and two bedrooms. The furniture was functional, the space tidy and sparkling clean. I looked around but saw no family photos, nothing to give me a sense of the woman in front of me. She moved past, closing the bedroom doors with a look that told me to mind my own business, then ushered me to the couch.

She sat across from me in silence, the two of us studying each other for a moment. Her expression was wary, examining me with a look that resembled motherly concern. She pursed her lips and then spoke.

"You eaten?"

The words were so unexpected that I laughed, a welcome emotion. My eyes threatened to water and I blinked back the tears, shaking my head at her. She stood, briskly moving to the kitchen, having bacon and eggs sizzling in minutes. I leaned back on the couch, trying to process my current situation. My mind meandered down different paths, all which ended at similar dead ends—me, deceased, my funeral sparsely attended. Running seemed to be the best course of action.

I turned, wanting something, anything to distract me. Martha stood at the stove, flipping bacon. She seemed relaxed, a calming presence in my new state of anxiety. "Have you worked for Brad long?" I asked. Silently, she went to the fridge, bending over and pulling out a carton of orange juice. I almost repeated the question, but she answered while pouring us both a glass.

"Honey, I been working for Brad since he was twenty-six, but I've known the boy since he was a teenager. I worked for his father before him." She brought the two glasses to the coffee table and slid one to me, setting the other in front of a recliner. I pushed off the blanket and stood, following her to the kitchen. She fixed two plates, passing me one, and we took our food back to the living room, sitting back down. It was weird to be sitting this close to Martha, in her apartment. She was a lot less scary up here, but that was probably thanks to my meek demeanor. The other morning I had been all bitchy attitude. Now I was a scared Chihuahua. A Chihuahua that was incredibly grateful for her kindness, especially given our volatile history.

"Do you like working here?"

She smiled, tilting her head at me, her full face smooth, impossibly ageless. "Oh yes. Me and Brad have worked ourselves into a comfortable life. It takes time, for two people to find their place, and we've gotten so we understand each other just fine. I give him his privacy and he gives me my space."

"Have you ever been married?" I got up and grabbed the orange juice, pouring more for both of us.

She laughed and shook her head. "I'm a loner, Julia. Besides, Brad handles any heavy lifting or odd jobs around the house, and that is enough to keep me from missing a man around." She took a bite of bacon and sat back, rocking. "So. What's our boy done now?"

I toyed with my eggs, thinking about how to answer the question, not knowing what information to give. She watched me, clasping her hands on her large stomach, her head tilted, face calm. "I've been in Brad's life a long time, Julia. There was a reason I left his daddy. I believed in Brad, believed in the good in his soul. I saw a lot of things at his daddy's house, kept a lot of secrets for that family. Secrets I'll be taking with me to the grave." She nodded at me, a stern brow arched, and continued her rocking.

Something about the way she spoke made me think that the secrets she kept might be of the caliber of this. And I needed to talk to someone, needed to unload. I took a sip of orange juice and met her unmoving gaze. "Brad hasn't done anything. It was something I did."

"You? You have a lot of stress on your face for something *you* did. What, you fail a midterm or something?"

I laughed, setting my juice down on the coffee table, shocked at the sudden urge I had to burst into tears. I swallowed hard. "No. I was snooping, listening to something I shouldn't have—and then Brad's partner, my boss, was killed. Now the people who killed him are after me." My voice broke on the last sentence, and I tightened my eyes, determined to hold my emotions in check.

She sighed deeply and closed her eyes. "Oh Lordy," she said, shaking her head. "And let me guess, he's going to try and save you."

I shrugged. "I don't know. He wants me to stay up here for a bit. You think I'm in danger right now?"

She, for some reason, found this inexplicably funny. "Up here? Lord no. No one is gonna harm you on this property, I can assure you of that. This is sacred ground, as far as most of the criminals in town are concerned."

We sat in silence for a minute, me trying to pick up the pieces of what she had said. "What do you mean?"

She exhaled, pushing the arms of the chair, and stood, tottering over to the kitchen and running water into the sink. She spoke over her shoulder, without looking at me. "Julia, I know you think you and Bradley are going to skip off into the sunset, and be together forever, but what you don't get is that every woman who's walked into my kitchen during the last five years has thought the same thing, has had the same stars in their eyes. And he has left each one of them before they get too close, before they get any piece of his heart. And as good as he protects his heart—he protects his secrets even better. And that man has a whole heaping lot of secrets." She turned, a dishrag in hand, and wiped her palms, looking dead in my eyes.

"And death threat or not, I'm not sharing any of his secrets with you. It ain't my place. I'm sorry, but some things you got to get from him, or go without knowing." She stared at me, silence between us; then she turned and started washing dishes.

I sank my head back on the soft couch. After a few minutes she wandered over and clicked on the small TV set on a side table, flipping through the stations till she found the one she wanted. On the small screen a preacher stood at a pulpit, gesturing wildly and shouting words of redemption and praise. I watched as she settled into her chair, pulling an afghan over her legs.

Sitting in her cozy living room made me think of home, and my parents. I stood, pulled out my cell and glanced at Martha. "I need to call my mom," I said softly, over the words of a sermon.

"You can use my guest room, if you'd like," she said, nod-

ding with her head to a closed door and preparing to hoist
herself to her feet.

"You sit," I whispered, moving around the couch and heading for the room. "Thanks." I dialed as I walked, quietly
opening the door and pressing Send before I stepped inside.

For a woman who had initially seemed inhospitable, she
had certainly made her guest room comfortable, with a recliner, neatly made twin bed and thoughtful items placed
around the room. I curled up in the chair and listened to the
phone ring in my ear.

To SAY THAT I am an independent daughter would be putting
it nicely. In actuality, I pretty much walked across the graduation stage, accepted my high school diploma, then left town
in a cloud of dust, happy to never look back, adios familial
responsibilities and obligations. That might be a *bit* of a dra-
matization, but not by too much. And now, after three years
away from home, college had become the justification of the
bridge between my parents and me.

When I was a child, my mother blamed the emotional distance on my intelligence. She referred to me as an "old soul,"
blaming our lack of connection on my mature, wise-beyond-
my-years outlook. In my teens, our distance was blamed on
hormones, my friends or my heavy academic schedule. It's not
that she and I fought; we just didn't speak, at least not about
anything emotionally fulfilling. We were two opposite souls,
coexisting in a home with my wonderful father, who roboti-
cally went about his day while trying his best to not irritate
my mother.

A death threat seemed like a valid reason to break the silence. I'd spent the first three years of college acclimating my
mother to accept occasional calls as normal college student

behavior. Initially, our lifeless conversations occurred weekly, then biweekly, then monthly. It had been a while since I had called home, longer than usual. I leaned back in the chair, trying to think of the last time we had spoken. It had been over two months, the extended silence my doing. I hadn't yet figured out how to break the news to her that I had ended my engagement. Mother had adored Luke, my ex-fiancé, and would not take our breakup well. So I had handled it as immaturely as possible, by simply avoiding the conversation.

The ringing stopped and voice mail picked up. I frowned, wondering what to say, then left a generic message, asking them to call me back.

Thirty-Five

An hour later, I again sat at Brad's kitchen table. He had come up to Martha's, finding her reading and me pacing. Now, after fifteen minutes of discussion, I looked at him with something akin to panic.

I had told him everything I knew—Broward's angry words, Genovese, Magiano, the connection I had made to mob activities, the voice mails I had left Parks. In return, he had told me nothing. It was beginning to really piss me off, and I told him so, my hysteria held off by my anger.

He groaned in exasperation, leaning back and looking to the ceiling as if for help from God. "Julia, the little that you know—that alone almost got you killed! Are you stupid enough to want to know more, to endanger yourself further?" He slammed his fist on the table, his dark eyes smoldering.

I stood quickly, my chair scraping against the stone floor, and snarled at him across the table. "According to you, I'm on the kill list regardless. I think I deserve to know what the fuck I'm being killed for! And you! In case you forgot, with all the hit men, and dead partners, and police interviews—I'm in *love* with you. *You*, who I apparently know *nothing* about. I know you think because I'm young that I don't know what love is, that I attached myself to you because of your big dick and fancy house, but that is bullshit! I know that I should run, run far away from your untamable sex drive, your Mafia friends and your pain-in-the-ass self. That is the logical, sane thing to do. But I'm not! I'm sitting here, in your fucking kitchen, waiting for the next person to walk in and blow my brains out! For you, you selfish prick. Because I love you!" I was screaming now, my mind emptying out through my mouth, my throat hoarse from the effort, and I leaned on the table, taking a deep breath, waiting for his response.

He looked at me, started to say something and stopped. Then, "Julia, you don't want to fuck with these people."

I sat down, looked at him across the table, begged him with my eyes. "I need to know more."

He cradled his head in his hands, then looked at me. "All you need to know is that Broward was helping one family gain power. It was supposed to be done discreetly, without alerting those who the power was being taken from. Something went wrong, and the situation was discovered too early. Broward was collateral damage, killed to erase all evidence of their involvement. He was a weak link, someone who would have yielded easily to persuasive questioning."

Persuasive questioning. *Torture.* "So now I'm the weak link," I said softly.

He nodded, his face grim, handsome features almost pained in their seriousness.

"And you are involved…how?"

He ran a hand through his thick hair, and the traces of gray in it picked up the light. "I have a lot of…connections to local organized crime families. I was originally approached for a family takeover a couple of years ago. I was not interested, wanted no part of it—plus, corporate structures are not my area of expertise. When I refused, they looked elsewhere."

Genovese. "Broward."

"Yes. I've heard about a few other clients of this variety he has taken on. I approached him, several times, telling him to refuse the business, to get out of this situation, but he has always shut me down. Whether it's because of our history, or his own ego, I don't know." He blew out a burst of air and looked at me, frustrated. "From the sound of the conversation you overheard, I wouldn't be surprised if it was me he was speaking to. We just argued last week about it."

I nodded, absorbing the new information. "Will they know I'm here?"

"They'd be idiots not to, and they are not idiots. Dangerous, impulsive, but not stupid. By now they know everything about you, and that is the biggest problem we have."

"Will they use you to find me?"

He laughed wryly. "Not in the manner you might think. But, Julia, you are looking at this the wrong way. There is no way to hide. If they don't already, they will soon have your Social Security number, your car registration and know when your next period is due. There is no point in hiding. There is only one thing to do."

"What?" Hope had entered my voice, a small glimmer, and I was afraid of giving it too much credence.

"It's something I have to do on my end. It's better if I don't tell you any more." He rose, taking his empty glass to the sink. I ground my teeth in frustration and rose, following him and grabbing his arm.

"And what, I'm just supposed to be a sitting duck while you 'try' something out without clueing me in on it?"

He growled, grabbing my wrists hard and pinning them together behind my back. His face, inches from mine, was tortured. He stared in my eyes, reading them, then lowered his
mouth to mine, hesitantly at first, then harder and deeper, his
hands releasing my wrists and sliding down my waist to my
ass, which he gripped tightly, a hand on each cheek, squeezing
and kneading the muscles there. I felt his emotions through
his mouth, his kiss possessive, protective. I wrapped my arms
around his neck and he lifted with his hands, picking me up
easily. Our kisses frantic, I wrapped my legs tightly around
his waist, my hands in his hair, and he carried me to the table
and laid me down, leaning over me. His mouth left mine, me
gasping, my hands reaching for him, but he held me down
and trailed his lips down my body, pulling up my tank top
and exposing my breasts and pink nipples.

Hot breath hit my skin as his soft lips traveled, down my
neck to my breasts, him planting small kisses along the way.
He took his time on my nipples, being impossibly gentle with
them, and I arched my back, pushing into his pelvis and lifting
my breasts deeper into his open mouth. A small cry left my
lips as he grabbed my tits, pressing them together and sucking them into his mouth.

"Please," I whispered, frantically reaching down, grabbing
his jeans, trying to unbutton them, my hands grabbing and
pulling anything and everything, the overwhelming need to
have him inside me ruling out any logical thoughts in my
head. "I need you."

"I don't have—"

I cut him off, moaning the words of my beg. "I don't care.
Now. Please. I need you to fuck all of this insanity away."

He lifted his head from my breasts and yanked open his
fly, bunching my skirt around my waist and moving aside

the cloth of his underwear. His cock popped out, hard and ready, a drop of precome glistening on its tip. I practically swooned, and before I could move, he was pressing the tip of it on my wetness, past my panties and shoving the thick girth all the way in.

I gasped, entering some unworldly plane of delirium. The release of having him bare inside me, of having his strong, massive body over me, my legs spread and back flat on his kitchen table, was mind-blowing. He moved inside me, his mouth at my ear, hot breath on my neck. My hands pulled at his T-shirt, pulling the cloth over his head, exploring the tight muscles on his back, my body craving more, more, more of him. He moaned in my ear, fucking me faster, our skin slapping together, filling me completely, then leaving me wanting. Fill, want, fill, want. Words came out, jagged in my ear.

"God, I need you, Julia, so fucking bad."

It wasn't enough for forever, but it was enough for right now, and I held him tight and squeezed my muscles around his cock, him moaning in immediate response. At that moment, in his arms, I didn't think about the danger, or my job, or any of the shit that was falling down around us. He gave me what I needed, and I took what I wanted. I came, dissolving in his arms, screaming aloud, releasing my fear and frustration in a wave of exquisite pleasure. The orgasm was strong and beautiful, and I went limp when it ended. He slowed his strokes, breathing hard and kissing my face, lips and neck.

"I love fucking you," he whispered, still moving inside me, slow and delicious, burying himself with every stroke. His words awakened my spent muscles and I moved, pushing against the table with my feet and rolling him over, straddling him for the first time, and gasping at the feel of him from this angle, his whole cock inside me. I rode him, pumping up and down, his hands traveling over my torso, his face strong and possessive beneath me. I leaned forward, my hair brushing his face, and buried myself deep on his cock, grinding my clit against his pubic bone, moaning at the pleasure it brought me. He took over, wrapping his arms around me and fucking me from below, fast and hard, our bodies slapping, slick and furious. The orgasm came, jarring me, taking my breath, an explosion of my world, and I screamed his name as his cock carried me through it. The last waves were still subsiding when he jerked out of me, his voice terse and quick.

"Suck it."

I moved off him, as quickly as I could in my final stages of euphoria. Burying my fingers inside me, I moved them in and out while I took him in my mouth—gagging on his width, and sucking hard and fast, my free hand resting on the rough fabric of his jeans, still on.

He came, filling my throat, his hand on my head with gentle pressure, his voice calling my name over and over until he was limp and drained. I rolled over, spent, next to him on the hard table, my skirt bunched and twisted around my body, my panties discarded somewhere on the floor.

I laid there for a solid minute, then rolled on my side, resting my head in the crook of Brad's arm, tracing a line on his abs. He spoke, his hair muffled in my hair.

"That was incredible." He kissed my head, then laid his head back on the table.

"Yeah. But it doesn't help my current predicament." I sighed, tucking my hand into his jeans, into the hardness and warmth there.

"It's going to be okay, Julia." His words were reassuring, his tone terrifying. It spoke of desperation and fight—as if he would somehow force the fate of my future. This shouldn't be his fight, but I was powerless in it, an easy pawn that could be swiped off the game board without consequence. I said nothing, rolling over and hugging his hard body, wanting the strength it provided.

Thirty-Six

I needed a distraction, and Brad needed twenty-four hours to take care of whatever his cockeyed plan was. We argued, a discussion bordering on a serious fight, about his refusal to share his plan with me. It was an argument I lost, his face stern and unyielding. I was almost grateful. I didn't know how much more information I could take. To be safe, we decided that I should stay in the house, out of sight. A ridiculous plan, but I didn't have a better one. I called Becca, asking her to come by and hang out, promising mimosas if she would come and keep me company. I would have asked Olivia, but she would have sniffed out trouble before she even walked in the front door. Becca was a lot less observant.

She arrived thirty minutes later, her silver Mercedes convertible pumping out music loud enough to cause the closest blueblood to have a heart attack. Becca doesn't leave the house unless she is perfectly coiffed, so I wasn't surprised to see her trot up the front steps wearing designer jeans, four-inch heels and a sequined gold top. Martha answered the door with a grunt, and I stepped out of the kitchen and waved Becca in.

Seeing me, she squealed and jogged over for a hug, passing right by Martha's death stare of a welcome.

"Look at you, you sexy thing!" she said, giving my just-had-sex-in outfit a once-over. Evading her judgment, I grabbed her hand and pulled her through the house. Martha called to me as I was rounding the bend of the hall.

"Don't think I'm going to be waiting on you two!"

I paused midstep, jogging back to the kitchen and grabbing the carton of orange juice and two cups she held out. She pursed her lips at me, and I grinned, bounding back down the hall and catching up to Becca.

"She seems nice," Becca said, nodding in the direction of Martha.

I grinned. "She is," I said, shocked at my own response. Maybe it takes drama to bring two people closer. I ushered Becca into the den, checked out the wet bar and found a bottle of champagne. Popping the cork, I poured us both glasses and settled into a plush recliner. She examined the champagne, then stood with her glass, walking around the room. I took a generous sip and leaned back in the chair.

"This house certainly is manly," she announced, checking out the framed sports paraphernalia housed in the built-in cabinetry. "Where's the bearskin rug?"

"You're hilarious. I'll be sure his decorator calls you for tips."

She shrugged, smiling at me over her glass. "Hey, he has good taste in women, right? That's all that counts." She raised her glass in a toast, and I leaned forward, clinking mine against hers.

"Amen. So, what's going on with you and Trey?" Trey was Becca's latest boyfriend, a tennis-playing premed major who had all of the family credentials that Becca's parents required.

"Ugh." Becca flopped into the closest chair, kicking off her heels and tucking her feet under her butt. "He is such a spazz. Did I tell you he took me to *Applebee's* yesterday for dinner? Applebee's. Like we're fucking high schoolers." She gestured wildly, as if the Apocalypse were imminent now that she had been forced to eat with the middle class. I stifled a laugh and nodded somberly, trying to emphasize with her difficulties.

"So anyway, I think I'm going to break it off with him. He's just so…young, you know? I need someone like Brad, someone mature. Has Brad ever taken you to Applebee's?" She didn't wait for a response, just sighed exasperatedly and sipped her champagne. "What about you two—how's everything going?"

I played with my glass, trying to figure out how to answer the question. I answered, as truthfully as I could. "It's going great, Becca. Things are different with him, different than any other guy I've dated. I've never had a more stressful relationship—so much has gone on with us, but despite all that, I think he might be it for me." I blushed, hating the words as they came out of my mouth.

Her mouth dropped open. "It? Like *love*? Are you sure? You've only been exclusive, what? Two weeks?"

"About that, and I am. When I'm with him, it feels natural, like he is the other part of me that I have been missing out on this whole time. He is so…everything. He makes every other guy I've ever met seem lacking."

"Wow. This is huge. I thought after the whole Luke debacle, you had decided to be single for a while. Now you are all ready to settle down for good?"

"Don't tell Olivia. She'll get all weird on me."

Becca nodded, her eyes bright. "Don't worry. That is so great, Jules, I am so happy for you." She got up, leaning over to give me a quick hug, then perched on the arm of my chair. "So...does he have any cute friends?"

BRAD MADE THE call, to a number he hadn't dialed in over nine years. The phone rang so long he expected voice mail, but then a gruff male voice answered.

"It's Brad. We need to talk."

"When?"

"Tonight."

"Come to the house. We'll talk there."

"Alone."

A sigh. "If you want."

Brad ended the call and tapped the phone to his lips, thinking. His father's voice hadn't changed much in nine years.

WE FINISHED THE bottle of champagne and then trekked to the front door. I hugged her goodbye, promising to set her up with a hot rich lawyer soon. Closing the door behind her, I turned to head upstairs and almost ran into Martha's large mass.

Arms folded over her chest, she looked at me with something akin to skepticism. "So, that's your friend, huh?"

I grinned at her, dipping sideways and around. "She's...different. Don't judge me because of her."

"Now what are you trying to say? I don't judge anyone."

I stopped, spinning around, and gave her a look of skepticism. "Oh, puh-lease. I know Becca is an airhead. But she's my airhead, so leave her alone."

She snorted, and I laughed, heading to the kitchen, which I had now decided, with its large teak table, was my favorite room in the house. Heading to the fridge, I opened the door and stuck my head in.

Brad's refrigerator was the most beautiful thing on the

planet. Other than its Sub-Zero fanciness and brilliant blue lighting, it was perfectly organized, with matching stacks of Tupperware containers filling its shelves. Martha had the food organized by day, and though today's spot was empty, yesterday's leftovers included shrimp salad, pork tenderloin and baked macaroni and cheese. I was starting to see why, after fifteen years, Brad kept her around. That, and the fact that she apparently guarded a treasure trove of secrets. I grabbed the mac and cheese container and scooped half of it onto a plate, popping it in the microwave.

Martha settled in on a stool, watching me. "Now, you know I'm about to fix dinner. You could just wait."

I licked the cold remnants off the spoon, watching the plate rotate in the microwave. "I'm just getting a snack. Don't worry, I'll eat your delicious dinner, too. What time are we eating?"

"Oh, whatever time that boy gets home. Have any idea when that will be?"

"I don't think he's eating with us. He said he wouldn't be back till late."

"Oh. Well, in that case I'll make jambalaya. You like jambalaya?"

"Of course. I'm not big on spice, though."

"Oh, mine isn't spicy, just good. I've been wanting jambalaya for months now, but Brad doesn't like it, and it doesn't seem right to do all that work for just me." She slapped the counter, happy, and heaved to her feet, headed for the fridge.

Thirty-Seven

The doorbell rang at 6:00 p.m. Martha and I were in the kitchen, window shades drawn, laughing over a story she was telling about Brad's teenage years, when we heard the chimes. We both froze, the grape I was about to eat dropping to the floor. A look came over her face, hard and determined, and she grabbed my arm. "You wait here."

"What?" I hissed. "Don't answer it!"

She waved me off, grabbing a hand towel and wiping her hands on it as she walked to the door. "Who is it?" she drawled, Southern and unintimidating.

"It's Stevie." The voice was muffled by the heavy door, but understandable.

"Stevie? Joe's boy Stevie?" Martha demanded, standing by the door with her hands on her hips.

Every gangster movie I had ever seen flooded through my mind, and I wished she would move away from the door before they shot through it. I tried to wave at her, but she ignored me completely, focused on the door.

"Yes. Let me in, Martha."

She walked away, and pulled out her cell. Going through the phone, she pressed a button and waited, the phone to her ear.

"It's me. Stevie is here. You want me to let him in?"

There was a pause, and then she spoke. "Okay." She hung up the phone and opened the door, peering through the crack created by the safety chain. An alarm somewhere in the house started, a slow chirp, gradually increasing in speed. She seemed pleased with what she saw and she closed the door, removed the chain and then opened it again, ushering in a tall man with a muscular build, dressed in a black polo and dress pants, a large gray gun strapped to his belt. Martha shut the door behind him, relatching the chain and locking the dead bolt, and pressed a button on the alarm pad.

She turned to the stranger, smiled widely and held open her arms. "Stevie, I haven't seen you in ages! Come here for a hug." It was the most enthusiastic welcome I had ever seen her give, and I moved closer for a better look.

The man's ugly face, scarred in places with a crooked nose, broke into a wry smile. He bent over, hugging the short woman tightly. I stood awkwardly behind them, waiting for an introduction. They separated, Martha holding him at arm's length for a moment, looking him over critically. "You look thin, Stevie. We need to start having you over for supper, or at least get you a woman who'll feed you."

He laughed, and turned to me, extending his hand. I stepped forward, shaking it, his grip firm and strong. *Safe.*

"I'm Julia."

"Stevie. I'm Brad's cousin."

"Here to protect us?" I asked.

Stevie glanced quickly at Martha, who hustled between us with a laugh. "Come, let's move to the kitchen! I've got food in the skillet that will burn." Stevie gestured for me to go ahead, and we walked into the kitchen, which smelled of grilled sausage and chicken. I sat at the counter, but Stevie glanced around, uneasy. "I'm going to check the house out," he announced, and left, his hand resting on his gun.

I watched his exit, then turned to Martha, my brows raised. "What's his story?"

"Oh, Stevie and Brad have been close as brothers ever since Brad was born. They're only four months apart in age. Brad said he sent Stevie over to keep an eye on us, just in case someone decides to stop back by. I doubt anyone will, but it's nice to have an extra person in the house, especially one with Stevie's skills."

She seemed ridiculously relaxed, given the situation. She added spices, chopped veggies and hummed under her breath. I told her my thoughts and she laughed.

"Girl, I've seen a lot of things working in this house, and it always ends up all right. Besides, if it's my time to go, it's my time. But listen, I changed the diapers on most of these boys. They ain't gonna touch me with a ten-foot pole." She set down the wooden spoon and turned to me. "Now, you? You I worry about. There's nothing stopping them from blowing your pretty little brains out."

My eyes widened, and I stared at her. "Is that your way of making me feel better?"

"Honey, it's me being honest. I believe women need to know what they're up against. If you want sunshine blown up your ass, you picked the wrong black woman." She turned back to the stove and turned up the heat, adding some more oil to the hot pan.

Thirty-Eight

Brad drove his car through the city streets, weighing the few options he had. He was dressed in a gray pin-striped suit, his shoes polished. His father would expect nothing less for a dinner at home.

The car took the curves easily as he left the city and moved into the streets of old money, condos and skyscrapers stepping aside for brick pavers, Rolls-Royces and heavily staffed mansions.

The estate had been in his family for over three generations. It was a fortress, surrounded by a fourteen-foot stone wall, stylishly covered by boxwood hedges, with security cameras positioned at regular intervals along the wall. The estate, for its pretentious address and luxury appointments, was small, only two acres, for ease in monitoring. Brad pulled up to a small guard shack and nodded to the uniformed man, a longtime employee, who manned it. Two other uniforms came from the shack and circled the car. Brad pressed the button, releasing the trunk, and waited as they shone their lights in the car and glanced through the trunk. Finally, the large, electrified gate in front of his car swung open, and he pressed on the gas.

STEVIE FINISHED HIS SEARCH of the house and entered the kitchen again, checking all of the windows and the locked door. He finally relaxed and sat at the island. Martha glanced over from the pot she was tending. "We could have just told you there was nobody in the house. And I checked all the doors and locks myself."

"Nothing wrong with a second set of eyes," he said softly, looking into her caramel-brown ones. She sniffed disapprovingly, and went to the fridge, getting the pitcher of tea out and pouring him a glass.

He smiled, looking like a teenage boy, and sniffed appreciably. "How soon before the food is ready?"

"Aw, I'd say about twenty minutes. Can you wait that long, or do you need a snack?"

"I can wait." He took a big gulp of tea, then studied me over the rim of the glass. "So. What's a pretty thing like you doing with the big ogre?"

I turned to him, a smile in my eyes. "The big ogre being Brad?"

"Of course. He doesn't know how to treat a lady. Now, me, I could give you the finer things in life."

Martha laughed, her spoon hitting the counter. "Like what? A Milky Way bar and a six-pack of Miller?"

He groaned, his hand to his heart. "Martha, how am I supposed to impress her when you paint me in that light?"

Martha laughed and grabbed three plates from the cabinet. "Stevie and Brad always thought they had some magic quality with the ladies, used to call it 'the Force.' Stevie's never mastered charm like Brad has—but that doesn't stop him from trying it on every female he sees."

"Oh, just 'cause you never fell victim to it doesn't mean it's not there. I just went easy on you, didn't want to give an old woman a heart attack."

"First of all, I wasn't *old* back then. Second, every time you boys got into trouble, you'd be sitting in my kitchen, trying your best to charm your way into me sneaking you some food—so don't tell me you haven't tried to use it on me!"

"Did they get into trouble a lot?" I interrupted them, curious.

"When they were younger it was mostly just kid stuff—BB gun fights, sneaking into movies they had no business seeing, throwing oranges at cars. Remember that guy in the Corvette?" Martha's eyes twinkled at Stevie, and he laughed, shaking his head. "Brad and Stevie were on a curve by the house, with about twenty oranges they had stolen from the groves around the pool. Every time a car would come around the curve, *blam*—they would peg the side of it with an orange. Now, most of the oranges were ripe and would splatter all over the side, scaring the bejesus out of whoever was driving and making a huge mess in the process."

Stevie broke in, taking over the story, his eyes lit with excitement. "So around the corner comes this red Corvette-beautiful car, so hot that we got distracted, just staring at the thing. Brad finally snaps out of it and grabs an orange and throws it at the car. There were two sounds at once," he said, holding up two fingers to illustrate the story. "A horn—the driver laid hard on the horn, alerting everyone within two miles. And brakes. That guy slammed full force on his brakes, squealing and leaving burnt rubber *all* over the place." He laughed, slapping his hand on the table. "The guy driving the car was one of these bald ugly guys, probably right in the middle of a midlife crisis. He threw open the car door before it even fully stopped and started screaming bloody murder and running for us."

"What did you do?" I leaned forward.

"Took off! Brad was trying to carry the orange bag with us, but it was heavy and bouncing everywhere, so finally he dropped it, and we split up, running in opposite directions. We were on residential streets by then, in Brad's fancy-ass neighborhood, so we stuck out like sore thumbs. And this guy was *fast*. I had slowed to catch my breath when, out of nowhere, the guy tackled me."

Martha held up a hand, stopping his story, and looked at me. "I'm gonna stop him right now before he starts blowing smoke into this story. Stevie starts crying like a little girl, screaming that they got the wrong guy, that he doesn't have anything to do with oranges—basically admitting to involvement every time he opens his mouth. The guy wrestles him onto his back and pulls back his fist, telling him that he better fess up and give him both his and his friend's name, or else he's going to beat the hell outta him. That was back when a grown man could beat up a kid and, as long as he deserved it, no one gave two shits. So, what do you think Stevie did?"

She had a hand on her hip, another one on the counter, and was staring at me as though she expected my prediction. "He told them?" I ventured hesitantly.

"Well," Stevie said, jumping back into the story. "As scared as I was of this middle-aged freak of nature, I was ten times more scared of Brad. But I wasn't quick-witted enough to come up with anything on the fly."

"So this idiot," Martha said, "just flip-flopped their first and last names."

"Hey—" Stevie broke in. "I was under pressure! I blurt out that I'm Steve Magiano, and that it was Brad Magiano who threw the orange, and that I had nothin' to do with it."

Thirty-Nine

The names hit me like the middle-age Corvette owner's fist, and my face must have shown it, for Martha flinched, then busied herself pulling out silverware.

"Magiano? You mean De Luca. Brad's last name is De Luca. Right?" I stood, breathing hard, and stared at Martha and Stevie, who had both found other items in the kitchen fascinating.

"I fucking need honesty right now." My voice was rigid and I saw Martha glance quickly over at me, and then look away. "What about women needing to know what they're up against, Martha?"

"It's not my place," she said quietly, as subservient as I had ever seen her, pain in the eyes she quickly averted from me.

"And you?" I turned my wrath on Stevie, who was desperately trying to get a little more tea out of his empty glass.

He set down his glass and turned to me, his face unreadable. I could tell from his eyes that I wasn't going to get any information from him, and he felt no shame at that. This was a man who had no issue with confrontation, or with withholding information.

Just minutes before, the kitchen had relaxed into a comfortable atmosphere, filled with the smells and noises of good cooking. Laughter, sizzles, pots banging. Now it seemed cold and foreign. I glared at both of them, then whirled and stormed up the stairs, hearing Martha's sigh behind me. I flew onto the landing and turned, looking into Brad's bedroom with the damn naked woman above his bed. She, in her black-and-white hotness, caught my fury. I strode in, climbing onto the bed and grabbed the large, canvas-wrapped frame and yanked it off the wall.

DOWNSTAIRS, MARTHA AND Stevie heard the sounds as Julia tore the portrait to shreds, slamming it against the door to break the wooden frame. He raised his eyebrows at Martha and she shook her head, turning off the burners and covering the rice. Dinner was finally ready, for all the good it did now.

"I always told that man his secrets would undo him." Martha set three plates on the counter, and spooned rice onto each one.

"You act like he ever had a choice," Stevie said, walking to the fridge and refilling his tea. He lowered his voice. "He was born, he grew up, he walked away from it as soon as he was old enough to make the decision. Why does it matter what she knows? You and I both know she won't be around long, either by execution or him tiring of her. And she won't tell anyone. Not now that she knows who he is."

"I don't know," Martha said, heaping jambalaya onto their plates. "This one might be different. I fought it, didn't want to see it, but something is different in his eyes when he looks at her. And from the evidence—don't eat at that table, I got to clean it—she can keep up with him sexually, which is a feat unto itself."

"So, what are you saying, he's in *love*?" He spat out the words, incredulity coating the question.

"Maybe not yet, but it could get there."

"Brad doesn't fall in love. Even with Hillary."

"Well, I told that boy marrying Hillary was a colossal mistake. It's not my fault he didn't listen then. But he hasn't asked me now. Probably won't, given as hardheaded as he is. But I will tell you, if that girl gets herself killed, I'll be upset. And Brad? He'll start a war the likes of which the Magianos haven't seen in a long time."

I LAY ON the soft sheets of the guest bed, and fumed. I was mentally exhausted, and the stress of the day weighed on me like concrete bricks, pinning me to the mattress. To make matters worse I was hungry. But I'd be damned if I sat down there with those two and ate. I could smell the jambalaya, the scent somehow making its way up the staircase, down the hall and through the thick wooden door. I pulled the covers over my head and tried to push away the thoughts that were drilling through my head.

So Brad is a member of the Magiano family. Those are the "connections" he mentioned. Hell of a connection. The Magianos, who killed Broward and tried to kill me. I'm sleeping with the fucking enemy. Even worse, I'm in love with the enemy.

I rolled over, curling into a ball, snapshots of the last few weeks shuttering through my mind. He had opened me up so much, pushed me so far past my sexual boundaries, stolen his way into and consumed my heart. At a time when everything had gone to hell and I didn't know where to turn, he had been my constant, my strength. The man I had trusted my safety to. And now this. Brad Magiano, not De Luca. A first name I loved combined with a last name I despised. The man I had turned to was the one I should have run from. I didn't know what bothered me more, the new danger facing my body or the risk I had brought to my heart.

Forty

"She has to die," Dominic Magiano said in Italian. "I'm sorry, Brad, but she knows too much." Words Brad felt he had overheard a hundred times before. Proper regret placed on the syllables, but compassion never truly behind them.

Brad faced his father in the darkness. They stood on one of the many outdoor terraces of the home where he had grown up, facing the subtly lit and landscaped gardens. He said nothing, listening to the sounds of the night.

"Are you close to her?"

"Yes." He said the word quietly, not needing to add anything more. Despite the estrangement, his father knew him well enough to understand the weight behind the response.

The old man stepped forward, a crack of light uncovering his features, features that had aged since the last time Brad had been home. His father was a handsome man, with a full head of white hair, olive skin and strong, powerful features. His eyes differed from Brad's; they blazed blue instead of brown, and had never failed to find weakness in an adversary. But the skin around his eyes had sagged, and age spots now covered his skin. He looked like an old man, though Brad would never dishonor him by pointing it out. From Brad's reflection, the aging process had begun when his wife, Brad's mother, had left. Now, over twenty years later, there was little life left in his bones. *An old, stubborn man.*

They had eaten in the large formal dining room, a fire lit despite the summer month. His father, it seemed, was perpetually cold, an irritating condition for Brad, whose internal temperature was the exact opposite. They had been the only attendees to the meal, and sat at opposite ends of the ridiculously long table. Brad was grateful for the distance, if only because it put him farther from the fire's heat. The dinner was long, five courses, and they were served by Abigail, a longtime employee of his father's.

There had been little conversation, because Brad refused to discuss his father's business and his father had little interest in Brad's caseload. Brad knew that any discussion regarding Julia would wait until after the meal. Over beef tenderloin with new potatoes, Brad had asked about his brothers.

"Alfonso's wife is pregnant again. They moved out of that townhome, they live in the Glades now, close to Dante. I wish you didn't live so far away from the family. You isolate yourself, so far from the rest of us. You think you're better than us?" He pointed his knife at Brad, his features dark.

This was where the conversation always ended up. No matter how it started, whether it was discussing the Yankees, the weather outside or current stock prices, it always ended with that accusation.

And now the night had finally climaxed to this point, cigars and whiskey on the balcony, Julia's imminent demise.

He spoke slowly in their language, barely containing the

anger in his voice. "Explain to me why you would order a hit, to someone I know, without contacting me first."

"You assume too much. When I gave the order I did not know her connection to you. All we had was a name and location—her home."

"I'm not just talking about Julia. You killed my business partner without consulting me."

"It was business. He knew the risks, as did you when you refused the business. His work was sloppy. If it hadn't been, our hand wouldn't have been tipped before the takeover occurred."

"Do you not have enough power? Why are you going after other families?" He puffed on his cigar, blowing the smoke up into the night sky, willing himself to stay calm.

"You know this business. We grow or die."

"That's Alfonso talking. You letting him call the shots now?"

His father's features tightened. "Don't forget your place, my son."

"Don't lose yours. You still stand in control of this family."

His father's face tightened around the lit cigar. He sighed, old again, and looked at Brad. "What do you suggest I do with this girl?"

"Leave her alone. She'll keep her knowledge secret in exchange for safety."

The older man scoffed, shaking his head at Brad. "You know better than that. Women cannot be trusted. As soon as you leave her, or scorn her, or she catches you with a whore, she will tell. She will forget the danger and do whatever she can to make you bleed."

Automatic sprinklers started in the gardens below, and Brad

leaned on the railing and ground out his cigar in frustration. His father spoke again. "No. Death is the only way."

Brad straightened, turning to face his father. "I have stood aside and watched you ruin and take countless lives. You know my opinion of your business. I won't dishonor you by voicing it in your home. But this is one time I am not coming to you and asking for compassion. I am demanding her protection. You have cursed me with this family. Now let me have one benefit from its association. If you come for her, you will be sacrificing me."

The eyes of his father deadened, black holes on gray skin. "You've been away too long, Brad. You've forgotten how I respond to demands. You may be my blood, but you are also the biggest indicator of my weakness. And everyone watches me closely for weakness." He stepped forward, gripping Brad's shoulder with his hand. "It's the principle of it, Bradley. My priority is this family. A family you ceased being a part of a long time ago. And she risks that priority. So, as I said before, death is the only way." He released his grip and turned, stepping back to the railing and looking outward, away from his son.

Forty-One

Brad came home at 1:00 a.m. His cousin and Martha were in the den, Stevie watching TV and Martha dozing in a recliner. Brad leaned on the door frame, his hands in his pockets, and asked Stevie the question with his eyes.

"She's upstairs. Asleep, in the guest room." At his words Martha stirred, then opened her eyes, seeing Brad and nodding hello.

"The guest room." Brad's tone was quiet, questioning.

Martha swung the recliner closed and stood, stiff-legged, and came over to Brad. "There was a slip of the tongue, Brad. She knows who you are."

Brad's eyes showed his anger, but he patted Martha's shoulder and kissed her head. "Thanks for keeping an eye on her. You go on to bed."

Her shoulders slumped, she walked over to Stevie, kissing his cheek and squeezing him hard. "See you soon, Stevie. Don't be such a stranger." Then she left, and Brad followed her to the back door, waiting at the window until he saw her enter her apartment. He locked the door, then swung by the fridge on his way back to the den.

He rubbed his brow, stress evident on his face, and met Stevie's eyes across the room. Walking forward, he set two cold beers down on the table, pushing one to Stevie. "Figured you might want one."

Stevie grinned, and used his shirt to open it, taking a big sip. "Didn't want to take one earlier. Thought you might want me sober."

"You thought right." Brad sank into a big leather chair, putting his shoes on the table and opening his own bottle, tossing the cap toward the corner trash can. It missed and Brad wearily closed his eyes, resting his head against the worn leather.

"So, what's the verdict?" Stevie asked.

Brad opened his eyes in response, lifting his head and his bottle. He took a sip and then played with the liquid on his tongue, staring forward, thinking. Stevie let him think, knowing that he would get an answer eventually.

"I am in a bit of a predicament." Brad spoke slowly, deliberately, his deep voice filling the quiet room.

"If you need help, you know you have my loyalty."

"This is not your fight."

"It's not yours, either." Stevie leaned forward, dropping his voice to almost a whisper. "She's pussy, Brad. I know you hate collateral damage, but you need to let this one go. They will make it quick. She won't suffer. And then all of this, the Broward mess, the family rift, the takeover complications, will disappear. And you can go back to your clean life and continuing pretending that you're not *numero due* of the Magiano dynasty." His eyes searched Brad's and Stevie shook his head in disgust at what he found there. "Don't give me that look. You know this world. I don't know that girl, and I have no loyalty to her. My loyalty is to you, and I love you like a brother. You standing up on this—for her—it's going to rip apart every bit of this life you've worked so hard for. She's a fuck. Maybe a hot one, but one who ended up in the wrong place at the wrong time. These girls come and go— you know that."

Brad spoke, steel in his words. "Because you're one of the few friends I have, I'm not going to break your fucking face for that statement. I'm also not going to dignify it with a response. Except for this. She's not just pussy. I don't know what she is yet, but she means something to me. You're right. I know this world, and I know the risks involved. And I'll tell you the same thing I told my father. If they come for her, they will have to go through me. And I have no problem dying in that fight." His eyes cold, resolute, he drained the rest of his beer and stood, walking toward the kitchen. On his way out, Stevie spoke.

"Martha was right." His voice was bitter, quiet, and Brad dropped the bottle into a trash can and turned to face him.

"Right about what?"

"You *love* her." He spat out the words as if they were dirty.

"No." He shook his head quickly, looking away.

"Christ, Brad, you've known the girl, what, a month or two?" Stevie stood up, walked over to Brad, looking into his face, which was growing darker. "You, with the heart of steel and the unending supply of ass. You're supposed to be the smart one!"

Brad's right fist connected with Stevie's chin in a strong uppercut, his left hand grabbing the gun out of his holster. In one smooth motion, he flipped the gun around and cocked it, pointing it at Stevie's head. The wounded man recoiled, and he glared at Brad, not bothering to wipe the blood pouring from his split upper lip. They faced each other, two experienced men in the game of war, one unarmed and knowing his weakness.

"Get out."

Stevie laughed, cold and hard. "You need every friend you got right now."

"I don't need any more bullshit right now. And you're bleeding all over my fucking carpet."

Stevie walked slowly around him, eyeing the gun, leaving the study and heading for the front door. "When you're over this shit, I'm gonna want that gun back." Then he left, slamming the door behind him.

Brad locked the doors and reset the alarm. Then he turned off the lights and walked upstairs.

HE CHECKED THE master bedroom first, hoping that she had moved there and was waiting for him in bed. But his bed was empty, the room silent. He turned to leave and then stopped, seeing something. Pieces of wood and ripped canvas scattered the floor and bed. He stepped forward, trying to distinguish the items in the dimly lit room. Then, realizing what they were, he swallowed a smile and headed to the other bedroom.

He opened the guest-room door quietly, stepping over a tray of untouched food and walking silently into the dark room. Julia was sleeping, her breathing quiet and regular. She lay at an awkward position, her arms splayed, head tilted up by too many pillows.

He watched her sleep, his mind thinking over Stevie's accusation. Was it possible? Or was this his knight in shining armor instinct? He had felt things for her, had told her as much this morning. But it was way too soon for love.

He felt out of sorts, a sensation that he was not used to and was uncomfortable with. He was used to being in control, to manipulating circumstances so that everything flowed to his liking. Staring at her, frustrated, he let the thought move around in his mind. *Love.* The thought floated, flipped, then settled. Maybe they were right. And in the realization, he saw light at the end of the tunnel.

Forty-Two

I woke from the weight of his body, pressing on the bed as he pulled back the covers and climbed in. I felt cold air, then hard warmth pressing against my back, his arms wrapping my body and pulling me close to him. He moved one of the pillows underneath my head, and my neck relaxed into a more comfortable position.

"I'm mad at you." I spoke through the layers of fabric but didn't pull away. Our bodies felt too perfect in the warm bed.

"I know," he whispered, planting a soft kiss on my neck. "As you deserve to be. But go to sleep now, and lecture me in the morning."

"I'm starving," I said, my tired stomach growling, reminding me of my missed dinner. Thank God I'd had some mac and...

"Do you want me to get you something?" Brad asked from behind me. But I didn't answer. I was already back asleep.

MORNING CAME, WITH the normal warmth of sunshine filling the room, smells of bacon cooking and sounds of Martha downstairs. I kept my eyes closed, and tried to avoid thinking, tried to pretend for a little longer that everything was normal. Unfortunately, my mental defense system was weak and out of practice. My eyes opened, revealing the well-appointed guest room, and Brad stirred behind me, sensing my movement. I rolled over, still nestled in the cocoon of his arms, and stared up at him. His eyes, heavy with sleep, blinked, and he looked at me warily.

"Good morning." His voice husky and dry.

I skipped the pleasantries. "Brad Magiano."

"Yeah, um, Martha told me that you found out about that." His eyes held no shame but twinkled with something close to mischievousness.

"And that's funny? You being part of one of the largest crime families in the country? The family that's hunting me down like a wounded deer?"

"Hey, it's better than me *not* having connections to the family that's hunting you down."

I frowned at him, pushing away from his chest. "Stop being cute. This is a major problem. I would have left your house last night if I didn't think I would be gunned down in the street!"

He grabbed my arms and tried to tug me to him, a movement I wormed out of, propping my body up on an elbow. "I'm serious! What the fuck? You are the fucking enemy, and I have been sleeping with you." The Julia Roberts reference popped out unassisted, and I hated the joviality it inserted into the conversation. But his face straightened, and I saw the seriousness enter his eyes.

"Julia—I know I should have told you. There is no excuse for that, and I'm sorry."

I waited, expecting the declaration of no excuse to be followed by an excuse. "So? Why didn't you?"

He groaned, lying back and staring up into the ceiling, avoiding my eyes. "I changed my name when I was seventeen, when I left that life. I have no connection to my family other than traditional obligations. Their business, their lifestyle, I left all of that behind, as much as I could. Sometimes, like now, it is inescapable. I had hoped to handle it without you ever finding out." He blew out a breath and turned to me, his eyes finally meeting mine.

I narrowed my eyes at his, rolling away from him and standing up. "So you *would* have kept this a secret! You never planned on telling me!"

"It's not who I am. It's what I was born into, and what I made the conscious decision not to be. I've been pigeonholed by it my whole life. I didn't want that from you." His eyes, frustrated pools of exposure, captured mine, and he held me there as he stood, the bed between us.

"So you didn't know about the threat? About Broward, about me?"

"I'm not in their circle. I wasn't consulted or aware of any of those actions. Please know that." I saw truth in his eyes, in his desperation for my approval.

"It doesn't matter. I understand you not starting the relationship with that tidbit, but when the shit hit the fan—when one of *your* family showed up to kill me—*that* is when you should have told me this. We have enough hurdles to overcome in the relationship, Brad. Big hurdles that already scare the hell out of me. Your family…I don't know how I would have taken that under normal circumstances. But now, in these circumstances…it's a deal breaker, Brad."

He physically swayed from my words, his eyes closing and head dropping. He stayed that way for a moment, solid, unmoving steel. Then he raised his head and met my eyes. "A deal breaker."

"Yes."

"You. The woman who raised holy hell in my kitchen, who professed her love for me, love that seemingly had no bounds. You, who wormed her way into the life that I have so carefully constructed. Do you think I *want* this?" he asked harshly, his arms dropping, two tightly coiled expression of frustration.

"Want what, exactly, Brad?" I spat out the words, stepping forward until I hit the bed. "What exactly have I done to make your life so damn hard?"

"I didn't want a relationship! Didn't want to fall in love or be committed, or be required to share the intimate details of my life! But I'm here—with you, a curse of a woman who has taken all of my fucking walls and shredded them like fucking tissue paper in your tiny little hands! It's been so easy for you, so effortless—and now, in the face of my darkest truth, you're done. My family, the bane of my existence. A force I have battled my whole life, a fight I have won—and it means nothing to you."

I opened my mouth, tried to cut in—to end this horrid rant—but stopped at the look in his eyes. It was desperation, it was rage, it was pure, uncontrolled anguish. I shut my mouth and did nothing but stare at him wordlessly.

"It's not your fault," he said quietly, his frame collapsing, the light fading from his eyes. "You're young. You don't know what love is. And this is a lot for you to handle." He turned, running a hand through his hair, gripping his head with both hands, before releasing it and glancing back at me. "I grew up around this. I forget what it's like for an outsider. I'm sorry." He stepped to the door, opening it quietly, and then he left.

IT WAS TOO MUCH to take in my raw and confused state. The only thing I did know, among the fear, and stress, and frustration, was that the one solid presence I had, the man I loved, was leaving. The one thing I should be holding on to, I had pushed away. I ran after him, pushing open the bedroom door, seeing him on the landing, his body turned, our eyes meeting. He looked beaten and confused, a look that contradicted every ounce of the man I knew.

"I'm sorry," I whispered. "I was wrong." He raised his head slightly, wariness on his face.

"I mean…" I stumbled, stepping forward until I stood in front of him, short in my bare feet. "You were wrong—you should have told me. But I was wrong for pushing you away for it. I do love you." I rose on my toes, running my hand softly along the curves of his face, his eyes closing, face turning down to mine. "I need you right now, need you to tell me that everything is going to be okay, need you to be on my side of this. When I found about about your family, I thought that you were with them, against me. And I couldn't take any more unknowns. I'm sorry."

He leaned down, catching my mouth, the kiss soft and forgiving.

I closed my eyes, sighing into his mouth. "But no more secrets." I pulled away, opening my eyes, seeing relief in his, his body moving, arms wrapping around me, pulling my body tight to his, his mouth lowering to mine, a tentative kiss that turned deeper at my acceptance. He gripped my body and walked us both backward, until my back hit solid wall, and he braced his arms on either side of my head, locking me into his frame, his hard body grinding against mine.

When his mouth finally released mine, my hands tight in his hair, I looked up, shifting against him and eliciting a quick breath from his mouth. "So? Did your fabulous plan work last night?" His earlier joviality had to have been caused by something.

"I'm working on it."

"Well, I don't want to be a nag or anything, but I do want to live, to graduate, to grow old with someone."

"I know. Don't worry, I will protect you. From now on, relax."

I sighed, leaning against the ridges of his body, resting my head on his chest.

"What happened to the print?" His chest vibrated with the words.

"The what?"

"The print. Above my bed."

I snorted. "Sorry. It was a little dated anyway, don't you think?"

He laughed softly, pressing his lips against my hair. "You gonna replace it?"

I wrinkled my nose, trying to imagine me, naked, on a fur rug, stretched out over Brad's bed. "We can find a nice landscape or something to fill that space." I heard Martha holler something from downstairs, and I straightened, leaving the warmth of his arms.

"Come to bed," he commanded. "I have plans for you." I felt his hand move up, sneaking under my tank, and I ducked away, under his arm, eliciting a frown from him.

I ignored his delicious body, lit by the morning sun. "I am about to start chewing on *you* if I don't get something to eat. You can have your way with me after breakfast, if your ridiculous libido can make it that long." I stepped backward toward the stairs, his expression changing and mischief entering his face. I spun and sprang to the stairs, thundering down them, his feet just steps behind, and we burst into the kitchen—scaring the crap out of Martha, my butt hitting a stool before he could get me.

I smiled at him smugly, grabbing a fresh strawberry from a fruit plate and popping it in my mouth. He wore dark pajama pants, no shirt and a bemused expression. It was unfair how incredible he made the combination look. He took a seat next to me and we said good morning to Martha.

Martha didn't waste time in shelling out breakfast—warm French toast, bacon and cheese grits. I scarfed it all down, and she had seconds ready before I even had a chance to ask.

"I grabbed that plate of jambalaya still at the top of the stairs. You didn't eat it last night?"

I shook my head sheepishly. "I was still pouting when you came up. I didn't realize you had food."

Her mouth thinned into a line that could only be described as petulant. "That was good jambalaya you wasted."

"I'm sure it was. Any left over that I could eat for lunch?"

"I'll think about it."

"Think about whether there is any left over?"

"Think about whether I'll give you another chance at it."

We grinned at each other and she put another piece of toast on my plate. I looked at Brad. "So, what's the plan for today?"

He smiled at me, surprisingly cheerful despite our bleak situation. "Let me make a call. Then I'll let you know."

He stepped outside, onto the deep back porch, his grin disappearing, a somber fix settling on his face. He walked down the steps and through the grass to the pool. Sitting down on one of the chairs that lined the blue water, he pulled out his cell. He looked at it a moment, thinking. He had gone to bed last night confident, his arms wrapped around Julia, content in recognizing his future. One with her. A woman who had unknowingly consumed him. Love, an idea he had tossed out with every other conventional theory, had tackled him unprepared. Tackled and possibly trapped him. Julia's blowup had terrified him. In coming to terms with his feelings, he hadn't considered the possibility of her leaving him. Now, having stared into that reality, knowing the effect it had on him, after only this short relationship...how would he handle it after six months of dating, or marriage, or kids? He had practically been brought to his knees upstairs. There was no way he'd survive it if he fell any further. She was so young. He barely knew love, almost missed it when it came and he had years of experience on her.

She had bent. When he had lost it, failed to control his emotions, she had wavered. What would she do next time? When he failed her, when he stumbled. She would run, leaving him broken and alone.

But this wasn't a typical situation. He could either risk his heart or risk her safety. And, when it came down to that, the choice was easy. He closed his eyes, affirming his decision. Then he made the call.

His father didn't answer, the automated voice mail picking up instead. Brad ended the call and waited, sitting in the sun. After a few minutes his phone rang, showing a blocked number.

"Hello."

"What is it, Bradley?"

"There has been a new wrinkle you should be aware of. Tell the boys to hold off the bloodshed until we can talk."

"Every hour that passes is more risk, you know that. I cannot extend any more—"

"Tomorrow morning. I'll come over for breakfast. If you don't think the information I give you then is worth your time, you are free to act. I will never give you my blessing, but I am asking you to listen to this information."

There was silence, crackly, then his father's gravelly voice. "Tomorrow morning. After that you will have exhausted my courtesy."

"I understand." Brad pulled the phone from his ear and ended the call.

THE MAGIANO PATRIARCH hung up the phone and looked into his reflection in the ornate gold mirror in his study. He looked older, his skin grayer than it should be. He decided to sit outside this afternoon, to get some sun. He needed to take care of himself, to ensure that he would be around for a long time. Long enough to convince Bradley to return to the family, to take his rightful place as head of the organization. He was the only one intelligent enough to keep it powerful. His other two sons had allowed power to corrupt them, had lost sight of proper business sense in the illicit world of blood, competition and status. Legitimizing the businesses would weaken them, but that would be Brad's choice. He needed to mend fences with his son before it reached the point where Brad would have that powerful decision to make. This girl threatened that possibility, with both her life and her death. Brad had always needlessly involved himself in rescue plights, had always stood in the way of the family's proper conduction of business. But this was a different type of stand. For Brad to put himself into the equation, to throw his life on the line, put him in a difficult predicament. Difficult, but an easy decision all the same. Family came first, and she was not family. He could not risk the entire family for one son and his temporary girlfriend.

He spoke softly, but the two men in the next room heard the words. They appeared instantly, and waited to hear his orders.

"Follow them. Make sure they don't do anything stupid. Keep a constant eye on them—I want to know everything that happens between now and tomorrow morning."

Forty-Three

Brad came back into the kitchen, the light not quite as bright in his eyes.

"Everything okay?" I asked.

He walked over and kissed me on the head. "Everything's fine," he said. "What do you feel like doing today?"

I looked at him, surprised. "What *can* we do today? Aren't we under house arrest?"

"No. Your day will be free of danger. What do you feel like doing?"

"Well, at some point I'd like to discuss with you the whole situation we are in."

He waved that off. "Other than that. I promise, we will sit down and discuss that."

"Okay...I don't know. I hadn't really thought about it. I need to do laundry and stuff."

He stared at me. "Laundry and...stuff?"

"Yeah, like ironing, grocery shopping. I have to get ready for work tomorrow morning."

"First of all, we don't know if you're going to work tomorrow."

I held up my hand, stopping the stupid list he was starting. "*Wait*—you mean because I might be dead tomorrow?"

"Well…you might be in danger."

"Okay, so not dead *yet*. And the whole update-me-on-the-current-status-of-my-own-mortality conversation is something you just kinda…" I waved my hand dismissively. "…tossed aside as something that we will do later. Whether you and your manliness realize it or not, I'd like to have *some* sort of input in the plot for my survival." I had sidled over to him during the course of my speech, and I ended the statement by poking his iron chest with my finger.

He grabbed my finger, his eyes dark. "Don't do that."

I fought a grin and yanked my hand out of his. We faced off in the kitchen, his hands on his hips, my expression stern, before he broke. Sighing, he wrapped his arms across my stiff body, pulling me to him for a hug.

It was an unexpected gesture, and I fought the embrace and stayed fixed, immobile, refusing to bend to his manly charm. He tried to wrap my arms around him, but they dropped, limp like spaghetti, unwilling to cooperate. He laughed at my stubbornness, his hands becoming playful, running through my hair, down my noncompliant arms, grabbing and squeezing my clenched butt. That broke me, and I smiled despite myself.

"There you go," he said, nuzzling my neck. "I know that you want to know what's going on. But all I can tell you is that you are safe. They have promised to stay away until I speak with them in the morning. And in the morning, I will play a card that they don't expect, and one that they will have no recourse against. I promise you, it will be fine."

"What, some secret body hidden somewhere? You're going to blackmail them?"

He scowled at me. "Nothing so barbaric, Julia. I'm the good

son, remember?" He held up a hand, stopping my thought process. "Just let me handle it. Please. I ask for one day of secrecy."

"I thought we weren't going to have any more secrets," I grumbled into his chest. I didn't like it, but twenty-four hours of freedom was more than I had fifteen minutes ago. I relaxed a bit in his arms.

"It's a good secret. So, what do you want to do today, other than laundry or some other menial errand?"

I stood on my tiptoes and put my mouth on his earlobe, biting it gently, then releasing it and giving him a suggestive smile. He grinned down at me and then dipped me back, nibbling and kissing my neck. Then he threw me over his shoulder and bounded up the stairs.

"I'm leaving for the day!" Martha called, up the stairs to Brad's retreating back. "You hear me?" Not getting a response, she shook her head, then wiped her hands on a dish towel, grabbed her purse and headed out the door, locking it securely behind her.

BRAD DEFTLY NAVIGATED through the broken pieces of his ex and threw me down onto soft sheets. He pulled my legs to him, grabbing the waist of my skirt and sliding it and my panties down, leaving me bare and exposed.

His mouth was instantly covering me, his tongue making incredible sensations that caused my toes to clench and my breath to catch. And when I came, five minutes later, it was intense, all of my tension and emotions spilling out, turning into delicious ecstasy and liquid, amazing pleasure.

He kept his mouth on me, gradually softening the pressure from his tongue, until he did nothing but hold me in his mouth, my body occasionally twitching in postorgasm aftershocks. When he did lift his mouth, I lay useless on the bed—drained of any coherent thought or muscle response. He grabbed my skirt, using it to wipe his mouth, and I frowned at him through my euphoria. He landed next to me, and I rolled over groggily, reaching for him, for his hardness.

He pushed me away, and I frowned at him. "Not now," he said. "You can take care of me later."

I pouted, but relented, watching him walk to the closet. "Have you decided what you want to do today?" he called, sifting through clothes.

"Got any well–hung friends?"

He glanced over, a grin on his face, and I stuck out my tongue playfully.

"I could certainly arrange that, if that is what you are in the mood for." He emerged from the closet, dressed casually, pulling a baseball hat onto his head. Pressing me back onto the bed, he ran his teeth over my neck, nibbling on the soft skin until I giggled.

"Stop—seriously!" I pushed him off and propped myself up on one elbow. "Ummm…what about an afternoon movie?" I glanced at the clock.

He frowned, sitting next to me and reaching for the drawer of the bedside table. "So, no afternoon gang bang?" Pulling out a watch, he slid it onto his wrist and fastened the buckle. Not waiting for a response, he leaned over, giving me a quick kiss on the cheek before standing. "A movie sounds good to me. We can do some shopping and grab lunch first, if you want."

The word *shopping* instantly perked me up. "That sounds good." I rolled out of bed and grabbed the bag of clothes I had packed. I rummaged deep in the bag, finding my makeup pouch and my toothbrush. I grabbed both and joined Brad at the long counter, and we brushed our teeth in companionable silence.

"You ready?" he asked, after rinsing thoroughly.

"Five minutes," I mumbled, through toothpaste bubbles.

He flashed a grin and headed downstairs. I flipped through the makeup bag, grabbing powder, mascara and lip gloss. Three minutes later, I stuck my phone in my pocket and bounded down the stairs.

Brad was on the phone, standing by the full-length windows that showcased the large backyard pool. Hearing my heels on the floor, he quickly ended the call and turned, whistling at my appearance. "You look great."

"Great, but penniless. Can we stop by my house? Last time I was there, I didn't grab my wallet."

"You don't need it."

"That is *so* sugar daddy of you, but I like to have my wallet. That way I won't feel guilty when I look at stuff. If you're paying, I'll refuse to look at anything and neither one of us will have any fun."

He shrugged. "Whatever. But I *am* going to buy you some things, so go ahead and start getting used to the concept."

"I didn't say I won't let you buy me stuff—just said I want my wallet also." I grinned at him, sticking out my tongue and heading for the back door. He followed me, pressing the button for the garage doors, and we headed outside.

"Wait." I grabbed his arm and he stopped, his car about to pull out onto his street. "Should we have a gun, or something? Some kind of protection?"

Brad pulled out, shaking his head at my question. "I do have a gun, in the center console, but I always have that there. No, we don't need any protection today."

The situation reminded me of a gun I had seen before, in the bathroom of his master suite. "So, you have two guns?"

He glanced over at me distractedly. "What? What do you mean?"

"I saw a gun in your house before, in the bathroom. And you said you always keep this one here, in the car. So you have two guns?"

He found my question amusing, and shook his head. "I'm not sure which gun you saw in my bathroom, but I probably have ten in the house, scattered about in different locations. Martha knows where they all are, as does Helga, who you still need to meet. I'll have them show you the locations, just so you don't accidentally knock one over at some point in time. Do you know how to shoot?"

I found *that* question amusing and grinned at him. "I grew up in south Georgia so, yes—I am well aware of how to shoot. Though I have more experience with shotguns and rifles than I do handguns. Why do you have so many?"

He shrugged. "I grew up in a house where guns were everywhere. If someone is going to come into my home to harm me, they are going to be armed. I'd like an even playing field."

I nodded at that, my nerves still on edge. He glanced over, his eyes sharpening when they met mine. "Julia, relax. We are safe. One thing my family does is keep their word. You don't have anything to worry about today." He smiled at me and gripped my knee reassuringly.

Today. I sank into the soft leather, the contoured seat fitting my body perfectly. *Yippee.*

Forty-Four

We stopped by my house on the way, Brad's car, as always, looking ridiculous parked in my neighborhood. Seeing as it was before noon, my house was quiet, everyone still asleep, and he came inside with me.

"Why don't you grab a few things while we are here?"

I heard his suggestion from my bedroom, and stuck my head out of the door. "Like what?"

"Something dressy. In case we go out tonight."

I shrugged, flipping through the rack in my closest and snagging a simple black dress that would cover any fancy destination he felt the need to take me to. *Or a funeral.* The thought stopped me cold and I grabbed my wallet and ran out, running into him in the hall. "Brad—what about Broward's funeral!"

He frowned down at me, taking up way too much of the skinny hallway. "What about it?"

"It's today! At three. We have to go." I couldn't believe that, in the course of everything, I had forgotten about the funeral. About the fact that my boss had died. I had shoved it aside as if it could hang out in the back of my mind without proper consideration.

He shrugged. "So? We'll skip it."

I flinched at the suggestion. "Skip it? We can't skip it. What will people think?"

"What people? Broward? He's not going to care."

I pushed him into the living room, away from my sleeping roommates, and cocked a hip, giving him my best stern look. "I'm well aware that Broward won't notice our absence, but everyone else will. I was his intern, and you were his partner. We are expected to attend."

He put his hands on his hips and stared down at me. "Julia, I don't give a fuck what people think. Some people might *think* that it's disrespectful for me to attend, given that I had relations with his wife. *She* may not want me there. And besides that, we have bigger issues going on."

"With the whole 'someone trying to kill me' thing? Because you just said I was safe." I tried to glare at him, but my smile broke through.

He kissed my head and hid his grin as he escorted me out the door. "Point made. But we're not going. I'm sorry. Thanks for yielding to my wisdom on this."

"Oh, I'll find a way for you to pay me back later," I intoned, climbing into the car as he held the door for me.

"I'm sure you will," he said with a grin.

WE PULLED INTO the Hillsdale Mall, the current favorite of local yuppies, and Brad circled around to the Neiman's valet.

"I can literally *see* a parking spot," I pointed out as he unbuckled his seat belt and reached over to unclick mine. "Right there! Like, ten feet away." He smiled at me, ignoring my logic, and climbed out, accepting the valet ticket from the teenager who opened his doors. I climbed out, expelling a big breath of air, irritated by the waste of money, and accepted Brad's outstretched hand. "Look at it! *Right* over there. Beautiful spot," I grumbled as we passed through the brass doors, held open by a suited Neiman's associate. Brad ignored me, and we came to a stop at the escalators, the bulk of the store surrounding us.

"Should we go upstairs to Women's Fashion?" he asked, returning the flirtatious smiles of the Cosmetics girls.

"No, we can just walk through to the main mall—unless you have something you wanted to look for."

"I think I owe you a pair of shoes."

"For what?"

"The elevator—a couple of weeks ago. You seemed quite upset about it at the time."

"Oh." I laughed. During a time when I was refusing to speak to him, Brad had inadvertently flooded an elevator in an attempt to foster communication. The stunt had ruined one of the few pairs of designer shoes I had actually purchased— ninety percent of my shoe wardrobe was donated by Becca— and I had dissolved in tears over the loss.

"Manolo Blahniks—if I recall?" he said, smiling down at me.

"Yes. I *will* allow you to replace those." That pleased him, and he grabbed my hand, pulling me to the left, and we zigzagged through jewelry and perfume counters till we ended up at the section of my dreams, the Neiman's shoe section. The softly lit cubbyholes showcased designer shoes as if they were Cartier watches, the attendants carried trays of champagne and there were pedestals of shoes everywhere, each more tempting than the next. It was how I imagined heaven to be.

We spent about a half hour in the section. I found the suede Manolos that had been ruined, and tried them on, holding up my foot and critiquing them. They didn't look quite the same. Maybe it was because I was envisioning the pair I had at home, the pair I had taken the hair dryer to in an attempt to dry them out. They now sat, sad and pathetic, high in my closet, with spots marring the coloring. I frowned and looked around. Then I saw *them*.

True love can be described in a variety of ways. However you describe it, I was in love with those shoes from the moment I saw them. I think I gasped a little—something made Brad look up from his phone, and he followed my gaze to the simple black heels high on the pedestal. He gestured to the attendant, and she brought the pair over, pure magic in her fingers. The pair was basic and classy Christian Louboutin—red sole, high stiletto heel, peep toe with an ankle strap. Elegance in the lines, in the leather, in the details. Small silver studs accented parts of the shoe, giving a slight edge to the classic details. I sighed softly, and Brad ended his call and told them my size.

I looked at him, troubled. "I didn't look at the price, but I can pretty much guarantee you they cost double what my Manolos did."

"I didn't see you orgasm over the Manolos."

"I kind of did, before. Back when I originally purchased them. Before I knew true love."

"I don't care about the price."

I wanted to argue with him, wanted to take the replacement pair of suede heels that were already on my feet, but I couldn't resist. I wanted them too badly to let pride and— what did my mother call it?—"social graces" stand in my way.

"Okay."

He laughed at my easy surrender, and wrapped an arm around me, kissing my neck. "You want to try them on?"

"Better, just to be safe."

Fifteen minutes later we left Neiman's and headed to the food court. We decided on P.F. Chang's, and lucked out with an immediate table, though it was crammed into a tight corner. Brad studied the small table with apprehension, then sat, his large body dwarfing the minute table. Add the ridiculously large bag that Neiman's had put my shoe box into, and we were short on foot, arm and table room. I stifled a laugh and smiled at Brad, the discomfort visible in his eyes.

"Want to wait for a bigger table?"

"No, I'll suffer through," he said, picking up the menu and looking it over.

We ordered, and once the waiter left I met Brad's eyes across the table.

"Uh-oh," he said, watching me carefully.

"What?" I asked innocently.

"That look. What is it?"

"I just have a lot to ask you—and this is the first time in a while we've been alone, undistracted..."

"I can think of something to distract us." He grinned, deviously at me, a dimple showing, and reached under the table, his hand grabbing my leg.

"Stop that!" I whispered, tossing the crispy noodle I had in my hand at him.

"Fine. As much as I will regret this—what do you want to ask me?"

"I know you hit the main points this morning, but explain to me again your relationship to your family." I stared at the menu, certain that he would be glaring at me from the other side of the table.

"You *would* pick a crowded restaurant to have this discussion in."

"Skim over things. I don't need to know where the bodies are buried."

"Fine. My father, Dom Magiano, is the head of the family. I was groomed to take over, but early on didn't...conform as expected."

"It's hard for me to imagine you conforming to anything."

"Well, imagine me as a rebellious teenager. At seventeen, I had a big argument with my father and I moved out, lived with my aunt's family for a few months, then found an apartment. I applied to college, and from then on was estranged from my family. Not estranged in a typical American sense—the Italian family structure will allow for some disassociation, but only within reason. I still attend family events, weddings, birthdays, as well as the major holidays. But as far as the family business goes, which is *everything* to my family, I have no part of it."

"Do you like your family?"

He looked at me quizzically—and in that moment, the waiter reappeared, setting our soups and appetizer on the already crowded table. When we were alone again, I tried to rephrase the question.

"Do you respect them, enjoy their company, have fun when you are with them?"

"With my family there is always respect. To not respect is to *disonore*, or dishonor both yourself and the other party. But I understand what you mean, though it will take a while to answer the question. Our family, I respect. They are extremely tight-knit and extremely loyal. There is great love in our family, and we are family first, business associates second and friends third. But I do not respect what they do. I understand why they do it—the need for violence in that business—but feel that the business structure could change to reduce the violent aspects. The big argument with my father, when I was young, was over legitimizing the businesses. I feel that he could remove the 'mob' aspect of our holdings, while still remaining profitable. He disagrees with that transition for several reasons, many of which are valid, and some of which actually reduce violence instead of feed it. But my father's motives are not identical to his sons'."

"How many sons?"

"I have three siblings. Two brothers and Maria."

"I interrupted you. Please go on."

"I always enjoy spending time with my family—and in true Italian form, it is a large one. I have over twenty cousins, and they are as close to me as my brothers. We all grew up together, a 'pack of wolves' my mother called us, and we were inseparable. I was the only one who left, and while I don't harbor anger toward any of them, there is a group of relatives who has great bitterness for me."

"Why?"

"For my independence, my life of freedom without fear of arrest or death. My wealth, though money has never been a problem for any of them. They feel slighted—rejected—like I have been disloyal, which I understand, though I have never crossed or harmed them by my independence. There are also some of them who have a streak of mean, of evil, if you prefer to think of it that way. They enjoy the brutality of the business. Unfortunately, the business, the money, the contacts—it all equals an environment where hatred and sadism can grow and expand, like kudzu, taking over anything good. Leo is part of that group, the angry, mean ones."

"Leo?"

"The man who came to your house."

"To kill me."

Darkness flickered in his eyes, and he nodded. "Yes."

"If family is so important, so sacred, why would they not leave me alone, as a favor to you?"

"Because of business. You are not part of our family. You are an outsider, a loose end. Someone who threatens the freedom and way of life of our entire family structure. They don't know you—they only know me. And my track record with women is..." He shrugged.

"Crappy."

The response brought a smile to his face. "If you want to put it so eloquently. Crappy. So, they assume that what typically happens with my other relationships will happen here—that I will grow tired of you, dump you—and in response you will do everything in your power to—what was the phrase my father used?—make me bleed."

I didn't like the idea of his family carelessly discussing our relationship and its certain demise when they didn't even know me. Clearly, I had already been judged and found wanting, therefore condemned to death. It felt like the fucking Middle Ages.

I slumped in my seat. "Unfortunately, I see their rationale. I wouldn't put much stock in you keeping me happy and unscorned either."

He laughed and grabbed my limp, depressed hand, bringing it to his lips. "Don't worry. I have a plan that will supersede all of their rational thinking."

"What is it?"

He started eating his soup, nonchalantly shrugging at me over the bowl. "Can't tell you yet. But it's a good one."

"What if it doesn't work—what if you can't convince them?" A little bit of panic had entered my voice.

He met my eyes over the spoon. "I'm an attorney. Convincing people is my job."

And, as far as I knew, he was extremely good at it. It was the only positive thought I could find, so I latched on to it with a death grip.

"Plus," he added, watching me, "they won't have an option. My father will know that when I speak to him."

I DISTRACTED MYSELF with eating, and we both gorged ourselves, finishing off beef and broccoli, honey chicken and lettuce wraps by the time we left. We wandered through a few more shops, but were both dragging our feet, and we finally headed back to the red-vested valet.

"What next?" he asked, when we were back in the leatherwrapped comfort of the car.

"Home," I mumbled, leaning back into the seat and stretching out my full stomach.

He pulled out of the mall and gunned the engine, heading for the interstate, and the car lowered itself, hugging the pavement as we flew along.

"Shit," I said, ten minutes later, as we came in the back door.

"What?" he asked, shutting the door behind him.

"I totally forgot about the movie!" I said, disgusted with myself.

"Why don't we watch one here instead—use the theater room?" Brad suggested, grabbing a bottled water from the fridge.

I frowned at him. "You have a theater room? Where?" I really needed to do a better job of snooping. Apparently there were entire sections of the house I had yet to explore.

He laughed, tossing me a cold bottle of water. "Yes, oh young one. Come on, I'll show you."

"What movies do you have?" I asked.

"You can look through them and see. If you don't see a movie you like, we can head back out, catch a later one."

I unscrewed the water's cap, nodding my agreement. Two minutes later, I was standing in the theater room, mouth agape.

To say that Brad had a movie collection would be a gross understatement. Imagine an entire video store—back when those still existed. That would be close to the selection that the damn man possessed. The walls of the theater room—walls that I had dismissed in my initial glance—were spring loaded. If you pressed the edges they popped open slightly, and you could then slide them to the side, revealing floor-to-ceiling shelves, all the height of a Blu-ray disc case. I rolled my eyes, amazed at the wealth of movies in a format that was relatively new. Brad handed me a large binder that was a catalog, the movies organized by genre, with small images of the covers and brief descriptions for every film, along with a notation of where they were housed. I quickly realized it would take hours to peruse the damn thing, and instead flipped to the index, scrolling down the titles.

The first two I suggested—*Bruce Almighty* and *Collateral*—Brad rejected, but the third he agreed to, and I followed the indicated shelf/section notation and pulled out *Good Will Hunting*, handing it to him.

We settled in, side by side, in the love seat–style theater seating, and I tilted my head toward the wall, now closed, the cases hidden from view once again. "You know that's OCD at its finest."

"That's called organization. Can you imagine trying to find a movie without a system in place?"

I squinted at him, trying to imagine the big man painstakingly organizing the thousands of movies, cataloging them in proper order. That didn't mesh with the Brad I knew—the Brad who couldn't sit still for five minutes without his leg jiggling, or pulling out his cell phone. "And you organized it?"

"Do you *think* I organized it? You know me better than that." He turned up the volume, the previews beginning, and put his arm around me, pulling me to him. "One of the interior designers handled it all. I told her I like movies, to get me a big collection. They kind of went overboard, but I don't mind."

"I just can't believe we were about to *pay* to watch a movie when you have so many choices here."

He laughed, and squeezed my arm affectionately. "God, you have issues."

I looked up, kissing him on the neck. "I can only see one issue that I have right now. One *big* issue." I poked his side.

He looked wounded. "Not me!"

"Shhh—we're missing the movie," I whispered laughingly, and snuggled close to him, pulling a soft fleece blanket over my body. Brad pressed a button on the remote, dimming the lights, and we settled in, forgetting for a brief moment the danger hanging over my head.

Forty-Five

Brad sat across from the two girls, his expression pained.

"Let me get this right," the brunette said, her intelligent eyes peering at him with distrust. "You are *proposing* to Julia tonight. You haven't bought a ring, you don't have anything romantic planned and you have dated her for a grand total of, what, three weeks?"

"It's been almost two months—"

"No, no, no," she interrupted him, waving her hand. "I'm not counting all the time where you were chasing her, and you were both single, and you were probably fucking half the town at the same time. I'm talking about committed relationship time."

Three weeks was probably overstating *that* qualifier, but Brad wasn't going to bother pointing that out.

The other one, a petite beauty with breast implants, a nose job and, in Brad's opinion, entirely too much makeup, slapped the girl's arm, interjecting herself into the conversation. "Well, I think this is *the* most romantic thing ever! Do you have any friends—single friends? I need to find a guy like you, one who is ready to settle down."

"Becca, he is *not* ready to settle down. That's the whole problem!" The aggressive one, who he thought was named Olivia, whipped out a finger, pointing it at Brad. "Why? Why propose now? Why not wait, get to know her a bit?"

He wanted to leave, to say "screw this" to the two spoiled brats in front of him, get up and continue on his way. But these were Julia's friends, her *best* friends, and he needed to stack the deck with every card he had if he wanted Julia to accept. He weighed how to communicate his intentions without bringing up the predicament they had found themselves in. The attorney in him looked at the angles available, the weaknesses of the jury. Reason might work with the pit bull; emotion would win the Barbie's heart. The problem was, all he had was emotion. A foreign tool in his belt. He spread his hands in a helpless gesture and tried his best pitiful look. "Because I love her. And I don't want to wait. I know, unequivocally, that she is the one for me." The word *love* rolled off his tongue, convincing and believable, so smoothly that he almost missed its significance and weight. Love. A concept he had avoided for so long, and which now felt so right in his heart. Expanding, pushy, it took up unnecessary space, crowding out so many hostile emotions—anger at his mother's abandonment, at his family's business, at his own stubborn independence—he had harbored for so long.

The tiny one practically came in her seat, dissolving into a sea of emotion and grabbing his arm in support. The brunette simply snorted, the word *bullshit* stamped clearly across her features.

It took fifteen minutes, every iota of debate experience he possessed, Becca chiming in her support at every opportunity, but Olivia finally cracked. And, after their crab cakes, fruit plates and a bottle of champagne were finished, the two girls and Brad walked across the street and entered the jewel-encrusted, chandelier-lit elegance of Lorenzi Jewelers, in search of the perfect ring.

Forty-Six

Brad already regretted his decision to involve the girls in this process. They had fully settled in at Lorenzi, taking charge as soon as the manager had gleefully greeted Brad and shown them to a private lounge. They now sat on velvet chairs, fresh champagne in hand, and critically surveyed the options. Every five minutes, a new black velvet tray with five carefully chosen rings was presented, and they would pick apart each ring one by one. It had now been over an hour, and they were no closer to a decision than when they first walked in.

Brad paced in the small room, occasionally taking calls, drinking sodas and trying to quell the nervous ball in his stomach. Nervousness was a foreign concept and he hated every ounce of it.

He already knew the ring, had it pictured perfectly in his mind, but hadn't seen anything close to it in the ten or fifteen trays that had paraded by. Julia was unique, different. He didn't want to take a normal setting and stick a huge stone in and be done with it. He wanted something exceptional, something that, when she saw it, she wouldn't be able to say no. Something that, if he wasn't enough, the ring would push her over. He was confident in his sexual prowess, but his relationship skills were rusty at best. He didn't have the option of fucking her into an engagement. Tonight, all he would have was himself and the ring. And he wasn't sure if he, alone, was enough.

He ground his teeth in frustration. The jewelry associates didn't seem to understand what he wanted or weren't listening to him. He tilted his head at the manager, and they moved into a side room.

"You aren't listening to what I am asking for."

The man practically quaked in front of Brad, perspiration running down his face, his hands nervously clasping and re-clasping in front of him.

"I am, Mr. De Luca! You want an elegant, refined setting—something antique, with a large stone."

"Then what the hell is this?" He gestured to the velvet boxes, stacked to the side of the girls. "There isn't a ring in that bunch that I haven't seen a thousand times before! They are all the same, just slightly tweaked! Is there *anything* else in this store—something you have set aside that you haven't brought out?"

"Did you see the marquis setting we brought out, it has—"

Brad cut off the man's pitch with one smoldering look. "I saw it *all*. How long would it take for you to design one?"

"Design, sir?" The man acted as if it were a foreign concept.

Brad clenched his jaw and tried to maintain his cool. "I assume you do custom pieces?"

"Well, yes, Mr. De Luca, of course. But I thought you wanted to propose tonight."

"I do. It's four. Five hours is enough time. I'll give you until nine."

"But, Mr. De Luca, it's Saturday."

"Money never seems to have trouble getting over that hurdle. Give me twenty minutes and a pad of paper—then tell me if my expectations are unreasonable."

He had the manager bring out all of their available large, loose diamonds, and the last three years of catalogs. He flipped through the catalogs, tagging certain settings, then sketched out a rough drawing of what he wanted. He called everyone back in and showed them the sketch and the stone that he had chosen.

There was silence for a full minute, as the girls and suited men looked at the black-and-white sketch. Brad inwardly groaned, hating that he had involved anyone other than himself in this process. Then Olivia beamed, gripping Becca's arm and smiling brightly at Brad. Becca gave a little squeal and hugged Olivia, and then the closest jewelry associate enthusiastically.

"It's perfect," Olivia said, walking to Brad and giving him a strong hug. "She will *love* it."

Brad turned his gaze to the manager. "I have faith in you. Make it happen." He stood, slapping the pale man on the shoulder and heading for the door. The man nervously followed him, speaking quickly and waving his hands frantically.

"Mr. De Luca, I don't really feel comfortable guaranteeing—"

"Mr. Thompson, you have the stones, and the tools. I will be happy to pay whatever is needed for you to call in the staff necessary to create the ring. Olivia or Becca, do you know her size?"

The brunette looked up, startled. "Um, sort of. I know she's worn one of my rings before. You can measure my finger." A female employee materialized and beelined for Olivia, reaching for her left hand.

Brad glanced at his watch and pulled out his wallet. "I have to go. Ladies, it was a pleasure. I greatly appreciate your help. Mr. Thompson, I will expect the ring delivered once it is ready. Please call my cell and we can coordinate a meeting location then." He pulled a black credit card from his wallet and passed it to the man. "Go ahead and authorize this for whatever you need. I'll stop by tomorrow and complete any paperwork that you will require."

He nodded to the group and headed to the door, feeling very satisfied with himself.

BRAD HAD LEFT the house, saying he needed to meet Clarke to sign the new partnership documents, but had promised me a late dinner at Cypress. I had never been there, but I assumed if Brad was taking me, it was probably a white-tablecloths type of place. I grabbed my black dress and hunted through Brad's closet until I found an iron. The best thing about the dress was it went perfectly with my new shoes, and matching them was all I cared about anyway.

I soaked in Brad's jetted tub, dimming the bathroom lights and turning up his thermostat. I had found some bubble bath in a decorative basket in the guest bathroom, and poured the entire bottle into the tub. I was a little unsure if you could use bubble bath in a tub like this one, with three different kinds of jets and more buttons and handles than anyone would ever need. My concern was quickly validated by the huge mountain of bubbles that formed within minutes, pouring out of the tub on all sides. I spent the first five minutes of the bubble brigade with a bucket I found in the air conditioner closet, scooping and dumping the bubbles into the shower. After five minutes, with more bubbles billowing out of every available jet port, I gave up scooping, and turned off the jets, settling for a normal, plain-Jane soak with a mountain of freesia-scented bubbles everywhere.

Even without the jets, it was a great bath. The tub was huge, big enough to accommodate Brad, though I couldn't picture him surrounded by light purple bubbles. I closed my eyes in the near darkness, letting the hot water penetrate my core. I looked forward to tonight, to seeing Brad, to wearing my new shoes and later on, to having his hands on my body.

It was surreal to dress for an event, to be excited, when you know you should be panicking. Surreal to put faith in a man that everyone thought would cause me harm. Granted, "everyone" didn't know the full story. Then again, I didn't even know the full story. I wouldn't for quite a while. It would take years of lunches, midnight chats, holidays, family gatherings, cuddles and fights. Years. And I didn't know if Brad was a "years" type of guy.

I did know that I had professed my love, and he had said nothing. The blowup, the moment when his face had shaken and his voice had wavered, that had told me more than anything. In that loss of control, I had seen vulnerability, love. I recognized it, but he—he was a long way from it.

ON THE WAY HOME from Lorenzi, Brad stopped at a flower stand set up in the back of a Ford truck. A tarp provided some cover, and buckets of flowers occupied three parking spots of an old Exxon gas station. He ducked under the tarp, coming face-to-face with an ancient, hunchbacked man who was missing a few teeth. Brad reviewed the limited selection, and picked out almost all of the orchids and lilies, having the man wrap them together in cream tissue paper and plastic. Giving the man three twenties, he ducked back into the car a few minutes later. Setting the flowers on the seat, he pulled out his phone and called his assistant.

"It's Sunday night." Rebecca's voice was clipped, and in the background he could hear the loud chatter of a bar.

"Exactly. You should be home, heading to bed early, so that you can give me a hundred and ten percent tomorrow."

"You should know by now that I never give a hundred and ten percent."

"Good point." Rebecca was his secret weapon, hidden from the public eye; she was a three-hundred-pound powerhouse that H.R. had felt comfortable entrusting to him. She was a late sleeper, and rarely in the office before noon, but she made up for it by working late, being available on weekends and handling his odd requests without a blink of the eye. The woman was efficient to the point of being lazy. She handled tasks in half the time of others, so always seemed to be idle. But the best, and most valuable trait she had was calling him on his bullshit and standing up to him when needed.

"I need your help tonight."

"That's a shocker. Look, tonight's not good. I put a lot of effort into looking hot tonight. And there's this guy, he's a little guy, but I'm fairly certain he's packing where it counts, and—"

"Rebecca! I don't want to know about your social life. I'm asking you to please pass up on the toothpick you are about to sexually molest, and be available tonight."

A big sigh loudly sounded through the phone. "W-H-A-T could you possibly need? I'm not calling any hookers for your horny ass."

"I need a nine-thirty reservation at Cypress."

"That's going to be impossible. Too short notice, and you know they only have, like, five of the tables you like."

"That's why I'm calling you and not trying to do it myself."

His stroke to her ego worked, and after a moment of silence, she sighed again. *"And?"*

"Lorenzi is making a custom ring for me. I need you to coordinate with the manager and go over there and stay on their ass. I have *got* to have that ring by ten tonight, ideally sooner."

She was suddenly a lot more interested and he could hear what sounded like the clatter of heels, the bar sounds subsiding. "What kind of ring?"

"You'll find out soon enough. Just make sure it is done, and that I don't get ripped off too badly. I expect some bleeding, just don't want to hemorrhage."

"I'm going to skip the interrogation for just a minute, but don't think it's not coming. Okay, so you want me to breathe down their necks and make sure that they give me the ring, and then you want me to bring it to you at Cypress before ten."

"No. I don't want you bringing it. Have them bring it. Just make sure they leave the store, with the ring in hand, in time for me to receive it. Text me when they leave. I won't be able to talk to you tonight, so I want to answer any questions you have now, so you can handle it all for me later. Do you have any questions?"

"I'm going to have to wait until I get to the jeweler to see if I have questions for you on that end. If you want me to properly do my job and help you, I'm going to need more information."

"It's an engagement ring. I've picked out the stone, and sketched out the design. The only questions they may have will be regarding the smaller stones. Just get the best of everything. I don't want an engraving or anything like that." He stopped talking and waited.

Her reaction was quieter than he expected, and a little confused. "Why are you designing an engagement ring? Is this for your brother?"

"No."

"It's for *you*?" Her voice was indignant and disbelieving.

"Yes."

"I'm confused…" she said slowly.

"It's for Julia."

"Broward's intern? You're proposing to Broward's intern. The girl you *just* started seeing. The one who refused to fill out the questionnaire." She enunciated every word, drawing the sentence out slowly, idiotically.

"Yes. Any other questions that *pertain* to your completion of those tasks?"

"How many people in your Cypress reservation?"

"Two."

"Have you told your father about this?"

"I'm not going to dignify that question with a response."

"Are you out of your fucking mind? This is so far out of De Luca–ville that I don't even know how to respond. You have rendered me fucking speechless."

"Well, that is a first. Thank you for your help. Text me if you have any dire emergencies."

"Don't you hang up on me, Brad. We are not even half through—"

He hung up the phone as gently as he could, given it was a cell, and set it on the seat, his home coming into view. Pulling into the drive, he parked in front of the garage, got out and shut the door, turning to face his house, the exterior lights illuminating the large trees in his yard. Inside, various interior lights were on. It felt good, coming home to someone. He had appreciated his freedom for so long, embraced it with a passion almost desperate. It would take a while to fully release that, to get used to not doing whatever he wanted. But while he had once yearned for independence, now he saw the possibility of something different, and he wanted it badly. Marrying her felt right and he was an impulsive but decisive decision-maker. Plus, it would protect her. The one golden rule was that children and wives were untouchable. His family would have no choice. As his wife she would be guarded, part of the inner circle. He strode up the driveway and headed for the back door.

Forty-Seven

It was almost six when I heard sounds downstairs. I wore one of Brad's T-shirts and had my hair pinned up, putting on mascara. I stopped, listening, then walked to the landing. "Brad?"

"Yeah. I'm coming up."

Happiness flooded through me. I trotted down the stairs, meeting him halfway, a hand-wrapped bouquet in his hand. A huge smile broke out on my face at the sight of him, and I threw my arms around his neck, kissing him firmly, trying to keep the mascara stick away from his shirt. "Hey, baby," I said.

"Hey, beautiful. These are for you."

"They are gorgeous! Thank you." I kissed his neck, then bounded up the stairs, screwing the mascara closed, meeting him at the top step. I took the bouquet from him and sank my face into them, inhaling the sweet fragrance.

"There are vases downstairs, I'm not sure where, but Martha uses them a lot."

"I'll find one. Come into the bathroom. You can talk to me while I put on makeup."

He followed me into the master bath, stopping when he saw

the mess of bubbles I had halfway cleaned up. I had hoped that most of them would evaporate, but that plan hadn't worked out too well for me. He raised his eyebrows and looked at me.

"Sorry. Your bathtub attacked me with bubbles. I'll clean it up later. You should probably know, I'm not very...tidy."

"I could have guessed that."

I raised my eyebrows at that, but turned back to the mirror, finishing up my mascara.

"You look beautiful." His voice was soft, and I turned, facing him, studying his eyes. They were, as always, dark and unreadable, watchful, intelligent. I smiled tentatively at him and he stepped forward quickly, his hand stealing around to cup my neck, his eyes on my face. He kissed me, hard and possessive, then softer. My mouth opened and his kiss deepened. He released me and we parted. He grinned, his eyes on my mouth, and then on my eyes.

I turned back to the mirror and fished through the makeup bag, found the earrings I had worn the night of the party and started to put them on.

"Wait," he said, reaching a hand out and stopping me. He walked into the closet, making noise for a few minutes, then returned, carrying a black velvet box. "Wear these."

I took the box gingerly—it was old and worn on the edges. Larger than a ring box. I opened the lid, revealing a pair of diamond and sapphire earrings. Each earring had a large round diamond, with an oval sapphire dangling beneath it, surrounded by tiny diamonds. They were beautiful. I studied them, wondering about them, and looked up at Brad.

"They were my mother's. The first, and only, piece of jewelry I ever bought her. My sister has all of her other pieces. It's not a gift, just a loan."

An unnecessary statement, but I understood him making it.

"I thought— I didn't realize your mother had passed. When you said that you hadn't spoken to her..." My words trailed off and I looked up, seeing the pain in his eyes.

"Three years ago," he said, taking the box from me and removed an earring, handing it to me. I took it carefully, the weight of it surprising me. It was, by far, the most expensive thing I had ever touched. I put it on, and looked at myself in the mirror, Brad's watchful face above mine. "I'll take good care of them tonight."

He wrapped his arms around me and kissed my neck. "I'm not worried. I'm not letting either of you out of my sight."

I smiled softly and fingered the remaining earring, bringing it up to my other ear. "Which one of us is more precious to you?"

He frowned at me. "I can replace the earrings. You, I cannot."

I turned and looked up at him. "No?"

"No."

He snuck a quick hand up my shirt and I flinched, knocking his hand back down and spinning back to the mirror, glaring at his reflection. He shot me a grin and smacked me hard on the ass, then turned to the shower, turning on all of the jets and then pulling his shirt over his head. Finished with my makeup, my ears brilliantly adorned, I left the bathroom and headed to the bedroom to dress.

Forty-Eight

Cypress was as opulent as I expected, but much smaller. We were greeted by a dignified older man who led us on a winding path through several candlelit tables. The room was pear-shaped, an illuminated pianist in the center of it, and the back, curved wall held four curtained alcoves. We were taken to the farthest one, and he pulled back the curtain to reveal a square table, set for two. We stepped up into the alcove, which turned out to be cozy but not claustrophobic. A window occupied the top half of the back wall and gave a stunning view of the downtown skyscrapers. Other than the view and a lone candle, the room was dark.

"Do you want the curtain open or closed, sir?"

"Open, for now. And would you ask the waiter for bottled still, please?"

"Certainly. Enjoy your dinner."

The man gave a slight bow and left. Brad smiled at me, reaching over and grabbing my hand on the white tablecloth. "You look beautiful."

"Thank you. You look very handsome yourself, though I am sure you are aware of that."

"Have you been here before?"

I grinned at him over the candle. "I will save you useless questions on any future dates by informing you that I have not been to any local restaurants that have an à la carte menu."

"That does save time."

"How many times have you been here?"

"A few. This is probably my third time."

I scrunched my forehead at him. "It's quite a romantic place."

"Yes, it is."

"You don't seem like a romantic type. Seems like you would avoid anything that hints of commitment."

"You're wrong on that logic. I am very romantic. It's part of my whole Don Juan persona. It's much easier to fuck women when you wine and dine them."

I raised my eyebrows at him while a waiter arrived and poured us chilled glasses of bottled water. "You do seem to be good at the whole wine-and-dine act."

We ordered drinks and a selection of appetizers, and once the waiter left, I turned back to Brad. "So, is this whole act to try and get lucky later?"

He looked wounded. "I thought part of the whole 'girlfriend' deal was that I was guaranteed to get lucky every night."

"Oh no." I shook my head at him. "That isn't part of the deal at all. Mood swings, PMS, grouchiness, you are guaranteed that. But sex is a constantly negotiated perk."

"That sucks. No wonder I'm a bachelor."

"Of course, I was going to wait and spring the bad stuff on you later, so I'm thinking you do have a chance at getting lucky tonight."

"Gee, thanks."

"No problem." The pianist started playing a Frank Sinatra tune and a peaceful lull fell over our table. I watched Brad across the table, his features strong and quiet, his eyes watching mine, his mouth twitching. He was in a good mood, but seemed jittery, nervous, which was very odd. He was normally confidently in control, reassuringly so. He checked his watch.

"Something wrong?"

"No. Just wondering where our drinks are."

I frowned. Impatience was also out of character, as much as nervousness. At that moment the waiter arrived with our drinks. After setting them in front of us, he bent over and whispered something in Brad's ear. My eyes narrowed as I watched the exchange, watched Brad's eyes lighten and his chair slide back as he stood.

"Julia, excuse me for one moment."

"Wha—?" I didn't get a chance to finish the question, since I was now alone in the alcove, the settling curtains the only sign that he had even been there. I watched their exit, two suits winding through the tables and disappearing down the hall we had originally entered through. *Weird.*

THE PALE LORENZI MANAGER stood by the host stand, with Rebecca's large frame parked beside him, her arms crossed, expression stony. *Shit.* He had told her not to come. Brad didn't stop, but nodded with his head to indicate that they should take this outside. He waited until their party of three passed through the heavy swinging doors, then nodded a greeting to them both. Rebecca didn't allow the jeweler to speak before she launched into a whispered tirade at Brad.

"Do you know how much this ring costs? Jesus, Brad. I negotiated a chunk of it off, but we are still talking about serious cash. For some chick you started boning a few weeks ago?"

He ignored her and addressed the man. "How did it turn out? Let me see it."

"It turned out fine. I was there, Brad—I made sure it was perfect—but we seriously need to discuss this!" Rebecca was pissed and getting even more worked up, pushing a blond tendril off her forehead and moving closer to him.

He turned to her, silencing her rant with his eyes. "Thank you for your help tonight. You can go now." Her eyes blazed at his statement, and he knew she would make him pay for it later. She started to talk, but he held up his hand. "Now. Go. I have to go back inside. We'll discuss this later."

She threw up her hands and wheeled around, storming over to her car and yanking the door open. Brad focused back on the jeweler, who had a ring box and loupe out. Brad took the box, opened it and examined the ring closely. It was a platinum setting, two thin strips of small diamonds that arched together and held a brilliant three-carat princess-cut diamond. It looked like an estate piece that had been passed down for generations. It was just as he had envisioned and he clapped the pale man on the shoulder, almost knocking him over in his enthusiasm.

"It looks perfect. Thank you. Did Rebecca take care of the payment?"

"Yes, though I feel like I have been through a wood chipper." The man sniffed disapprovingly.

Brad grinned. "Working with her can do that to you." He shook the man's hand and tucked the box into his suit jacket, then nodded goodbye and headed back into the restaurant.

OUR APPETIZERS ARRIVED while Brad was gone, so I snacked on lamb tenderloin, beef carpaccio and shrimp cocktail. I was on the verge of getting annoyed when he appeared again, ducking under the curtain and giving me a smile.

"Don't smile at me," I muttered, my mouth full of lamb.

"What?"

"You can't just mysteriously disappear mid-romantic meal."

He reached over and speared a piece of carpaccio with his fork. "No? That's not part of a traditional romantic meal?"

"No, it's not. And stop grinning at me. You're supposed to look remorseful, apologetic."

He shrugged, his mouth now full of shrimp. "I apparently suck at romantic dinners. It's good that you're finding this out early on so the bar can be set low."

He was so damn disarming it was annoying. I watched as he polished off the rest of the appetizers, glad that I had gotten my portion while he was gone. "So? Where did you scamper off to?"

He wiped his mouth with the cloth napkin and scowled at me, taking a sip from his drink. "I don't exactly scamper."

"No, you don't. My mistake. Where did you lumber off to?"

"Be patient. You'll find out soon enough."

"I'm not a very patient person."

"So I'm finding out." He was way too cheerful. Something was up. And his nervousness was gone. Whatever the waiter had taken him away for had apparently relieved his tension.

"Do you take drugs?" The question popped out before I could stop it, though, now that it was hanging out there, it seemed like something that I needed to know the answer to.

"Drugs?" He seemed confused.

"You know, coke, heroin, speed, anything deemed illegal in this country?"

"You are the hard-partying college student. I should be

asking you that question. I am, how did you put it when we met?...Old."

"Yes, you are old. Ancient, in fact—but don't be evasive."

"No. I don't do drugs. I am prescribed and take Adderall, if you want to consider that a drug. You?"

I snorted, offended. "No!"

"Your roommates obviously have a strong relationship with weed."

"My roommates are idiots. Lovable idiots, but still. I've smoked weed before, but it doesn't do anything for me." He raised his brows. "I mean, I don't get high."

"Three weeks ago you didn't have orgasms either, but that turned out to be false."

"Oh my Lord, you are never going to let me forget that, are you? Anyway, we—" I broke off when I saw the waiter hovering outside our curtain. I nodded to him and he stepped into our room and began the menu presentation.

The restaurant served veal—which I had never had, so, at Brad's urging, I ordered that. He, predictably, ordered a steak and a variety of side dishes, and two minutes later we were alone again. The candlelight played on his strong features and he looked at me, waiting for me to continue.

I searched my thoughts, trying to remember what I had been saying. "We need to discuss tomorrow."

"What about it?"

"I'm going to pretend that your family killing me is not a concern and skip to the next stress point—Burge."

He shrugged. "What's stressful about it?"

"Well, to start, I need to convince him that my position is needed, that he shouldn't drop me as an intern. Plus, I have to fake my way into doing everything that I told him I can do."

He held up a hand, swallowing a piece of buttered bread. "What do you mean fake?"

I avoided eye contact, reaching for my glass and taking a sip. "Well, I kind of exaggerated what I had been doing for Broward. So that Burge would consider me useful, needed."

"Kind of exaggerated, or did exaggerate?"

I rolled my eyes at him. "Don't give me grief. You are the office's biggest bullshitter."

"Apparently not. What did you tell him you could do?"

"Operating agreements, basic filings, meeting minutes."

He shrugged. "Those are basic enough tasks."

"That I don't know how to do." I hated saying the words, but felt that they added credibility to my stress.

He waved off my concern. "Don't worry about that. He won't fire you."

"How do you know that? You were the one harping on me that I needed to make a good impression so he would ignore the inconvenience of taking me on."

He shrugged, piercing a piece of leftover meat with his fork. "He mentioned you on a call the other day. He likes you. He won't fire you."

"*Likes* me likes me?" I leaned forward over the table.

"What are you, twelve?" He grinned, wiping his mouth. "No, just normal likes you. If I was you, I wouldn't worry about *that*."

Something in his tone, a playful mockery, made me focus on him and I toyed with my bottom lip before taking the bait. "What do you mean?"

"What you look like at the office..." He grimaced, and I bared my teeth at him, causing him to burst out laughing. "Sorry! But you look..."

"Super hot? Sexy? Drop-dead gorgeous?" I helpfully supplied, giving him a lifeline that he didn't deserve.

"Dorky," he finished. "Adorably dorky," he added quickly at my dark face. "It's a good thing, will help you with your whole 'faked work experience' thing." He was saved by our food, brought by two tuxedoed gentlemen, and our table was quickly filled with large plates and delicious items. When departing, the waiters closed the curtains, cutting off our view of the room and wrapping us in privacy. The showcased view, savory food and sudden seclusion were distracting, and saved me from coming up with a witty response.

We topped off dinner with wine, crème brûlée and flourless chocolate cake. I was absolutely stuffed, and leaned back in the seat with a contented sigh, my eyes closed in bliss.

"Don't go to sleep on me." His words sank into my peaceful cocoon, a silky smooth tone that must have dropped half the panties in town at one point or another in time.

"I'm not."

"Good." I felt his hand on mine and opened my eyes. He stood, pulling back the curtain and waiting for me.

"We're leaving?" I hadn't seen him pay the check.

"Not entirely. Unless you're tired, I was thinking we'd have champagne on the roof deck."

I smiled up at him and rose, grabbing my purse. "You know you only have to mention champagne and I'll be there."

"I was counting on that." His hand on the small of my back, I ducked slightly to pass through the curtained opening, and we moved into the main restaurant area. The pianist was now singing "The Way You Look Tonight" and it felt surreal, winding through the tables, glasses chinking, jewels sparkling, Brad's hand on me, his masculinity invading my senses. He guided me to a discreet elevator that was open, waiting. We entered the industrial space—one not designed for patrons—wide, steel and filthy, smelling of grease and food. I stood close to him, not wanting to get dirty, and he wrapped a hand around my waist.

"Are we on the wrong elevator?" The setting was such a contrast from the splendor of the restaurant that I felt like I had just exited a movie set and was now backstage.

"Just think of it as adding to the exclusivity factor." The doors opened, and we stepped into a room smaller than my bedroom, with only a wall of electrical boxes and switches. A large machine vaguely resembling a giant air conditioner hummed to the right of us. Brad stepped forward, through an exit door, propping the door open as he held it open for me. I stepped through, and suddenly was out into the night air.

Forty-Nine

We stood on a rooftop. Brad had referred to it as the "roof deck"—but that was a bit of an overstatement. Roofing material was underfoot, and there was no railing to stop us from falling over the edge, pipes and electrical systems surrounded us. But the view was spectacular, huge buildings all around us, a rainbow of a thousand city lights before us. We gingerly moved forward, stepping along a small walkway, through two humming generators, until we stood on empty, unobstructed roof. Ahead, a small table had been set up, complete with a white tablecloth, two place settings and a candle. Next to it sat a silver stand with champagne chilling. To the left was ten-foot-high arched glass, the ceiling of the restaurant. I walked over and looked through the yellow glass, seeing the small round tables, black-coated waiters, and the illuminated pianist, all oblivious of our view. Brad stepped forward, standing beside me, looking down on the scene, difficult to see through the dirty glass. Something caught his eye and he moved down to a crouch, fiddling with a small window on the side of the arch. I started to ask what he was doing when, suddenly, there was movement beneath his hands, and I could hear the piano, hear "What a Wonderful World" softly drifting out from below Brad, through the window he just cracked.

"And you say you're not romantic."

He stood, dusting off his hands. "I have my moments." He put his hands in his pockets, looking at me across the roof. "You look beautiful."

I blushed. "Thank you." This evening had not gone as I had expected. An expensive restaurant, yes; this rooftop scene with a quiet, subdued Brad, no. It was not any side of Brad I had ever seen. I was suddenly nervous, off guard.

He stepped slowly forward, keeping his hands in his pockets, and watched me. Tilted his head to the side and really looked at me. I felt his gaze, penetrating, and averted my eyes, feeling bare and exposed. Then he cocked his head toward the table. "Shall we?"

I lifted my eyes, meeting his strong gaze, and nodded, walking over to the table, to the chair he pulled out for me. He stayed on his feet, undoing the champagne bottle and popping the cork, the sound of bubbles reaching my ears. I intentionally relaxed my hands, setting my purse on the rough, pebbled roof. *Why am I so nervous?*

Once he had poured our champagne, he sat down across from me and leaned forward, holding his champagne flute out. "A toast."

I raised my eyebrows at him. *More romance?*

"To the most wonderful woman I have ever met. May we spend the rest of our lives together."

"*That's* your toast?" My brow furrowed and I kept my glass raised, interrupting his sip of the bubbly liquid.

He looked at me, wounded. "You don't approve?"

"As I'm sure you have figured out by now, I have a very healthy self-esteem, bordering on egotism."

"Bordering on?"

"Shut up. Regardless, you have been with a disgusting amount of women, and will be with a hundred more before you die. For me to be the 'most wonderful' woman you have ever met, and you toasting to 'spending the rest of your life' with me rings a little..." I tilted my head.

"Fake?"

I made a face, trying to think up the right word. "Bullshitty."

"That's not a word."

"I'm pretty sure you can figure out what I mean by my non-word." I went ahead and took a sip of the damn champagne, which went down perfectly.

"Do you want me to work on a different toast?" He looked at me with amusement.

"No. I believed you earlier when you said I looked beautiful. I'll keep that part." I smiled at him over the rim of my flute. A breeze floated over us and I turned my face into the wind, looking out over the city lights.

"Happy?" Brad's voice was quiet in the night air.

"Very," I murmured. "But I feel a bit like Cinderella. Like I am in a wonderful, perfect world, and tomorrow morning it will all disappear. Which, I guess, it will." I set down my glass and looked at him. "Brad, you don't know if you will be able to protect me. You don't know what your father will say. Everything could change come morning, and I could be in danger."

He stayed silent for a minute, studying me. "You said a few days ago that you loved me."

God, all he ever does is change the subject. I sighed. "Yes."

"Why do you love me?"

"What?" I was caught off guard. Brad discussing feelings was taking this date to an even stranger place. "Is this you fishing for compliments or being insecure?"

He looked at me steadily, his strong build sitting back, one hand loosely on his glass. The man looked as if he'd never had an insecure thought in his life, and probably hadn't. "It's me wanting to know if you truly know what love is."

"Do you?"

He narrowed his eyes at me. "Now you are being evasive."

"Fine. I'll answer the question, then circle back to this train of thought." I sighed, taking a slow sip of champagne to buy myself time, trying to organize my thoughts and emotions into a communicable form. *Talk about putting myself out there.* I looked at him, silent and sure, waiting for my response. I was nervous again, and cursed myself for it.

I sighed. "At the risk of scaring you, I think I knew from the moment I met you. I didn't admit it to myself then, and my mind is fighting with me to even admit it now. You are so...different than anyone that I've ever met, and that isn't necessarily a good thing. I should not be sitting here now, should not have ever gone to lunch with you, to Vegas with you, should not have risked my job and my future to be with someone who should have been nothing more to me than a good fuck."

He watched me carefully, his dark eyes revealing nothing.

"That is what you were. The only man who ever touched me and made me physically need, made me wet and hot and viral. I have become your sexual slave and if, an hour ago, you had bent me over in front of that entire restaurant and wanted to fuck me, I would have done it." His eyes changed during my speech, flashing in the darkness, and I felt his virility steal over the table, the vocalized words making me wet, and I clenched my legs together under the table.

"I lusted for you and that is why I didn't stay away from you like I should have, like every reasonable bone in my body told me to. But in fucking you, in you taking my sexuality and warping it, expanding it, I lost myself, my barrier. And somewhere in all of that, I fell. I was unguarded and unprotected and my heart latched on to you and made every pore in me yours." I wanted to pull my eyes from his, but he held me still, exposed.

"It's not because of your money, or your looks. It's your essence. I love your sense of humor, your honesty, your ability to piss me off and make me laugh at the same time. I love how you are respectful to Martha, and how you will risk your safety to keep me safe. I don't ever want to experience anything again without you next to me. You change a situation, make an ordinary event incredible." I stopped suddenly, out of words and too bare to create any more. I closed my eyes briefly, then opened them and stared into his, scared of his reaction. "Does that scare you?"

He was still, and when he spoke, his words held restrained emotion.

"There is very little that scares me, Julia. But you certainly do. I think I have, for a long time, feared love. The last person I truly loved was my mother, and it did nothing to protect me from her abandonment. Since then, I've avoided love. Not deliberately, but I've set myself up for failure through my actions. Whether it was this crazy situation that brought us together, or my own inability to screw this one thing up, somehow you slipped past that defense." He paused, his eyes on mine, dark prisons I was unable to break from. "Julia, I have fallen hard. Fallen madly in love with you." The words hung across the table for a moment, and I waited in the stillness, not wanting to break the moment, his bareness breathtaking and terrifying in its sincerity. "I didn't admit it to myself until last night, and am just now fully coming to grips with it."

He bit his bottom lip, the causal gesture tantalizing. "I didn't expect to ever really fall in love. I hoped, one day, that I would find someone who could satisfy me sexually, and also provide a home, possibly children. But I didn't expect to fall in love with her. I expected to have affection, to love her in the sense that I love Martha. But what I have with you is different. I don't really understand it yet, so I'm not going to try and put it into words, not yet. It is going to sound strange, but I don't particularly like the feeling. I don't like not being able to control every part of a situation. I don't like feeling vulnerable, unsure. You are a gamble in that you are young, you could fall out of love as quickly as you fell in it."

He held up a hand, stopping the protest that was about to leave my lips. "I am, as you have so eloquently put it, ancient. You may, ten years from now, decide that I am too old for you. You may decide that you settled down too young, that you missed out on other opportunities. You just got out of a two-year relationship, an engagement. You haven't had any time to be single, to have a normal college experience. That may not seem important to you now, but it could later." His brow furrowed and he looked at me intently. "I've never really cared if a woman 'broke up' with me. With you it is different. I am a gambler, Julia—I love the thrill of it. But with my heart, with my life, with you, there is too much at stake."

I frowned at him, trying to understand the meaning behind his words. "So, what are you saying? You are *breaking up* with me? Because you love me?"

He laughed softly, shaking his head. "No. I just want you to really think this through. I want you to understand what is at stake for me, and for you to really look at what you are giving up by being with me. I want you to really ask yourself if what you are feeling is love. Because for me, I have no doubts. I hate it, it scares the hell outta me, but I know it is true. I know that my life, from this day forward, will be incomplete unless I share it with you. I'm asking if you will be my wife."

His wife? This was so unexpected that I blinked, my jaw literally dropping as my mind tried to comprehend the statement.

"Julia, will you marry me?"

I was so flustered I hadn't even noticed him standing up, walking over to me and kneeling at my chair, a small box in his hand, unopened. He looked at me gravely, with such intensity, his handsome face waiting, expectant.

It was like time stood still, as if even the piano player took a break midsong. I was still adjusting to the fact that he had admitted love, to being "in love" with me. This was too much, too overwhelming, and I stared at the small box in his hand, in terror, afraid to open it, afraid that it might contain something beautiful that would be the final crack that would cause this whole beautiful glass ball to break into a million pieces. I understood what he was doing, understood what my saying yes would mean—to my situation, to the danger that threatened my life. Marrying him would protect me, but chain him. Possibly chain us both, and it was too soon. There was too much unknown about each other. Yes, I loved him. I was surer of it than I had ever been of anything. But did he really love me? Or was this a gallant form of chivalry that had invaded his senses, chloroformed his heart?

He shifted, waiting, his face growing stressed, and I stared at his eyes, the depths I loved, though I could never tell a damn thing from them.

I moistened my lips, my eyes stuck in the channel between us, then spoke.

"No."

Fifty

His eyes blinked, but stayed on me. "No?"

"No. I'm sorry."

He looked down at the rough roof beneath his knee, then hefted himself to his feet and sat down across from me. He gave an exasperated smile and looked at me, waiting.

"I would love to marry you, and to be your wife. But I want you to propose to me for the right reasons—not because we are in a bad situation. Am I correct in my understanding that getting engaged is your plan for keeping me safe?"

"Are you even going to look at the ring?" He set it on the table in front of me, pushing it forward, his eyes excited.

I glared at him. "Are you listening to me? I'm not going to look at the ring."

"Why not?"

Grrrr. "Am I correct in that you are proposing so that your family does not hack me into little pieces?"

He grinned, still not getting the idea that I was rejecting him. "They don't 'hack.'"

"Answer the question."

"I am *in love* with you. Something I never expected, didn't want, but am now ecstatic over. You know me well enough to know that when I want something, I go after it. I love you, and want to let everyone know it—want to make our relationship permanent."

"And…it would also conveniently fix our problem." I folded my arms at him, the damn black box in front of me *screaming* for attention. I fought against looking down, against giving credence to its screams.

He shrugged. "Well, yes. As my wife, you would be untouchable. Protected."

"Under lock and key."

His eyes narrowed, a hard edge coming to them. "I don't know what you mean by that comment. I have no desire to put you up in a big house and leave you alone, if that is what you are referring to. I want a partner in life, not a trophy in my case."

"And you will be faithful?"

He reached forward, grabbing my hand and clasping it in both of his, pulling my eyes to his, dark and solemn. "Julia, you are incomparable. I know what I risk in straying from you, what I would lose if you left me. I promise to never kiss, caress or fuck another woman without you there, watching it happen. And I promise to allow you to be as unfaithful as you want, as long as I am there to make sure you're satisfied." His mouth curved into a grin and he brought my hand to his mouth, kissing it gently.

"Or flirt."

"What?"

"You can't flirt with women either. And by the way, you really do suck in the romance department. Hallmark will never put that last paragraph on a card." My mouth moved without order, and I found myself grinning back at him. He nudged the box again, practically pushing the damn thing into my lap, his eyes lit with anticipation. He was like a damn kid at Christmas. I looked at him expectantly, and he frowned, then understood what I was waiting for.

"Oh. Right. No flirting. Do you want me to kneel again?"

I exhaled, frustrated. "You are treating this as a joke."

"And you are way too serious about this—this is supposed to be a happy time. I am finally throwing off my stubborn bachelor ways and professing my love to you. You should grab the damn ring and run for the closest altar." He reached forward, plucking the box from the table and opening it in one quick motion. Then he held it forward, and leaned across the table at me. "Julia, please. Ignore the bullshit and the drama going on in our lives. I truly believe that I was made for you, and there is not a woman on the planet that is more perfect for my troublesome self. I know you deserve better than me. But please, give me a chance to be a husband worthy of you, and I will spend my life becoming the man you deserve. Please, Julia. Marry me."

His intense eyes, with darkness that I never could decipher, stared at me, and I saw truth in their depths. My eyes flickered from the heat of his stare, and I glanced down at the ring. I expected the ring to weaken my resolve, to be the final straw that broke the camel's back. I expected that I would not be able to resist a diamond. It was a gorgeous setting, a perfect, breathtaking stone, but I wanted more. And looking back into his eyes, I found it.

I wanted him. Needed him. And in that desperation, I wanted to push him away, badly. Because in that vulnerability, there was certain heartbreak. But in the ring, in the engagement, there was safety. And I needed to be smart.

I exhaled slowly, decisively, and nodded. "Yes." I held up my hand when he rose, his face lit with excitement. "Wait." He stayed standing, but leaned forward, resting his hands on the table, waiting for me to finish.

"I'll accept your proposal," I said carefully. "But I'm not getting married. Not for at least a year, long enough for me to feel like you will be faithful to me. I'm not worried about us being happy, about us having enough love, about you being 'the right one' for me. I worry about you not being happy in a monogamous relationship, whether we are engaged in a swinger lifestyle or not. I just need time to make sure that you will be loyal, and will be happy being loyal."

I paused, trying to keep a smile from my face. "But to appease your bloodthirsty family, and because I can't imagine life without you, I will accept your proposal."

I was in his arms before I could take a breath, his arms around my body, his mouth on mine. He lifted me, spinning me around, and I laughed when he finally let me come up for air.

"Thank you," he said, his mouth at my ear, voice gruff. "You have made me so happy." Then he bent me back into a Hollywood dip, and my eyes found his in the dim light. "I love you," he whispered.

"I love you, too," I said, smiling up at him.

"Will you wear the damn ring now?" he said, pulling me back to my feet, the rooftop spinning a little, city lights and night sky everywhere.

I smiled and rolled my eyes. "Well, if you insist."

And then my unromantic future husband knelt again on the rough rooftop and, with the sounds of Sinatra floating through the night air, put the ring on my finger and made it official.

Epilogue

We rode back to Brad's house, the new engagement ring sparkling on my hand. It shone at me in the dark car, claiming
me as its own, and I slid it off, then back on, just to prove to
myself that I could. He reached over and grabbed my hand,
squeezing it reassuringly, and I looked over at him. His profile was strong, beautiful, mine. It felt odd, having security
in our relationship. And at a point when I had just come to
terms with the feelings I had for him.

"So. What's next?" I spoke over the music, and he reached
forward and turned it off.

"Tomorrow morning, I will speak to my father. If you feel
comfortable enough, I'd like you to be there."

"Me?" I blinked, considering the situation.

"Yes, you. He will love you, I promise."

"Did he love your first wife?"

"Hillary?" He shifted in his seat. "Ummm..."

"Oh my God—he hated her."

He grimaced, an overdramatic expression that turned into
a smile as he started to laugh. "He, uh, wasn't fond of Hillary.
But you are different. He'll like you."

I crossed my arms, pulling my hand from his. "Really."

He groaned, hanging his head a fraction too long, and I glanced worriedly back and forth between him and the road. "He is going to love you because I love you."

"Ah, no. That didn't work for Hillary."

"You are different than Hillary. She was reserved, collected."

I straightened in the leather seat. "I'm collected."

He laughed, reaching for my hand again, and I moved it away. "No. You are lovable, funny, quirky and feisty, but you are not collected. You are classy. I'm not saying you aren't a lady, but you have an air of energy and spunk that keeps you from being collected and reserved. It is why I fell for you, and why my father will, too. He didn't like Hillary because he didn't think she could make me happy. He was right, but I would never admit that to him or myself until it was too late."

I blew out a puff of air and allowed his hand to find mine. "What if he shoots me?"

"My father will not shoot you." My scrunched face must have showed my disbelief. "I promise! Now, come on, I want to take my fiancée to bed." He put the car in park and leaned over, asking for a kiss. I grumbled slightly and met his lips, pressing mine chastely to his. He grabbed the back of my head and pulled me harder to him, taking my breath and my senses and communicating more sex, desire and need in one kiss than anyone I had ever met. I pushed him away, gasping for breath, laughing a little. "Fine. Take me to bed, if you must."

"How kind of you." He eyes held a glint of the devil I knew lay inside him. Then he blinked, and there was nothing but arousal and desire.

We started on the stairs, not the interior ones, but the wide, stone steps of the back porch, a passionate kiss against the column that led down to the ground, small groans emerging as he stripped off my dress and examined me closely, my back arched against hard stone, his hands traveling down between my breasts, worshiping them each in turn, his mouth quickly following the path of his hands.

I begged for him on those steps, soft pleas that went unfulfilled, his focus on me, his hands and mouth, that soft mouth that held such a wealth of carnal knowledge, taking me to that sweet, perfect arc. I came, my legs trembling around his head, my hands gripping rough stone, my new stilettos digging into the strength of his back.

Then we moved, him carrying me through the house, my bare breasts resting against his suit, his eyes on mine, a small smile tugging on those lips.

The bed was our next stop, soft down pillows where stone had just been, that magnificent cock finally let loose on my eager body. I rolled, I bent, I rode and I was conquered, six times in all! It was a long and lengthy session of firm hands, soft kisses and positions I had never even dreamed off. And in the end, I wanted to watch, and with his eyes on mine, furious, dark depths that reached in and grabbed my heart, throwing out all reason and restraint on their treacherous path, he finished, my hand taking the final steps to bring his body to the point that I had already traveled so many times that night. And as I watched him, as he marked my body with his ownership, I focused on those depths, those intense, dark eyes that led right to his soul, and the realization of the night's events hit me hard. This man, this beautiful, incredible, strong man, was close to being mine. Completely and forever mine.

That night, after a long, hot shower, I lay in bed and stared up at the ceiling. Tomorrow held so much. My return to the office, his father's decision, the beginning of my second life as a fiancée. Hopefully, this engagement would stick. The diamond glittered at me in the dim room. It would have to stick. My heart couldn't survive a fall, not from the height that my feelings had climbed.

I closed my eyes, focusing on the sound of Brad's breathing, a strong, steady cadence that spoke of confidence and assurance. I borrowed some of his confidence, dreaming of tomorrow and of the security his father's blessing would bring. Of the changes that being Brad's fiancée, his wife, would bring to my life. *Me, a wife.* And I knew, as I finally fell asleep, that my life was never going to be the same again.

★ ★ ★ ★ ★

Acknowledgments

I owe this book, and any success it has, to a team of individuals.

First and foremost—the readers. Wherever you are, whether it be curled up on your couch or in the break room at work—you rock my world. Thank you, from the bottom of my heart, for taking a second chance with Brad and Julia. Your time is valuable, and I am so grateful for it. I was (and still am!) a passionate reader—and I never realized my worth as a reader until I sat on this end of a book. For every friend that you share a good book with, or for every review you leave online, you grow another pair of angel wings. Thank you.

The bloggers. I don't know how you find time for it—with work, lives and family—but you are my rock stars. As a reader, you helped me find those perfect, often-unknown gems. As a writer, you helped the readers find this story. Thank you so much for everything you do for us. You are all amazing.

My husband. Thank you for being the inspiration for Brad. It is also oh-so-helpful how you are always on hand to "inspire" me whenever the need arises. You are incorrigible and so much like me it is insane, but I love you, baby, forever and always. Thank you for giving me support and time to write, and for spoiling me incessantly.

My family. Thank you for giving me an ear when I need one, space when I need to write and advice when I don't know what to do. You are my core support and I love you all. Most of all, thank you for not judging me for writing hot, dirty, scandalous smut.

The team. Maura Kye-Casella, you are the best agent a girl could hope for. Thank you for always being available and for never pressuring me. Emily Ohanjanians, thank you for all of your work on *Blindfolded* and *Masked*—you took those books and strengthened them in ways I couldn't. Kate Dresser—thanks for jumping in midstream and breathing more life into *Masked*. You have been a dream to work with, thank you for being so flexible and insightful, all at the same time. And to the entire Harlequin HQN team—you have been brilliant, patient, helpful, timely and supportive. I feel as if I have joined a family; thank you all for taking me under your wing and showing me such love.

My God. Thank you for giving me these ridiculous, crazy ideas that somehow, when written on paper, seem to make perfect sense. Thank you for creating my soul mate and somehow making him just lovable enough to steal my heart. And thank you for keeping me focused. You keep the ideas coming, and I will keep putting them on paper.

Thank you all. Without you this book wouldn't be the book it is today. I appreciate you all and apologize for not telling you each and every day how much you mean to me.

Sincerely,

Alessandra